First paperback edition May 2018

For information regarding special discounts on bulk orders or for teachers, schools and librarians, address PB&J Literary Agency, 5580 La Jolla Blvd. Suite # 62 La Jolla, CA.   92037

Contact the author via PB&J Literary Agency at
pbjliteraryagency@gmail.com

richardholemanwrites.com
Facebook.com/RichardHolemanWrites

Discover Richard Holeman on goodreads.com

Also by Richard Holeman

Haloes are for Show-Offs

First Boy on the Moon

A Story by
Richard Holeman

For Petra
My first faithful reader

Acknowledgements

I could not have written this book without the generous and invaluable help and support of Donatella Velluti, who lovingly and wisely edited the original manuscript. I remain grateful for everything.

Thank you to Stephen Leigh and Kathryn Davis for proofreading the final draft.

I was gonna be
The first boy on the moon
The pirate king of summer
The terror of late June
Fireworks and sunburns
And ice cream trucks we hardly could afford
I had a necklace made of candy
And a broken broomstick for a sword
A superhero in the morning
And a cowboy
In the early afternoon
And later in the evening
I was gonna be
The first boy on the moon
Fireflies and bare feet
And somersaults in fields gone dry and brown
I had a best friend like a brother
And a homemade map for leaving town
But momma always kept an eye out
And she'd holler
If I didn't come home soon
I told time by the streetlights
I was gonna be
The first boy on the moon

Part One
June Bugs

One - A Ride Home from School

I was born in winter and I grew up to be a man who loves the wind and the cold much more than I do the sun, but when I was a kid, I loved the summer and all the promises it held. Fireworks and fireflies, hot dogs on the grill with beans and potato salad, late nights at the drive-in movies and all the low-budget adventures a kid could dream up. Summer was the year's longest, sweetest taste of freedom and not a moment was to be wasted. In the summertime, I could stay outside on the block, away from the apartment, until it got dark, and the days grew longer with each passing week until it didn't get dark until almost 9 o'clock at night. The summer days were long, but before they began, you had to endure the longest day of the whole year: the last day of school.

In June of 1976, I was ten years old and the country was gearing up for its two-hundredth birthday party. In the spirit of the bicentennial, Miss Winters' fourth-grade classroom had been pasted over with dime-store tributes to America.

As the big clock on the wall slowly counted down to the final bell, I sat at my desk in that star-spangled room and gazed out the big, open windows at the trees, the grass and the sky, where summer lay hushed and waiting for me.

In the circular driveway, big yellow school buses waited to make their last rowdy deliveries of the school year. Parents were parking their cars along the curb or milling around on the sidewalk, but I looked through them, beyond the street and into the distance, imagining all of the good times my best friend Jesse and I would have over summer break.

I had a lot of friends on the block where I lived, but none of them had ever been the kind of best friend to me that Jesse Gwinn had been, and that was no fault of theirs. Jesse was unique, even in our neighborhood of misfits and geeks. He was the buzz cut prince of our block, the leader of our gang of kids and he knew every single shortcut in town. We were all friends on our block, but Jesse and I were something more than friends or even just *best* friends.

We had been blood brothers since we nicked our palms with a pocketknife in 1974 and we would be blood brothers for the rest of our lives. Jesse was the kind of kid whose imagination and sense of fun made even a rainy-day good, so you can imagine what he could do with three whole months of sunshine. In my mind, I drifted up and away and out of the classroom, off with Jesse to the woods or down by the small, scummy pond we called Blackberry Bog or the fields beside the railroad tracks.

I was startled from my daydream by the loud BANG of a car exhaust backfiring and I saw a big, ugly Country Squire station wagon pulling up to the curb. The car was old, the paint was faded and cracked and the paneling was peeled and chipped. It came to a stop with another, smaller backfire and a puff of grey smoke coughed from the tailpipe, the driver-side door opened and my mother climbed out of the car and looked toward the school.

"Holy shit! We got a car!"

The classroom erupted in gasps and giggles and Miss Winters shouted, "Richie!" and I realized I had said it aloud.

I endured a brief scolding from Miss Winters, but with only seven minutes left in the school-year, I figured she wasn't going to do much and moments after she concluded my public correction and sent me back to my desk with a stern eye and a sharp, pointing finger, that blessed final bell went off with a droning buzz and we were free.

I rushed for the door, but in my excited haste to meet the summer out on the sidewalk and see our new used car, I had forgotten my book-bag. To go back to my desk and get it, I had to wiggle and push my way through the small mob of fourth-graders streaming out of the classroom, the result being that I was the last kid in the room, left behind by the stampede.

As I was leaving, Miss Winters stopped me. "Richie Holeman!" I turned in the doorway and faced her. "You clean up that foul mouth of yours over the summer, young man."

"Yes, ma'am. I'm sorry. I thought I was only thinking it. If I knew I was gonna say that *out loud*, I would have said 'holy crap'. I swear."

She sighed. "Have a good summer, Richard."

Instead of fleeing breathlessly from school and out into the open arms of summer, I was one of the last kids out of the building, walking out the big front doors on the tail end of the excitement. My brothers were already on the sidewalk with our mother, gawking at the used station wagon. Gary was begging to steer it around the neighborhood sometimes, Tommy was asking if he could ride in the foldaway seats in the very back and Mom was smiling and talking to one of the other mothers about the great deal she had gotten on the car.

Tommy saw me coming and said, "Hey, look! We got a new car!" and I walked around the car once and came back to stand on the curb between him and my mom.

"What a piece of junk," I said, and before I could laugh, my mother's hand shot out and her knuckles rapped me hard on the side of my head. My eyes blurred over with tears and Gary snickered and some of the moms and kids stared at me, but I didn't cry.

My mother glared down at me and said, "Get your ass in the goddamned piece of junk. Now!"

We piled in the car, Gary up in front in his position of privilege, Tommy riding happily in the jump-seats and me sitting sullen behind my mother, careful not to let my feet get under her seat or to catch her eyes in the rearview mirror.

The car *was* a piece of junk, but that didn't mean I wasn't happy we had it. Mom hadn't had a car in almost a year and we had all suffered without one. There had been no drive-in movies or weekend rides through the country. When mom did the monthly shopping, we boys would help her push the groceries home in a couple of shopping carts, then Mom would tell us to take the empty carts back to the supermarket. Sometimes we took the carts all the way back to the store, but mostly we abandoned them, banged up in the field or on the railroad tracks. Once a week, we had trudged to the laundromat and back, carrying our clothes over our shoulders in pillowcases and there had been no rides home from school on rainy days. All that would change now, for as long as the wagon continued to run, and life would be a little better, things would be a little easier. Mom would be a little happier.

Piece of junk or not, the radio worked and Mom had it tuned to the local am pop station as she drove through town. I sang along silently with The Captain & Tennille (*my momma told me, you better shop around)* and Gary asked Mom how she had managed to get the money to buy a car.

"It wasn't very expensive at all," she said and I resisted the urge to mumble under my breath. The turn signal clicked and clacked as Mom turned the big Country Squire into our neighborhood of four-unit apartment buildings.

"And Ben helped with the money," she continued, "With him moving in with us, he thought we should have a car, so he helped out with the money."

Moving in with us?

Ben Granberry was my friend Bobby Bozart's uncle. He had arrived one day in April, on a train from out of town, for a visit with his sister and never left. He was the kind of man my mother liked, with a greasy 50's haircut like my father had and, within a few weeks, he had been spending most of his time on our front stoop or at our kitchen table, playing cards and flirting with my mom, and then he began to sleep over some nights.

He didn't work and all day long, he filled the apartment with cigarette smoke and his yelling. He drank black coffee every morning until eleven and then he drank cheap cans of beer the rest of the day, and the only good thing about that was he usually dozed off early in the evening, snoring in Mom's bed with the television on.

"He's moving in? When?" I asked my mom, carefully, quietly.

She looked at me in the mirror. Her eyes were sharp. Looking back, I wonder if she had thought that if I had recognized the car for the piece of junk it was, maybe I had recognized Ben for the no-good drunk he was, but that day in the car, I didn't wonder what her thoughts were, only if she would smack me for asking. "That's right; he's moving in. Today. He's already brought his things over and I don't think you're stupid enough to have anything to say about that."

I was not.

From the back of the wagon, my eight year old brother Tommy said, "But where's he gonna sleep at?"

We had a three-bedroom apartment. Mom and Gramma had their rooms and me and my brothers shared the third one.

Gary turned in the front seat and looked over his shoulder at Tommy as Mom guided the car into an empty slot under the leaning wooden carport behind our apartment building. "He's gonna sleep in mom's room, dummy. Where'd you think he was gonna sleep?"

"Oh." Tommy thought that over for a moment. "So he's gonna be like a dad then?"

My mother's sharp eyes flashed in the rearview mirror once more, but this time they passed over me and settled on Tommy.

"No, he's not going to be like a dad, really. He's not moving in for you boys." Her voice and her eyes softened, the way they always did for Tommy. "But he'll help out and we'll all go places together. Like a family, yeah. It'll be...nice. You'll see."

Yeah...we'd see.

Two - Gramma's Good Advice

Ben was sitting on the front stoop of the apartment building, a beer in one hand and a cigarette in the other, when we came around from the parking lot. "Hey, boys," he said, "Did your mom tell you? I live with you now."

"Yeah...we heard," I said, brushing past him and into the apartment.

I heard him pop the tab off another beer can and he said, "So whatcha think of the car, guys? Got a really great deal on that thing," and Gary said, "It's neat, but Richard thinks it's a hunk of junk."

Thanks a lot, big brother.

I got a short glass of milk from the kitchen, careful not to fill it more than half-way because Mom was strict about the milk rationing, and I went down the hall to Gramma's room, where she lay on her bed, watching a soap opera on television.

Gramma had lived with us for as long as I could remember, ever since I was a baby. She had always been closer to my mom than she was my aunts, and both of *them* had husbands, so she lived with us. She helped mom take care of us and pay the bills and, when she could, she stood between my mother's temper and me. When she couldn't do *that*, she gave her love to me like a salve after the yelling or the spanking was over.

She was hugely fat and very unhealthy and she looked much older than her 56 years. She took insulin shots and a handful of different pills every day and she was sometimes in the hospital for days or weeks at a time.

Gramma's room always smelled of rubbing alcohol and the old-lady-perfume she liked to wear, but it was a refuge for me. Some mornings we would lounge in her bed and share a grapefruit with sugar, taking turns with a tiny spoon, scooping wedges of sour fruit from the rind, and most nights I would sit behind her in my pajamas and massage her back and shoulders with the alcohol that "soothed her aches."

Sometimes at night, when I left her big bed for my own small one, Gramma would say something to me that I thought was strange, spooky, and a little bit mean. In a quiet voice, she would say, "Richie, if you come in the morning and I don't wake up...I'm dead. But it'll be okay because all I want from the Lord is to let me die in my sleep."

I took her whispered warning to heart and often, especially in the early morning, I'd approach her bedroom door with caution, peeking in through just a crack to see if she was dead or awake, but this was late afternoon and I could hear The Young & The Restless on her television so I barged right in, interrupting Gramma while she was scolding some sad actress on the TV screen.

"Hi, Gramma."

Her eyes lit up, but they didn't leave the television. Gramma didn't stray from her stories during the juicy parts.

"Richie, Richie. Come up here on the bed and give your grandma a kiss." She patted the bedspread with her soft, splotchy hand. "Careful now and don't spill your milk."

She was a big woman and she nearly filled the huge bed herself, but she moved over on the mattress and made a space for me and I climbed up and lay next to her, leaning against her soft shoulder so I didn't slip off the edge of the bed.

"Well, school's out and you've got all summer to ride your bike and play with your friends. *And no* homework. I know you love *that*."

"I guess, Gramma."

She took the glass of milk from my hand and set it on the night table, then took my chin in her hand and looked in my face. "What's wrong, Richie?"

I shrugged. "I just said something true about the car and Mom got mad. That's all."

Gramma hugged me and said in a hushed, conspiratorial whisper, "That old car's seen better days, hasn't it, Richie?" and I whispered back, "It's a real piece of junk."

She patted my back and said, "Yes, it sure is, but it's the best your mom could get and it makes her happy, so don't you go saying anything about that old car to her that isn't nice. Okay, Richie?"

"Ok. I won't."

Gramma handed me the glass of milk. "Drink your milk and go on now and let me finish my stories."

I climbed down off the bed and before I left the room I said, "Gramma, why does Ben have to live with us?"

She looked at me and smiled the crinkly smile that I loved so much. "Well, Richie," she said, "Do you remember what I just told you about the car? That it's seen better days, but it's the best your mom can do and it makes her happy?"

I remembered. "Yeah, Gramma."

"Well, that man is kind of like that old car."

She giggled at her own joke and I smiled, too, but the look she gave me was wise and I knew that Gramma always gave her best advice when she was being funny.

In my room, I stretched out on my bed, wishing that Mom hadn't let Ben move into our apartment, remembering the first time I met him, back in April. I had disliked him instantly and felt a little bit bad about that, him being Bobby's uncle and only in town for a visit, but I thought he looked like a loudmouthed bully and the first chance he got, he proved me right.

He had only been around for a few days, but he made fast friends with my mom and that day, I was just home from school and me, Jesse and Bobby were riding our bikes up and down the sidewalk, bunny hopping off the curb and racing up the block. A man in blue jeans and a wrinkled white t-shirt came down the sidewalk with a beer can in his hand and a cigarette jammed in his lips. He had slick blonde hair combed up in a big wave and a faded rose tattoo on his arm, and he had his own kind of walk that was three parts shuffle and one part stumble.

Bobby skidded his bike on the sidewalk. "Here comes my Uncle Ben."

"*That's* your uncle?" I stopped my bike next to Bobby's and leaned across the handlebars.

"Sheeshomighty!" Jesse said, "He looks half-way drunk."

"Prob'ly more than half by now," Bobby said, "Heck, it's almost 4 o'clock." He stood on his pedals and pumped off the curb with a bounce and I followed him out on to the street, Jesse's shadow racing up beside mine. I heard my mother's voice, calling from the open apartment door.

"Well, hey, handsome! 'Bout time you dragged your ass down the block to see me."

Bobby's greasy uncle Ben said something to my mom that made me forget that I knew how to ride a bike.

"Shit fire and save a match, but ain't you foxy!"

He *called* my mother *foxy*!

I whipped my head around to see if my eyes could believe my ears, saw my mother and Ben meeting on the sidewalk in a soft embrace and calamity struck. My feet slipped off the pedals, one hand came off the handlebars and I lost control of my Huffy.

"Look out, Richie!" Jesse shouted.

I crashed into the back end of a parked Oldsmobile, slid forward off the seat of my bike, smashed my nards on the crossbar and tumbled butt over bicycle to the ground. My head smacked hard against the blacktop and I burst into wailing tears.

Bobby was sitting on his bike, his mouth wide open and his eyes staring down at me and I could hear he had started to laugh, but stopped himself. Jesse was leaning over me with his hand stretched down for mine and I took it, found my feet and rushed headlong for my mom, but I had been crying and my eyes were blurred. I tripped over the curb and fell again, this time into soft grass, at least, but the insult on top of my injury only started me crying again when I had almost stopped.

My mom turned and leaned toward me as I got up off the ground, stretched her open palms out toward me and pinched her mouth into a concerned little button.

Bobby's uncle turned toward me, too, but his mouth was a wide, dopey grin and he almost fell down himself flailing his arm around to point a finger down at me.

"Well, see, now...this is what happens when a little girl tries to ride a big boy's bike" His dopey grin burst open for a dopey laugh. My mother's concerned-button-mouth stretched into just the thinnest thread of a smile and I stood staring up at them both, tears running down my face, snot running out my nose.

Mom said, "Richie...you're alright. Go get your bike."

"Oh, he's fine!' Bobby's uncle said. He looked down at me and shrugged. "Oh, go on and quit your bawling, kid. We can get you a set of training wheels for that bike, you know. Hell, we can get you a sissy bar, too, if you're gonna cry like one."

I wiped my hands across my wet, dirty cheeks, stopped the last of my tears and stared up into Ben's scruffy, saggy face. He stared back at me and his eyes were milky and stupid, but they were mean, and I was afraid. "Jeez, kid, it's just a joke. You ain't gonna cry again now, are you?"

"No."

I looked hard into his eyes for another moment before he broke my gaze and I silently swore my most solemn swear, the most sacred vow I'd ever made to myself; no matter what, for as long as this big, stupid man was around, I would never cry in front of him again.

He tilted the beer can to his mouth, swallowed loud and said, "Go on then and get your bike like your momma told you."

My mother's eyes widened for a second and her eyebrows arched, but she didn't say *anything*.

I left my bike in the street and I stormed up the sidewalk and into the apartment, but I heard them all before I slammed the door.

"I'll get your bike, Richie!" Jesse hollered and my mom said, "He just needs a minute or two."

"He don't need a minute," Bobby's uncle grumbled, "A boy just needs a *man* around...to toughen him up a little."

That was how I knew, seven weeks before my mom asked him to move into our apartment that Bobby's mean, chain-smoking uncle was going to wreck my summer, maybe even my life.

Three - Spilled Milk

Over the next several days, summer unfolded, not with the triumphant flourish I had come to expect, but slowly, cautiously. I slept late in the mornings, sometimes until eight or nine, and some days, if I woke up and heard Ben's voice down the hall in the kitchen or through the screen-door from out on the stoop, I stayed in my bed even longer.

When I did get up and at it, I didn't linger around the house too long, except on Saturday mornings when my favorite cartoons kept me in pajamas and Cheerios until nearly noon. Most days, though, I shared a late grapefruit with Gramma in her room or raced through a bowl of cereal in the kitchen, staring at the back of the cereal box while Ben sat across from me, sucking coffee and blowing smoke. After breakfast, I was out the door and down the block or over the fence and, except to check in once in a while as Mom required or to grab a quick boloney or peanut butter sandwich for lunch, I didn't come home until the late evening sun descended.

One morning I woke up to the sounds of my brothers whooping and talking excitedly. Mom and Ben were talking with them and I could tell by my mother's voice that she was smiling and even Gramma was in on the conversation. These were not the sounds of a typical morning in our apartment. Something was happening and instead of lingering in the bedroom, I pulled on a t-shirt and socks and went into the kitchen to find out why everyone was so happy.

"What's going on?"

They all stopped talking and looked at me, and Gary and Tommy said, in unison, "We're going to Wildwood!"

"We *are*?"

"For three whole days," Mom said and she put her arms around Ben, lay her cheek against the back of his shoulder and hugged him from behind.

"Today?" I asked, excited, thinking ahead to the beach and the boardwalk, the cotton candy and taffy. "We're going *today*?"

Ben took a noisy slurp of coffee from his mug and said "Richie, if we were going today, your lazy ass would've been left behind."

I hung my head, but Gramma looked at him and said, "No, he would *not* have been left behind."

Ben mumbled something about "sleeping until almost ten" and my mom unwrapped herself from his shoulders to refill his mug and empty his ashtray. I had a brief, flashing memory of her when she used to work, leaving the apartment late at night in her waitress uniform to work the graveyard shift, pouring coffee and dumping ashtrays for the all-night counter-clowns that hung around the diner.

"We're not going 'til *August*, Richie," she sighed. "Not 'til August. We've gotta save up some money for the trip and get new tires on the car. It's something to look forward to."

August. Two months away. Plenty of time for something to go wrong.

"Do you promise, Mom?"

I was thinking back two summers, to a promised trip to Florida that never came because Mom had used the money she had saved up for our vacation to bail her boyfriend out of the county jail.

"We're *going*, Richie!" she scolded, "I said we're going and that's enough! I don't have to promise."

I retreated from her glare.

"Okay, sorry. I was only asking." I got a bowl from one cupboard and a box of corn flakes from another, filled the bowl and went to the fridge for the milk. "How come you didn't wait 'til I woke up to tell us?"

Ben snorted and said, "Wait for you to drag your butt out of bed? You wanna know what's going on and not miss out on things, start acting like a part of this family."

"*You're* not my family," I said and Mom spun around from the counter where she was making coffee and smacked me across the face with her open hand. A good, solid smack that set the side of my face on fire. I dropped the open carton and a puddle of milk pooled on the floor around my feet.

"Ah, Madonna mia! Goddammit, Richie!"

Oh, no!

She smacked two more times, once on the back of my head and again on my shoulder when I ducked away.

"I'm sorry! I'll clean it! I'll clean it up."

She stood over me, towered over me, and her voice was quiet, but there was possible thunder behind the clouds in her eyes.

"You'll clean it up? Are you gonna put it back in the carton and save me the money I'll have to spend now to buy more milk? Are you?"

"No. I'm sorry. You hit me and I dropped it."

"Because you have a smart mouth!" She grabbed a dishtowel from the countertop and knelt down to mop up the milk. "Go to your room, Richie. You're grounded for the day. Now apologize to Ben and go to your room."

I stared at her.

Apologize? For what? I wouldn't.

My brothers sat silently and ate their cereal with exaggerated crunching. Ben leaned against the wall with his coffee and his cigarette, staring down at me and Mom glared hard at me while she sopped up the last of the spilled milk.

Gramma said "Frances..."

"He'll apologize, Ma." That shut Gramma up.

I looked up at Ben and my eyes brimmed with angry tears but I kept my vow and willed them not to spill over. I would not cry in front of this man. Not ever.

"I'm *sorry*." Words that should have been spit.

"Go to your damned room," Ben told me. "Do like your mother told you to."

I went, and I slammed the door behind me.

Four - A Black Leather Snake

June crawled on toward July and we kids filled those long days with as much fun as we could get away with. All day long, our block was a rowdy circus of kids, small dogs, bicycles and balls. The girls drew hopscotch patterns on the sidewalks and the boys stole their chalk and wrote dirty words or drew silly pictures on the curbs and walls. We competed to see who could shinny the farthest up the streetlamp poles and we ran through the lawn sprinklers in our swimsuits, or even in our underwear, while our moms and the men sat in lawn chairs or on the small stoops, drinking beer, smoking cigarettes and laughing or cursing amongst themselves when they weren't hollering at the kids.

We lived in a rent-controlled apartment complex of four-unit buildings, spread out over the six noisy blocks that were our neighborhood. The apartment buildings faced each other in pairs across small concrete courtyards, every other building a different shade of pastel blue, yellow or pink.

In our building, my family and Jesse's had two of the apartments and the other two may as well have been empty, as far as we were concerned. Ol' Lady Hartel lived alone in the downstairs apartment next to ours and we hardly ever saw her. All I knew about Ol' Lady Hartel was that she was about a hundred years old, kept a pet parakeet in a cage and watched her television with the volume turned up very, very loud.

Upstairs, the unit next to Jesse's apartment belonged to a couple of college guys named Donald and Youngblood. Mom called them hippies, but they didn't have long hair, and they were gone all day at school, then gone all evening at work, so I never saw very much of them, either. Sometimes late at night, I could hear rock and roll music and smell sweet, tangy smoke drifting down from their open windows.

The Hodges brothers lived in the building across the courtyard and the rest of our gang were scattered up and down the block.

The neighborhood was our own small world, bordered by a tacky strip mall on one end and Grand Avenue, four-lanes wide and busy, on the other. Railroad tracks ran along the back of the neighborhood and on the other side of those two sets of twin silver rails there was an open dirt field where we rode our bikes and had rock fights. Our favorite place, though, was the small stand of woods where we spent most of our time, playing cowboys among the trees or chasing frogs in the pond.

When the streets of the neighborhood could no longer contain the wild children we became in summer, we spilled over the fences and into the woods or across the tracks. We built forts in the woods and slid on scrapped pieces of cardboard down the dirt embankment of the overpass, threw rocks at passing trains and played war in the soggy, swampy patch of bushes around the pond.

If we had a little money, from collecting returnable pop bottles or aluminum cans, we would listen for the ice cream truck and if we really wanted to get in trouble, we harassed the shop owners at the strip mall.

Summer was bigger than the neighborhood and, though our township was small, back then, it seemed like the whole world and when our sense of adventure and exploration outgrew the apartment complexes and the fields, we had outlying destinations around town, and we had our bicycles.

There was a big park across the river with a big sports field, a playground and a community center where kids could play board games in the afternoon. Closer to home, on our side of the river, there was the baseball park where we played pickup games when the Little League teams weren't using the diamonds.

The county library across town had become too long a ride for most of my friends once the Bookmobile, a big converted bus with shelves of books instead of benches and "County Library" painted on its sides, started making stops in the neighborhood, but I still took that ride often because the library had a better selection of books.

Several miles beyond the library, there was Kiddie World, the only toy store in the entire township. It was a very long bike ride to the toy store but at least a few times every summer Tommy and I, and sometimes a friend or two, would pedal the hour or so in the summer heat, brave the traffic crossing Main Street and spend a few hours just wandering the aisles of Kiddie World.

We couldn't buy any of the toys in the store, but we could look at them (*wow, check that out*) and we could dream (*wish I had one of these*). We could look ahead and plan our meager Christmas wishes and we could make a mental note of something we might ask for on our birthdays, but most importantly of all we could lie in our beds late at night and whisper for hours about the amazing toys we had seen and would someday afford. We would talk about toys until we fell asleep and dream of them until we woke.

One late afternoon in the third week of June, Tommy and I were riding home from an expedition to the toy store, pedaling our bikes through a neighborhood of neat houses where all the trashcans had been lined up along the curbside, waiting for the garbage men to come around and empty them the following morning. Now, my little brother Tommy was a notorious trash-picker and he couldn't resist the temptation of a full garbage can. More than once he had needed rescuing from a dumpster after its big steel lid had slammed shut with him inside, prowling through the rubbish in the dark.

Tommy had a good eye for the slight distinction that separated treasure from trash, and when he skidded his bike to a stop in front of a big, overflowing can, I knew he had spotted something.

I stopped my bike and looked back at Tommy. He was tugging furiously at something in the depths of the trashcan and he held it triumphantly above his head once he got it free.

"Wow!" he cried. "Look what I found!" Even at a distance, I could see his excited smile.

"What is it?" I called back to him.

He held up a long black strip that glistened like a snake in the glaring afternoon sun. It was a thick, wide leather belt with a big buckle and shiny snaps.

"It's a real police belt!" Tommy exclaimed.

It's dangerous.

"Tommy, you can't take that home."

He looked at me defiantly as he buckled the belt into a loop and hung it over his shoulder. "You can't tell me what to do, Richie. I found it. It's a police belt. I think it is, anyway."

He got back on his bike and started pedaling again and when he was half a block ahead of me, I started pedaling my own bike to catch up with him. If he got too far ahead and got home before me, without me, I would catch hell from Mom.

We got home and dropped our bikes in the yard. Mom and Ben were sitting on the stoop. Ben was drunk and Mom was reading one of her Harlequin romance books. I wondered if any of the men in those books sat on the porch and drank beer all day and didn't bother to shave their scruff for weeks at a time.

Tommy hopped up on the porch and showed off his trashcan belt, which Mom promptly took away from him. Tommy sniveled a little and looked at me and I knew that he could read my mind because I was reading his.

I told you so.

Later that evening, Ben used his pocketknife to cut the belt into three straps, each one longer than the other was, and he hung them from nails on the kitchen wall.

Five - The Bicycle Witch

By late June, the Little League baseball season was over, but Gary made the All-Stars team that summer so he had a few more weeks of playing ball and showing off his fancy team uniform. Tommy and I didn't play on any Little League teams. Mom always told me that she couldn't afford it or that I wasn't *really* interested in baseball, but I remember there was always enough money for Gary to join a team and that I might have been more interested in baseball, and better at hitting one, if I'd been allowed to play.

One year, when we were at the community center signing Gary up to play, I bugged Mom about letting me try out for a team, too.

"Oh, Richie," she'd sighed, "You know you won't be able to catch the ball good enough with your bad hand. Don'tcha know that, hon?"

My *bad* hand was my left one. I had been born with deformities to *both* of my hands, but the left was the worst of a mismatched pair, smaller than my right one and lacking a thumb. Mom usually didn't mention it unless she was using it as an excuse for why I shouldn't, couldn't or wouldn't be able to do something. When she did *that*, she always called it my bad hand.

"But, Mom. I play baseball all the time with the gang. I don't drop the ball that much."

She looked at me and shook her head and her eyes chased my argument away. "That's different, Richie. The boys on the Little League teams hit the ball a lot harder than your friends do."

After that, I never asked my mother again about playing baseball, or about joining Cub Scouts or the swim club or any of the other fun things that Gary got to do. I never got a fancy baseball uniform with tall striped socks and a cool cap that I could wear around town and I never slid into home plate, except in my imagination, but I spent a lot of afternoons and evenings at the baseball park because Mom loved to watch Gary play and she'd take me and Tommy along to root for him, too.

I'd cheer when my brother got a hit and holler "good eye, good eye" when he didn't swing at a bad pitch, but I'd get bored with the game and the chattering parents in the bleachers and wander off with the other kids who didn't play ball.

We had a game of our own, chasing foul balls that the players smacked over the fence and into the parking lot. You could turn in a foul ball at the concessions stand and the ladies working the hot dog steamer and the candy counter would give you a free cup of soda as a reward.

So many balls were fouled into the parking lot that most of the parents parked their cars across the street at the church to avoid dented fenders, banged up hoods and smashed windshields. We kids would spread out in the dusty gravel lot behind the bleachers and race after the balls when one came fouling over the backstop, but there were always bigger, slouchy boys hanging around who would bully us smaller kids and take all the baseballs. They would just about mug a kid for a lousy twenty-five cent Coca-Cola.

One night, Mom drove us all to the baseball park for Gary's All-Stars game and Jesse came along, too. We spent the first few innings in the bleachers, dutifully cheering for Gary and his team, but once our hot dogs and potato chips were only oily memories on our fingertips, we jumped down from the aluminum benches and ran for the empty parking lot.

"Hey, where you guys goin?" Tommy hollered after us.

"C'mon," I hollered back, "We're gonna go chase foul balls."

"Oh, boy! I'm coming!" Tommy stomped down the bleachers and his sneakers kicked up dust as he ran to catch up with us and I heard my mother shout, "Watch out for cars, boys!"

There were a half dozen or so kids scattered around the parking lot, mostly bigger boys, but we decided to stick together and agreed that if we got any balls to turn in at the snack shack, we'd take turns sipping the soda. We stood around in the lot, listening for the crack of bat against ball, looking up into the bright lights whenever we heard that sound in case a lucky foul came arching our way, and Tommy called out, "Look, guys! There's The Bicycle Witch!"

None of us kids knew her name and I didn't think any of our parents knew it, either. Everyone in town just called her The Bicycle Witch. She didn't live in our neighborhood. She had a tiny house with an overgrown yard and a crooked fence on a quiet street across the river.

The Bicycle Witch could be seen all over town, though, riding an old, creaky blue Schwinn, her long white hair flowing out behind her from under a big hat, and she must have *loved* baseball because she was at the Little League park almost every time there was a game being played.

None of us kids, except maybe Tommy, would ever admit to being afraid of her and most of us, except maybe Tommy, would deny believing she was an actual, real, live witch, but we all kept our distance from her and we never spoke to her. She didn't talk to anyone very much, either, but she would laugh loud and sudden sometimes, even if nothing seemed funny.

She always wore pants with a long skirt pulled on over them when she rode her bike. She seemed strange and spooky and some of the grown-ups said she was off her rocker, but I was never convinced she knew any spells or magic until that night at the baseball park.

She was pedaling her bike around the parking lot in a big lazy circle while we kids chased foul balls and each other across the loose gravel. She wasn't paying any attention to me and I wasn't paying any to her, but when a big, mean-eyed boy stomped in front of me for the third time, scooping up a ball that should have been mine, The Bicycle Witch stopped her bike on the soft edge of the lot and looked right at me.

"She's looking right at you," Tommy said.

"No, she ain't."

Jesse giggled and ribbed me with his elbow. "Yeah, I'm pretty sure she is," he whispered. "She's pretty much looking right straight *at* you, Richie."

I told them to knock it off and to quit teasing me, but I snuck a look directly at The Bicycle Witch and her big round eyes *were* peering out from under the brim of her red hat and she *was* sort of smiling at me. Then, she *winked*.

"Did you see that? Did you?" Tommy hollered, "She winked at you, Richie! The Bicycle Witch winked right at you!"

There was a loud crack, like a gunshot. The bleachers erupted in a mass cheer that choked itself off into a group groan as the baseball arched up and up, a bright white dot as it passed through the glow of the big lights, a dark sphere as it fell through the darkness and landed with a thud in the gravel right in front of my feet.

I stared down at the ball, looked up at The Bicycle Witch, then back down at the ball again.

A couple of the bigger boys started toward me, greedy grins on their faces, but I stooped down, scooped up the baseball, and ran off toward the snack shack with my little brother and my best friend laughing along behind me. We handed the ball over to the snack bar ladies (*One free Coke, please*) and the three of us stood in the shadows under the concessions stand's awning and passed around the small paper cup, sharing sips of the soda just as we had promised to do.

"Oh, my gosh, Richie!" Tommy said, his eyes wide with wonder, "The Bicycle Witch did that. She gave you that foul ball."

I shrugged my shoulders. "Don't be a dummy," I said, "She ain't a real witch. That was just coincidence."

I wasn't sure whether I was trying to convince Tommy, or myself, that The Bicycle Witch was just a weird old lady and not a witch, wicked or otherwise.

Jesse shook his head. "No, man...that was *magic*."

"What's *that*?" Tommy said, "Richie, what's a *coincident*?"

"It's when things happen at the same time just cause they happen, but it looks like there's a bigger reason for it," I said, "Something like that anyway."

"Oh, I get it," Tommy said, "It's when a witch gives you a baseball."

I swallowed the last sip of soda, crunched crushed ice between my teeth and looked across the parking lot at The Bicycle Witch. She was riding her bike in circles again and when she looped around and passed close by us, she looked at me for only the briefest moment, rang the bell on her bicycle's handlebars and let out a loud burst of delighted, kooky laughter.

Six - A Clean Bill of Sale

A few nights later, after dinner, while we were watching television in the living room, there was a pounding on the apartment door, so loud and sudden that it startled all of us. Ben went to the door and when he opened it, a woman I had never seen before started yelling at him and demanding the money he owed her or she wanted the station wagon back. My mother stood beside Ben in the doorway and then they went out on the stoop and closed the door behind them. They were shouting at each other, all three of them arguing loud enough that we could hear them through the closed door.

From what I could tell, eavesdropping from the sofa, the woman's name was Goddammit Linda and she had sold the Country Squire to my mom and Ben. She was mad because Ben still owed her a hundred dollars on the car and he hadn't paid her yet, or even called her on the phone about it.

She said if he didn't pay her the money in three days, she was taking the car and they could see her in small claims court. I heard Ben tell her that he had a clean bill of sale, the pink slip was in my mother's name, and Linda could go straight to hell. He said the car wasn't even worth the two hundred he had already given her and if she tried to take it back, he would get the cops on her.

Mom and Ben came back in the house and they were both red-faced and angry. "You kids go to bed." We turned the TV off and Gary and Tommy went to our room, but I went to Gramma's room to rub the alcohol on her shoulders and say goodnight.

"Gramma," I asked, "Can that lady take the car away if Ben doesn't pay her the rest of the money?"

Gramma sighed and said, "Well, I don't know if she'll be able to take it back but there's bound to be more than a hundred dollars' worth of trouble over that damned rusty old car."

I sighed. "We're not gonna to go to Wildwood this summer," I said, "I know something's gonna go wrong and ruin it."

Gramma kissed my forehead and told me we were going to Wildwood no matter what. "I promise you, Richie. Gramma will make sure we all get to go. It'll be our family vacation"

A few mornings later, Mom went out to go to the Stop & Shop and the car wouldn't start. It whined, coughed, and sputtered but the engine wouldn't turn over. Later that afternoon our neighbor, John, who everybody called a shade-tree mechanic because he kept most of the old cars in the neighborhood running, came by to look at the Country Squire. He told Ben someone had poured sugar in the gas tank and it had clogged up the entire fuel system.

John said the car would have to go to a shop because he had three other cars he was busy working on and he didn't have the time to clean out the station wagons filters and fuel lines. Ben cussed a blue streak and Mom said she knew it was Linda who put the sugar in the tank.

Later that morning, a tow truck came and hauled the old car down to the garage for repairs.

Mom went and picked up the car three days later and the repair bill was more than two-hundred dollars.

Seven - The Gumball Bandits

As June burned down to its last few days, Jesse and I made a fortunate discovery while we were playing in the fields across the railroad tracks late one humid morning. We spied something shiny, half buried in the dirt, gleaming in the bright sunlight and Jesse got down on his knees, dug it out of the ground. It was a cheap costume necklace, a long band of thin, plated copper bedazzled with hundreds of fake tin dimes.

"No wonder someone threw that thing away," I said. "That is one ugly necklace, pardner."

Jesse looked up at me and said, "No, man. I bet we can use these fake dimes in the machines."

I didn't think so. "They're not heavy like real coins, Jess. They won't work."

"Just c'mon with me," Jesse said. "Let's just go try a few."

We climbed the fence into the apartment complex and Jesse washed all the dirt off the necklace at one of the outside faucets. He yanked a handful of the fake coins off the chain and shoved the necklace down in the pocket of his jeans.

We ran through the apartment complex, around the corner to the strip mall and into Mr. Ratto's corner market. Just inside the door, there was a row of machines that dispensed cheap toys, fake tattoos, candy and gumballs. Jesse knelt on one knee in front of the machines, stuck one of the fake dimes into the coin slot and gave the handle a turn.

He grinned devilishly as the mechanism turned and we heard several gumballs drop into the dispenser, and his grin grew wider and even more devilish when the fake dime got jammed in the coin slot and he realized he could just keep turning the handle and getting more gum.

We got about thirty gumballs out of the machine before the coin jammed up the mechanism completely. He moved on to the rest of the gumball machines, turning each knob until it jammed and we fled the store, our pockets bulging with gumballs and sweet tarts.

All that week, Jesse and I went around town in the mornings, jamming our fake dimes into gumball machines and being run off by angry shopkeepers, our pockets full of sugary bounty. By the end of the week, we each had a substantial stash of candies hidden under our beds and we decided it was probably best if we didn't show our faces around any of those stores and gas stations for a few weeks.

One evening, my mother came out of my room with a shoebox in her hand and my heart sank. She had found my secret, sugary stash. She stood in the center of the living room, right in front of the television, pulled the clear plastic bag that held my gumball heist stash from the box and held it out in front of me. She shook it hard.

Busted.

"Richie, where did you get all of this candy?"

"From the stores," I told her, "Out of the machines. Me and Jesse got it."

"But how did you *pay* for it?" Her voice was a rising warning. "Dammit, Richie, did you steal this candy?"

"No, Mom. Not really. We used fake dimes. They got stuck in the machines and..."

She reached her hand into the bag, filled her fist with gumballs and candies and hurled them at me. They hit me in the face and the chest, bounced, and rolled all over the couch and the floor. A few strays hit Tommy who was sitting next to me on the couch and he scrambled away, out of the line of fire.

"You stole them!" she shouted, "That's stealing! Get your ass in your room!"

I moved fast but she moved fast, too, and before I could get down the hall and into my room, she was behind me with a length of Tommy's salvaged police belt in her hand, smacking me hard across the back of my legs as I ran. I leaped onto my bed and pulled the blanket up over my legs for protection, but that only made Mom madder and she smacked harder with the belt, making sure I would feel it through my thin woolen shield.

I was screaming and I could hear Gramma shouting from her room. "Frances! Frances, that's enough now!"

My mother swung the belt a few more times, her face red and her mouth snarled, and then turned and stalked out of the room, calling me a thief as she slammed the door shut behind her.

I cried myself to sleep and when I woke up, it was dark and my brothers were asleep in their beds. My legs stung, as if they had been sunburned. I went into the bathroom, ran cold water over a washrag, and soothed the red marks on the backs of my thighs and then I went to Gramma's room and climbed into bed next to her and fell asleep with tears on my cheeks as she snored.

Mom grounded me again, this time for three days. I stayed in my room and read comics, drew pictures and played with my toys. On the third day of my groundation, the very last day of June, Mom came into my room and told me if she ever caught me stealing again, I would *really* get a beating.

Light - Pancake Dine and Dash

Later that night, close to midnight, after we had watched a mystery movie on television, Mom said, "Let's go for pancakes."

It was something she did every once in a while; she'd just announce all of a sudden, almost always late at night, that we were going out for pancakes and we'd all get dressed and get in the car and she'd drive us to some diner or pancake house. We always got pancakes and chocolate milks and we never went to the same diner twice in a row.

On all of those midnight pancake outings, when we finished our milk and flapjacks, mom would send us boys and Gramma out to the car, one by one. A few minutes later, she would come out, get in the car and drive out of the lot in a hurry.

That night, though, we sat in the car and waited and after ten minutes or so, Mom still hadn't come out and Gramma seemed worried. A police car pulled into the parking lot and a couple of cops climbed out and went inside through the smoky glass doors.

When Mom came out, she was walking with the policemen and they stood beside the car with her for a few minutes. One of them shined his flashlight in the backseat of the car and Tommy waved at him. Mom was crying and I could hear her telling the cops how hard it was trying to feed three boys, and one of the cops told her to ask for help before stealing and the other one handed her some money from his billfold.

She got in the car and Gramma said, "Fran, what happened? Are you in trouble?"

I saw my mother's grin in the rearview mirror and she told Gramma that she hadn't gotten in any trouble at all.

"I just cried a little and told them the boys were hungry and they paid the check *and* one of them gave me twenty dollars."

Gramma sighed and Mom pulled the car out of the lot and when we got home, I lay in bed, the welts on the backs of my legs still stinging, and I thought about the value of gumballs and the consequences of pancakes and chocolate milk, but I couldn't fall asleep.

I snuck out the door, the way I always did when I felt restless at night and everyone else was asleep. I tiptoed around to the back of the apartment building and sat on the ground beneath the small tree that Jesse and I called ours.

We had been climbing and falling out of that tree since we were just little kids and just last year,

Jesse had broken an arm tumbling out of its branches to the sidewalk below.

I cried a little in the dark and watched the beetles we called June Bugs scurry around on the sidewalk and fly away into the streetlamp's glow, where they swarmed in black, buzzing clouds. Something moved in the shadows and I saw a mangy Siamese cat with only three legs come limping around the corner of the building. It was fat and its swollen belly swayed as it padded lightly along the edge of the building's concrete foundation.

It's gonna have kittens!

The cat noticed me and stopped in its tracks for a moment, then disappeared, slinking through an unscreened opening into the crawl space beneath our apartment building.

Mom hated cats. If she knew one was living underneath her floor, carrying a litter of kittens, she'd have Ben or the landlord, Mr. Dollasso flush it out for sure, but I'd already decided that I was gonna feed her until she had her kittens. I went back into the apartment, locked the door behind me and climbed back into my bed. Before I fell asleep, I decided I wouldn't tell anyone, except Jesse, about the stray momma cat.

Part Two
July on Fire

One - Just Like Lobster

July broke hot and humid over the neighborhood; we abandoned shoes and shirts for bare feet and sunburns, and excitement and anticipation spread up and down the block as everyone, kids and grown-ups alike, prepared for the biggest Independence Day celebration in the history of America.

In our neighborhood, the Fourth of July was always a big deal, not because we were any more patriotic than any other neighborhood, but because it was, like Halloween, one of the *cheap* holidays. There were no gifts to buy, no expensive turkeys or hams required and it fell soon enough after the first of the month that most of the moms still had a little money and food stamps left over to splurge on ice cream and soda pop.

Those first three days of July, all of the talk on the block was about the big Fourth of July cookout party. Whatever else we kids were doing, whether we were riding our bikes, running through the lawn sprinklers or playing baseball, we chattered about the party. We exaggerated about how we would stuff ourselves on hot dogs, drown ourselves in root beer and blind ourselves with sparklers.

Our mothers, over coffee in the morning or laundry in the afternoon, conspired about the food – Maria's frying chicken, Frances and Janine will grill the dogs, who's cooking burgers and will there be enough potato salad? Well, any one of us kids could have told them that on the Fourth of July, there could never be enough potato salad.

The men brought out the barbecues from the sheds in the parking lot and bragged about burgers and sauces, and some of them put an end to the hamburger arguments by proclaiming that burgers were for the brats and *they* would be grilling thick steaks or chops for themselves.

The Fourth was a big day any year, but in the summer of '76, it was a bigger deal than ever because it would be the good ol' USA's 200th birthday and, really, what could possibly be more patriotic than throwing a huge Fourth of July block party on the back of a government check?

On the morning of the Fourth, I rushed through a bowl of cereal and dressed in yesterday's cut-off jeans and rubber flip-flops. I dug around my room and found my Army surplus canteen under my bed. I was filling it at the kitchen sink and mom asked where I was going so early.

"Meeting Jesse down at the bog, Mom. It's the Fourth of July. We gotta get the crawdads."

Mom sipped her coffee and smiled. "Oh, yeah, I forgot all about that." I liked it when my mother joked with me and I knew she was pretending to have forgotten about the crawdads and I smiled back at her.

My mom loved crawfish and every Fourth of July, Jesse and I would take a bucket and a few slices of bologna and catch a haul of crawdads from the creek that fed Blackberry Bog. We would bring them home in the afternoon, and in the early evening, as the cookout was getting underway, Mom would put a big pot of water on the stove to boil and, one by one, she would drop the crawfish to their bubbly, boiling deaths.

Later, when we all gathered in the yard for our feast of burgers and weenies, potato salad and baked beans, she would bring the crawfish out in a big bowl. We would eat them dipped in melted margarine and mom would say, "God, that's good. *Just* like lobster."

"Ah, Mom, you didn't forget."

"Who says I didn't forget?"

"I say," I teased her back, leaning to look into the fridge. "Besides, you bought extra boloney."

"But only take four slices, Richie. We still need lunches, ya know." As I headed out the door, my full canteen sloshing against my hip and four slices of boloney in a plastic bag stuffed in my pocket, she called, "Bring home lots, Richie!"

I ran down the sidewalk, my rubber sandals calling their name (flip-flop! flip-flop! flip-flop!), crossed Jefferson Street against the light and climbed the wooden fence that separated the apartment complexes from the small stand of woods that bordered the highway. I struggled getting over the fence in my sandals and wished I had thought to wear my sneakers, but when I came tumbling down into the dust on the other side, I saw a quarter gleaming in the sun, tucked it in my pocket and called it a lucky day.

I followed the familiar path through the bushes, swatting at clouds of tiny black bugs as I went, and spied Jesse sitting on a mossy log on the far side of Blackberry Bog, his chin in his hands.

"Hey, Jesse!" I called out to him and he looked up at me as I took off my flip-flops and hung them on a low-hanging branch, but he didn't wave and he didn't call out. My bare feet sank and slipped in slimy mud as I made my way around the edge of the pond and sat down beside Jesse.

"Hey, buddy, I got the boloney and the canteen." He didn't say anything and I knew he had been crying because his eyes were pink and swollen and he wouldn't really look at me. "You bring the bucket?" I asked him, even though I could see the red plastic bucket sitting in the mud at his feet, because I didn't know what else to say and Jesse liked to talk about his hurts in his own time.

I knew better than to poke at it so we sat together quietly, the sounds of the pond and the stream and, further off, the highway, protecting us from silence, and then he put his hand on my shoulder and looked into my face. I didn't know what he was going to say, but I could see an apology in his eyes that meant he had hard news.

"I'm movin' away, Richie." *What?* "To a whole 'nother state." *What did he say?* "All the way to goshdanged Ohio."

"Ohio?"

I stared back at him. I could feel tears welling up in my eyes and we sat with our arms locked around each other's shoulders and bawled like babies.

We had cried together before, Jesse and I, or sat and held the other while one of us cried alone. We'd been best friends since we were little kids and there had been falls out of trees and rock fights lost and punishments harsh enough to make us dream of running away from home together, so, yeah, we'd cried together a time or two, but never the way we sobbed that day on the muddy bank of the pond. Nothing in our friendship had ever hurt like this. Even a beloved hamster's death didn't carry the finality of your best friend moving away to goshdanged Ohio.

After a few minutes, we had cried ourselves out and Jesse blew his nose into his t-shirt then took it off and passed it to me because I wasn't wearing one and I blew into it, too. We laughed and Jesse tossed the shirt into the pond.

"One less thing to pack," he said and sighed.

"When are you going, Jesse?" I asked him quietly, "And why do you even gotta move all the way to Ohio?"

He picked up a handful of muddy pebbles from the ground and tossed a few into the pond and then, as if that had been too much effort, he started dropping them one at a time between his knees, into the plastic bucket.

Plunk... plunk... plunk ...

"In August." He wiped his nose with the back of his hand. "Before school starts. My mom says it's 'cause she can get a job there, working with my aunt Lynne in a factory, and we can have a house and maybe even a dog, but really it's 'cause she hates my dad. She just wants to be far, far away from my dad."

I sighed. "It's *too* far, though, Jesse."

"You're my best friend, Richie," Jesse sobbed, "You're like my own brother and I'm never gonna see you again."

I tried to cheer him up, but in my heart, I felt afraid that he might have been right.

"Yeah, you will. You'll see me again, Jess. Your mom's gonna have to let you come back sometimes to visit your dad."

His tears stopped and he caught his breath.

"Yeah, sure, but he lives all the way across the county and it'll be like when I go to his house now. I won't see you, Richie."

I hugged my best friend and told him that he *would* see me again someday, no matter what, because Ohio is far, far away when you're a kid, but when you grow up you can go anywhere you want and someday I would ride all the way to Ohio on a big motorcycle and pull right up to his house.

Jesse smiled at that and said, "I'll have a motorcycle, too, and we'll ride off together."

"Yeah. Just like the Lone Ranger and Tonto," I said. "No... like Butch and Sundance."

"Yeah, like Butch and Sundance." He agreed. "But, Richie...what are we gonna do until then?"

I shrugged my shoulders. "I dunno, but if this is our last summer together, we're gonna *rule* this neighborhood!"

"Well, okay!" He slapped me hard across the back and jumped to his feet. "Let's go catch us some crawdaddies!"

I picked up the bucket and fell in step behind him. "Just like lobster..." I said and giggled.

"Sheesh... your mom."

We waded up the shallow stream and when we could see crawdads out in the open, we would reach down and catch them with our hands. They moved fast in reverse, scooting backward along the creek bed, but if you poked behind them with a stick and got them crawling forward, they were slow. You could reach down and grab them around the tail, careful not to get your fingers near the claws, which looked a lot more dangerous when I was ten years old than I know them to be now.

We caught them where we couldn't see them, too, with boloney tied to the end of a stick and pushed down below big rocks and under the edges of the bank. Those crawdads sure must have thought more of boloney than I did because they'd latch onto the end of that stick and we'd yank them up out of the water and into our bucket.

While we hunted crawfish, we talked about past adventures and the cookout party we would have that night and the fireworks Ben and John had brought home from a trip to Philadelphia the week before and we completely avoided the subject of Jesse moving to Ohio. August came fast every summer and this year it would be here soon enough, and we would have to say goodbye, but for now, we had the Fourth of July and the rest of the summer and about thirty crawdads in our bucket.

We had one slice of boloney left over and we split it in half and munched it as we walked back down the stream and around the edge of the pond. I got my sandals from the branch where I had left them, slipped them back on my muddy feet and we walked back up the path where Jesse climbed to the top of the fence so I could hand him up the bucket. He handed it down to me once I'd gone over and we walked through the neighborhood with the bucket sloshing between us, up the sidewalk to our building to show my mother how many crawdads we had brought her.

Ben was sitting on the porch smoking a cigarette and drinking a beer and mom came out and peered into the bucket. "Oh, you boys got a lot, didn't you?"

"Yeah, we got more than twenty." Jesse told her. He slipped his palm into mine, we shook our secret handshake and he said, "I better go wash up. See you at the cookout, Richie."

He stood there for a moment, looking at my face, and then ran up the stairs to his apartment.

"What's wrong with Jesse?" my mom asked, looking down at me over Ben's shoulder, "He down about something?"

I felt my lip begin to tremble

"Mom, Jesse's moving away. To Ohio."

"Awe, Richie..." She reached out and stroked my long summer hair and I knew I was about to cry.

"Well, don't get all emotional about it like you're a couple of little queers," Ben said from the porch. I rushed into the apartment because I knew those were tears I couldn't hold back.

I stopped at the door to Gramma's room, but I could hear her snoring over the sound of her portable television, so I went into my own room and sat on my bed, crying a little.

I finished reading a Justice League comic I had started the night before and tossed it onto the floor. I turned on the little bedside radio and, as I fell asleep to the biggest pop hits of the day, I reminded myself to tell Jesse about the cat living under our apartment building. I would tell him at the barbecue and we could sneak a few hotdogs away to feed her.

Two - Go'bless America

I was awakened from my nap by Tommy coming into the room, shutting the door hard behind him, and I sat up in my bed, disoriented the way you can be when you've slept too long in the middle of the day and into the evening. He tossed his baseball mitt (another of his trashcan treasures) into the closet and sat down hard on his bed. I rubbed my eyes and swung my legs over the edge of the bed. Dried mud caked my feet and streaked the blanket at the foot of my bed. Mom was gonna be mad. I looked across the room at my pouting little brother and, with a little more sarcasm than compassion, asked him, "What's *your* problem?"

"Nothin'."

"No, really, what's wrong?"

He sighed. "Just Gary and his dumb friends. I went to the field to play baseball with 'em but they wouldn't let any of us little kids play, so we started our own game, but then the big kids lost their ball on the highway so Gary took my ball. That's my ball."

"I know," I said, "I was there when you dug it out of the dumpster."

"Well, they took my ball and they still wouldn't let us play. They just made us chase foul balls and bring 'em back." He sighed again. "And not even a free soda!"

I shrugged my shoulders. "You're just lucky they didn't use you for third base."

"Huh?"

"Nothin'. Just tryin' to make a joke." I brushed the dried mud from the blanket the best I could and rubbed it into the carpet so my mom wouldn't see it. I looked at my bed and the blanket was still dirty, streaked with brown and red where my muddy feet had been. "Shit."

"Ooh… you cursed!" Tommy said in a low voice.

"Shut up. I'm gonna get in trouble when Mom sees my blanket."

"Just turn it over, dummy."

Genius.

"You're pretty smart for a trash-picker." I glanced out the bedroom window and saw that the sky was growing dim. "C'mon, help me. It's almost time for the cookout."

We turned the blanket over on the bed and tucked the edges under the mattress and I felt satisfied that Tommy's idea had gotten me out of a smack on the head or a belt on my butt. I told Tommy I would see him outside after I washed my feet and, before I went into the bathroom, I knocked on Gramma's door and pushed it open slightly.

"Gramma? You awake?"

"I'm up, Richie. Come help your gramma out of bed."

I went in and stood beside the bed and she hefted herself out of the blankets and rested her considerable weight on my shoulder until she got one hand and then the other wrapped firmly around the grips of her walker. She was breathing heavily from getting out of bed, but she smiled at me and all the wrinkles around her eyes deepened. "I'm alright, Richie. Let's go have a *time*. But first you go wash those dirty feet."

"I will, Gramma. I'll be right out."

I washed and dried my feet and rinsed out the tub, stopped off in my room to put on socks and my high-top sneakers and stepped out the front door of the apartment into the carnival atmosphere that was our block on the Fourth of July.

The sun was setting low and everything in the world was some shade of blue, except for the glowing coals in the barbecues and the sizzling white glow of the sparklers that the little kids held out in front of them like torches as they ran up and down the lawns. Picnic tables, card tables and even a few dining room tables were set up on the lawns, loaded with plastic forks and paper plates and bowls of potato salad and watermelon and beans.

In some of the yards, flags flapped in the breeze and music, country and rock and soul and oldies, oozed out of open windows and doors and into the street where it blended into the sound of one big song of summer, but it couldn't drown out the siren wails of Piccolo Petes, the bang of firecrackers and the whooshing launches of bottle-rockets. Fountains of colored light erupted all along the block and smoke hung in the evening air, sweet and tangy from the barbecues and stinking of sulfur from the fireworks the men and kids were lighting off on the sidewalk and in the middle of the street.

From the porch, I saw my mom at one of the tables with some of the other moms, playing cards (*Rummy. All they ever play is Rummy*) and drinking cheap wine and beer from paper cups. Gramma was sitting in her recliner (Ben had dragged it out in the yard for her) talking with Ol' Lady Hartel, eating a big dill pickle and smiling and calling out, "Happy 4th! Be careful now! Happy 4th!" to the kids rushing around her with sparklers held ablaze.

My brothers and Jesse and a few of the other guys were setting off fireworks on the curb while John and Ben stood over them drinking beer, and I jumped off the porch and ran down the walk to join them.

Jesse slapped my palm and Tommy smiled up at me from where he was knelt over a smoking, growing snake of black, stinky ash. He had a cluster of sparklers stuck in his shirt pocket and a handful of fireworks lay in the dirt at his feet. Even Gary grinned at me in the glow of the big, rainbow fountain Ben had just set off and John handed me a small sack stuffed with fireworks.

"Here, Richie, light 'em up... but don't blow your thumbs off, kid."

He started to laugh, but I just stood for a moment looking up at him. I was used to the kids teasing me about only having one thumb and I had long-since learned to ignore or even fight over those taunts, but when an adult made a joke about it, when a grown-up that I liked made fun of me, I was always surprised and sad. John's laughter died young and his eyes softened.

"Hey, Richie, I'm sorry, okay? That was a dumb joke to make." He hunkered down in front of me and handed me something he had slipped out of his back pocket. "I'm sorry I said that, Richie. Here, take this."

I looked into the palm of my hand.

"Holy wow!"

He had handed me what looked like a miniature stick of dynamite. This was no ordinary firecracker and it was absolutely something that was bound to earn me a beating, but it looked amazing, scary, and powerful and I tucked it secretively into the pocket of my cut-off Tuffskins jeans and smiled at John. "Jeez, John, what *is* this thing?"

His answer was low and conspiratorial. "Kid… *that* is an M-80. That thing really will blow your fingers off if you're not careful when you light it."

Sheesh…

"And don't you go lighting it off around here tonight," he warned me with a grin, "You hear me? You save it for some time when you're out in the woods with your pals, and if your mom catches you with it, you didn't get it from *me*. Capeesh?

"Yeah," I smiled, 'I capeesh."

"Have fun tonight, Richie. I shouldn't have said that about your thumb."

I smiled and told him I wouldn't hold it against him and I joined my brothers and my friends in the middle of the street.

For a brief, burning time we were a wild band of pyromaniacs setting fire to our own neighborhood, but when all our fireworks were spent, the matches we'd been allowed to have were tucked deep in our pockets and we were normal kids again, sitting at picnic tables or on the grass, stuffing hot dogs, fried chicken and watermelon into our sunburned faces.

I sat with Jesse and Tommy on the porch steps and we laughed with our mouths full of food when a drunken voice bellowed out from down the block, "Happy Birthday, America!" and another drunken voice answered back, "Go'bless America, but *fuck you*, Uncle Sam!"

Then the sky burst open in blazing streaks of light as the township fireworks began to launch up into the night sky from the park across the river. We never went to the park on the Fourth because we could see the fireworks from right here on our block and we'd lay on our backs in the grass or on the hoods of the cars, stuffed on soda and hamburgers, tired and stinking of gunpowder, and watch the black summer sky explode in colorful celebration.

Near the end of the fireworks display, I saw Ben get up from where he had been sitting on the lawn with mom and John and a couple other neighbors. I could tell by the way he staggered that he was drunk and I wondered what he was up to as I watched him creep across the lawn and stop behind Gramma's recliner. Gramma was staring up at the fireworks. I saw a spark of light in Ben's hands, and he tossed something burning on the ground under her chair.

BANGBANGBANGBANGBANGBANGBANG!

Gramma shouted and slapped her hands to her face and leapt out of her recliner as a whole pack of firecrackers exploded under her chair. She almost fell on the lawn, but she twirled her arms and landed on her butt in her chair and it looked a little comical, but it wasn't funny. It wasn't funny at all. She was crying and clutching her chest, Ben was giggling and holding his gut and I was running at him across the lawn to do… *something*.

He stopped me with a shove and I fell on my butt in the grass and he towered over me, leering down at me with a stupid smile on his face and said "Oh, what are you gonna do, Richie? It was just a joke, just a joke."

My mom rushed between us to check on Gramma and as she passed, she planted a hand in Ben's chest and pushed him firmly back from me.

"You stupid asshole! You scared the hell out of mom. What the hell is wrong with you?"

She knelt in front of Gramma, took her hand, and asked, "Are you alright, Ma? You okay?"

Jesse's mom brought a paper cup of water for Gramma to drink. Ben mumbled at my mom ("It was just a joke, Fran") and then slurred an apology at Gramma ("I'm sorry, Anna") and slunk off to sit in a lawn-chair and drink beer. He leaned back in the chair and lit a cigarette. He glanced at me and I *stared* back at him.

Someday, I'll be bigger and you won't want to be here when I am.

I felt a hand on my shoulder and, of course, it was Jesse, come to draw me away from trouble. "Man, that guy is such a creepo," he said in my ear. "C'mon, let's get some ice cream before we have to go inside."

"Alright," I said. "And we need a couple hot dogs, too. I gotta tell you something."

The party was dying down. The littlest kids had been put to bed and the moms were cleaning up the tables and the yards. Kids were scattered in small groups, saying goodnights and waiting for their mothers to call them in and the men sat in groups of their own, smoking cigars and cigarettes and pulling the tabs off cans of beer.

Jesse and I scored bowls of slightly melted vanilla ice cream, I grabbed a few cold hot dogs from the table, and we sat out on the curb. I told Jesse about the pregnant cat living under the building and he asked me what I was going to do about a stray cat and a bunch of kittens. I told him I was going to feed her until she had her babies and then *we* were going to catch them all and set them free in the woods. Jesse, being the truest friend a kid ever had, approved my plan with a grin and a slap of his knee.

"But we'll need cat food, Richie. She can't eat scraps every day."

"She can't? Why not?"

"Well, she can have the hot dogs tonight, sure, but I read in a library book or seen on Wild Kingdom that you shouldn't give people food to wild animals."

"Jesse!" I laughed. "It's a cat. It's not a wild animal."

"There are house cats and alley cats and wild cats, Richie," he explained, "Does she come to you when you call her or let you pet her? Does she sleep in a house?"

No, no and no.

"Then she's a wild cat," he said and I wondered how I could have known him all those years without realizing he was such an expert on cats. We schemed and planned for a few minutes on how we'd get the money to buy cat food and where I'd hide it from my mom, and when our ice cream was gone, I said, "C'mon, Jesse, let's go feed her."

We got up from the curb and started across the lawn and Jesse asked, "Does she really only have three legs?"

"Well, it's more like three and a half, but yeah. She's all mangled up."

"That's kinda gross," Jesse snorted and then I stopped in my tracks.

Ben was passed out drunk in the lawn-chair where he had been sulking. His head hung back over the chair and a can of beer rested between his legs. His mouth hung open and a burned-out cigarette dangled between his fingers and a devilish thought was born in my mind.

Jesse said, "Richie...what are you thinking of?"

I ignored my best friend's cautious question and I crept across the lawn. I had forgotten about the M-80 John had given me, but now I dug in the pocket of my shorts for that fat red bomb and the smuggled matches. I lit the fuse (*"That thing really will blow your fingers off if you're not careful when you light it*"), quickly tossed the M-80 on the ground under Ben's chair.

KAABOOOOOOOOOOOOOOOOM!

The giant firecracker exploded. It was the loudest thing I had ever heard, so much louder than I had expected, and I reeled around to look at Ben, certain I had blown him to Kingdom Come. He let out a loud, frightened "whoooooop!" and leapt up from the chair, the can of beer tumbling and spilling in the grass. He stumbled forward, knocked a barbecue over on the lawn and fell on his ass when he stepped back to avoid planting his bare feet in the smoldering coals.

Everyone was looking at him, and at me, and when he turned and locked his eyes on mine and screamed at me ("Richie, you little bastard!"), I stumbled backward in my hurry to escape, landing hard on my butt. He was drunk and he had been startled and ended up on his ass in front of everyone, but he was angry and he moved toward me faster than I thought he could.

He smacked my face then my mother was there, digging her fingers into his arm, pulling him away from me. She stood between us with her arms thrust out to shield me, screaming "Don't you touch my son! Don't you *ever* touch my fuckin' kid!"

Ben put his hands out in front of him like a coward. "You saw what he did!"

"And *you* did the same damned thing to his *grandmother*, you drunk idiot!"

Ben dropped his hands, balled them both into fists at his side and stared past my mother and straight into me.

"I'll tell you what, Frances; you better do somethin' about that kid or I'll pack my shit and move right the hell out on you."

I stood behind my mother, secure in her protection, relishing the moment that was about to come, when she'd tell that no-good drunk to go right ahead and pack his shit and get out, but she didn't do that. Instead, she whirled around and smacked me hard across my face. I stepped back, my face stinging red, my eyes wet with tears (*don't you cry in front of him*) and pointed a finger up at my mother.

"You…y-you…you *bitch*!"

I said it before I could stop myself, cursed at my mother for the first time in my life as if she wouldn't halfway kill me for it. Before I could turn and run into the apartment, she was on me, smacking me hard across the sides of my head, grabbing at the back of my t-shirt as I fled up the porch.

I tried to push the door shut behind me as I ran into the apartment, but it didn't stop her, only enraged her, and she burst through behind me with the devil in her eyes. In the living room, I fell and banged my head on the coffee table and she kicked at my legs until I got up and then she pushed me down the hall and into my room, hitting me on my back and on my ass as we went.

In my room, like so many times before, I jumped onto my bed and cowered against the wall, knowing she would beat me into the mattress for a few minutes, until her temper was satisfied, and then she would stalk out of the room, calling me names and slamming the door, leaving me in the darkness to cry.

When it was over and she had gone, when my tears had subsided and the stinging pain in my head and butt became a dull throb, I heard a soft voice outside, behind the apartment.

"Here, kitty. Here, kitty, kitty..."

I pulled the curtain back and peeked through the window. Jesse was standing on the sidewalk underneath our tree, tearing up a hot dog and tossing the pieces across the lawn to the three-legged cat. He looked in at me and raised his hand in a half-hearted wave then he ran around the corner of the building and I heard him stomp up the stairs to his apartment and close the door.

I lay in my bed and I could tell by the sound of his footsteps above when he'd gone to his room and then to his bed and I fell asleep wondering what in the world I was going to do when August came and Jesse moved away with his mother to goshdanged Ohio.

Three - Read All About It

When I woke up the next morning, the apartment was quiet. Gary and Tommy were already up and gone and I could hear Ben snoring in the room down the hall, sleeping late, sleeping off his drunk. From the living room, game-show excitement erupted on the television and I knew that my mom was sitting on the couch watching The Price Is Right. Mom loved that show and she had a big crush on Bob Barker. Sometimes she would talk wistfully about going out to California and being a contestant on The Price Is Right, maybe winning one of the big showcases or even a brand new car.

Gramma's bedroom door was closed. She probably wanted left alone to watch her stories and recover from the violence and excitement of the night before. I knew that later, when her door was slightly ajar, as it almost always was, I'd stop in to see her and she'd scold me for setting off the M-80 under Ben's chair, but there'd be a gleam in her eye that would say, "but you're a good boy for sticking up for your gramma."

I lingered in the bathroom for a few minutes, took a deep breath and went into the living room to face my mom. I stopped just inside the room, stood still at the end of the couch, and waited for her to look at me, certain that her mood was bad but not knowing just how bad, afraid to speak and interrupt Bob Barker and land myself in trouble again.

On the television, Bob Barker told my mom he would be right back after a few brief messages and the game show cut to a Tidy Bowl commercial that usually made me laugh, the one with the tiny man in a tiny rowboat drifting on the clear waters of a sparkling toilet bowl. Mom looked up at me, her brown eyes glaring from behind her glasses.

"What do you want, Richard?"

Not Richie, not this morning, but Richard. My father's name, my in-trouble name

"I was gonna go outside and meet Jesse. We got some stuff we wanna do."

"And?"

"Well... am I grounded, Mom?"

She sighed. "You ought to be, and the only reason you're not is because I don't think I could stand to look at you all day, every day for the rest of the week."

"Oh." I should have been happy that she didn't ground me, but freedom isn't so sweet when it's granted only because you're too bad a boy to have around the house.

"Not to mention, Ben's prob'ly gonna wake up hung-over and grouchy and maybe he doesn't need to see your face until he's had his pill and about a pot or two of coffee."

I thought about telling her I was sorry about last night, sorry for lighting the M-80 and for calling her the B-word, but I wasn't sorry and she knew it. I decided that any more talk of the night before would only give her an excuse to change her mind and imprison me in my room, so I took the chance she had given me and headed for the front door.

"Okay, Mom. I won't come home 'til lunch."

"Richie…"

I stopped with my hand on the doorknob. "Yeah, Ma."

"Why don't you get a sandwich at Jesse's or take one with you and just be home in time for dinner?"

"Oh. Okay." Crushed. Flat. "I'll eat lunch at Jesse's."

I stepped out the front door, briefly into the bright summer sun, and ducked into the dim stairwell that led up to the second-floor apartments. I knocked on the door to number 3 and Jesse opened it almost immediately.

"Hey, Richie. I heard you comin' up the stairs."

"I *know*, Jess." For six years, nearly every time I came to his door, Jesse had been telling me he had heard me comin' up the stairs. Sometimes when he came down to our apartment, I'd open the door as soon as he knocked and he'd ask if I'd heard him comin' down the stairs and, just to tease him, I'd tell him I hadn't heard a thing. "You got any ideas how we can make some money? Scrounge pop bottles?"

Jesse smiled and put his finger over his lips, letting me know his mom was within earshot so I wouldn't mention cats, kittens or cat food. He called back over his shoulder "Ma, I'm goin' out with Richie!" then said softly to me, "Just a sec. Need a few of these" and grabbed a thick handful of tissues from the cardboard dispenser that sat on top of the television set. He came out into the stairwell and closed the apartment door behind him.

"Tissues? You got a cold or something?"

"No, man, I ain't sick; these are for the… well, just wait 'til we get out of the stairs and away from our moms, at least. Jeez, Richie."

"Yeah, yeah, okay."

We bounded noisily down the stairs, off the side of the porch and around the corner of the building to the parking lot and carports.

"Some Fourth of July," Jesse said and it was all he needed to say to express everything he felt about the mean trick Ben had played on Gramma, my revenge on Ben and the beating I had taken afterward.

"Yeah, some Fourth," I agreed. "Thanks for feedin' the cat, Jesse."

"Yep. She gobbled those wieners up fast, Richie. We gotta get a big bag of cat food."

We were passing through the dusty shade of one of the big, open carports and I was about to ask Jesse why he brought the stack of tissues when a grown-up called out my name.

"Richie! Hey, Richie!"

We stopped and looked around and John was looking at us over the hood of a beat-up old car, waving us over to the carport.

John was always working on somebody's car in the parking lot or out at the curb, under a tree. He worked cheap and he fixed cars for cash, food stamps, cigarettes or favors and come the first and fifteenth of the month, when everyone got their welfare and disability checks or their social security payments, so many people owed him money for keeping their cars running that he didn't even need to have a job. He just hung around the block, smoking Marlboro cigarettes and drinking beer and listening to the country music station on the radio while he worked on some old pile of junk.

Once, I had asked Mom why John and Pinky didn't live in a better neighborhood since she worked as a nurse at the hospital and he could make so much money fixing cars. For a moment she had been mad, because she didn't like being reminded how crummy our neighborhood was, but she said, "Because what money John doesn't spend on his habits, he loses at the dog track."

I knew John loved the dog races, but I didn't know what his habits were and I didn't ask my mom because I liked big John and he liked me and I didn't want to hear anything bad about him.

Jesse and I walked over to where John had his big toolboxes open and his wrenches and sockets spread out on the asphalt under the front of the car and stood looking up at him.

"Hey, Big John," I said and Jesse added "How's the car fixin' biz?"

John frowned and lit a cigarette.

"It's a bitch is what it is, Jesse. Goddamned transmission's shot on this heap and that cheap-ass DelRusso wants me to fix it when what he needs is a new one. Hell, he needs a whole new car, if you wanna hear the truth." He wiped his hands on a greasy orange rag and leaned against the car. "Richie, what you tell your mother when she asked you where you got that firebomb?"

"She didn't ask me where I got it."

He whistled through his teeth. "Well, that's good, then. Guess she just figured it was something from your pack of fireworks."

"Yeah... prob'ly. See you later, John. Good luck with the bitch transmission." John was an adult you could curse in front of and he didn't think anything of it except maybe that it was funny. Jesse and I turned to get on our way and John said, "Hey, Richie."

I turned around to look at him as he was crawling back underneath Sal DelRusso's broken-down car. "Yeah?"

He looked at me, squinting, the cigarette dangling from the corner of his lips. "I think you did exactly the right damned thing with that M-80."

"You do? Really?"

He smiled. "Shit, yeah, I do really. You paid a hard price for it, that's for sure, but you did just the right goddamned thing. Don't let your mom hear I said it, but that Ben had it comin' to him."

John smiled and retreated to the greasy darkness beneath the car. "Now go on, fellas, get the hell outta here. Kill the fuckin' day, why don'tcha."

Jesse and I walked together through the big parking lot, keeping an eye out in the corners and near the dumpsters for empty returnable pop bottles. We hurried across Bloomfield Street and climbed over the brick wall into the alley behind the little shopping center on the highway. We snuck down the alley and came out at the end of the strip mall, near the row of three or four newspaper vending machines just outside the donut shop's big windows.

Inside the shop, a few people, mostly old men, sat at the little peach-colored tables, munching donuts, drinking coffee, and reading newspapers, but none of them seemed to notice us out on the sidewalk as Jesse pulled the wad of tissues out of his pocket.

I asked Jesse what he was planning to do with the tissues and he said, "Oh, man, Richie, I got a genius plan." He knelt down in front of the first machine and shoved a small wad of the tissues up the coin return slot. "You ever buy a newspaper out of one of these machines, Richie?"

"Sure I have," I told him, remembering Saturday mornings at the pancake house or late nights at the diner, when Gramma would slide a quarter across the table and send me out to the sidewalk for a newspaper.

Jesse had moved on to the next machine, and then the next, stuffing white balls of tissue up inside of the coin return slots. "Well, these machines are crapola," he said. "If you don't pull on the handle at just the right second after you put your money in, the latch doesn't open."

I knew where he was going with this.

"And you gotta get your quarter out of the coin-return and try again," I said as he clogged up the last of the machines.

"Yeah. Only today, all the coins that go down the return are gonna stop up behind those tissues. Later, say around five or six o'clock, we come back, pull out the tissues, and get the quarters. Did I tell you it was genius or what?"

I had to admit, it was pretty genius. "But if we get caught, they're gonna get the cops on us, Jesse."

"But we ain't gonna get caught," he told me matter-of-factly. "They don't come around to empty the money and put the new papers in until the middle of the night. All we gotta do is come back and get the quarters before dinner and we're home free." His eyes lit up. "And rich!"

I didn't think we would become millionaires by stuffing up the coin-returns of four newspaper machines, but we might get enough money to buy a bag of cat food.

CLANG, CLANG!

The donut shop's glass door opened, the big cowbell above it clanged and the donut lady stuck her head out to holler at us.

"Hey, you kids, what you doin' messin' around them paper machines?" Her thick glasses glared in the bright morning sunlight, icing and batter smeared her apron and flour dusted her hair.

"We're just readin' the headlines," I told her.

She frowned. "Well, you can't just hang around out there and read the paper for free. Why don'tcha buy one or go on home?"

Jesse flipped her the finger, hollered, "Why don't you buy a new hairdo?" and we were running back into the alley and scrambling over the wall, laughing as we dropped back into the neighborhood. We rested against the wall and I looked at Jesse and giggled.

"What?" he said, "What's so funny, pardner?"

"Why don't you buy a new *hairdo*?" I asked him, "Is that the best you could come up with or what?"

"Jeez, Richie," he said, "Did you see that hairdo? She looked like Cruella DeVille with all that flour in her hair."

We were both giggling as we ran off down Bloomfield Street.

Four - Hey, Kool-Aid!

We crossed the street to our side, still laughing, and for a moment, I felt sad and guilty for having such a good time when Jesse was going to be moving away in just a month, but then I remembered I had told him we were going to rule the neighborhood and I snapped out of my doldrums. I smacked him lightly on the back of his head and sprinted for the corner of our street, my best friend running behind me in mock pursuit.

We stopped under the big tree on the corner and stood bent over with our hands on our knees, catching our breath and Jesse said, "Hey, Ray's got his stand out."

Ray Laws lived in the building on the corner of our block. He was one year behind us in school and he was an okay kid, but he had a couple of annoying habits that kept him on the fringes of our neighborhood gang of boys. The first thing was, even in the third grade, he still picked his nose and ate his boogers. The other thing was; if he wanted to get your attention, he would hold his hand up in your face like a traffic cop and say, "Stop in the name of the Laws."

I glanced across the street and saw Ray sitting behind pitchers of red and blue drinks at his perpetually failing Kool-Aid stand.

Every summer, Ray would set up his stand on the edge of the lawn in front of his apartment building and sell Dixie cups of Kool-Aid for five cents from late morning until early afternoon. The problem was, though, that he gave away more Kool-Aid than he ever sold. The bigger kids would just come along and shake him down for a few cups, and the rest of us mostly got our Kool-Aid free because we were his friends. Ray also drank a considerable amount of his own inventory. Some people paid for their Kool-Aid, of course, and he would toss the nickels and dimes into a cigar box, but the poor kid never really made a profit. Even at eight cents a packet, Ray Laws just couldn't make a go of it in the Kool-Aid business.

I was hot and thirsty and I remembered the quarter I had found the day before on my way to meet Jesse at the bog.

"Wanna get a Kool-Aid, Jess? I got a quarter."

"Save that for the cat food fund," Jesse said and started across the street toward Ray's stand. "We're gonna sell that boy a kitten."

We are?

Jesse grinned. "You remember Ray had that cat? The one that got ran over in the street?"

I did remember. I still remember.

Ray and his sister had a big orange cat named Tubbs and his death a few months before summer had been a spectacular event on our block. A gang of us kids had been playing ball on the grass in front of Ray's building. His mother and sister had been sitting on the porch and Tubbs the cat sat with them, lounging in a spot of sunlight and swishing his tail. Louis Moretti had popped a foul ball up onto the porch and scared the cat.

Tubbs darted from the porch, streaked across the lawn and ran into the street where he was struck by a big sedan. The car came to a screeching stop and a lady got out, screaming "Oh my God! Oh my God!" while Tubbs flopped around on the blacktop.

Louis' dad had come out with a shovel, swung it and banged the cat once on its head. Tubbs stopped flopping and lay in the road like an orange mess while we kids just stared wide-eyed and open-mouthed at Mister Moretti, and Trina Laws cried out from the porch, "He's dead! He's dead!"

Ray saw us coming, broke out in a salesman's grin that spread his freckles out across his cheeks and called out, "Richie! Jesse! Ice cold Kool-Aid!"

I teased him. "How can it be ice cold? There ain't even any ice in the pitchers."

Ray frowned. "Well, the ice melted." Then he grinned again. "But it's still cold, guys. I'll give you two-for-one."

"Ray, we don't want any Kool-Aid. We aren't even thirsty," Jesse said. "We're here to sell *you* something!"

Ray poured himself a cup of the red Kool-Aid and downed it, finishing with an exaggerated sigh of refreshment. "I don't wanna buy anything."

Jesse said, "Ray, you don't even know what we're selling. How do you know you don't want it if you don't even know what it is?"

Ray stood up from the plastic kiddie chair he had been sitting in and came around the cheap foldaway table that he used for his Kool-Aid stand. "Okay... well, what is it then?

Jesse looked at me and grinned. "Richie, tell him what it is."

"It's a kitten, Ray. Don't you want another cat?" I said and Jesse chimed in with, "Yeah, since Tubbs got hit by a car and whacked with a shovel."

Ray's eyes lit up at the mention of a new kitten, dimmed briefly at Jesse's graphic reminder of Tubbs' gruesome death, then brightened again when I told him he could have the pick of the litter.

"Well, let's go see 'em then!" Ray said and started gathering up paper cups.

Jesse put a hand on Ray's shoulder and said, "Well, you can't see them on account of we ain't got 'em yet."

Ray stopped closing down his stand and eyed us suspiciously. "Whatta you mean you ain't got 'em yet? How can you sell kittens you don't even have yet?"

Jesse sighed. "We can sell 'em because we know we're *gonna* have them. Richie's got a three-legged cat and it's 'pregnated."

Ray looked from Jesse to me and I assured him that there would be kittens. "They just haven't been born yet, Ray. You can buy one and in a couple of weeks or a few months, when they're born, you can have whichever one you like best."

Ray thought it over and said he would really like to surprise his mom and his little sister Trina with a new kitten, but he couldn't afford to buy a cat because he'd only had the stand open for a week and business had been slow. "I haven't made much money yet, guys."

"That's why this is such a good deal," Jesse told him. "When you pay in advance, you can get a kitten from us for cheap, pal."

"Well, when are the kittens gonna be born?" Ray asked and I knew we had him. "You know you can't just take them from their momma when they're born, right? They gotta drink the momma cat's milk and open their eyes and figure stuff out first."

I told Ray that we couldn't say exactly when the kittens would be born because we didn't know exactly how pregnant the momma cat was, but that it would probably be pretty soon because she was really, really fat.

"So how come I can't just pay you when I can take the kitten home, Richie?"

Jesse answered for me. "Because we need the money to buy cat food to feed the momma cat."

Ray looked doubtful, but Jesse told him that if we couldn't buy cat food, the momma cat would probably starve and all the kittens would die inside her belly and Ray grimaced and said, "Jeez, Jesse, that's gross. How much do I gotta pay?"

"Well, how much you got in your cash box?"

Ray flipped open the cigar box, stuck his finger inside it and counted his coins. "I got a dollar and eighteen cents but I need some of it to make change with."

Jesse looked at me and I told Ray he could have his pick of the litter for just one measly dollar and he counted two quarters, four dimes and two nickels into the palm of my hand.

"Deal!" he said. "You guys promise you'll come and tell me as soon as they're born?"

"Yeah, we will, of course," Jesse said, "But one dollar is pretty cheap for a pick of the litter kitten so how 'bout a couple Kool-Aids?"

He picked up the pitcher of blue Kool-Aid, poured two cups and passed one to me. We tossed them back and drank them down and Ray said, "Hey, I thought you guys weren't even thirsty!"

live - Iag You're Dead

We left Ray at his stand with his pitchers of warm Kool-Aid, his paper cups and eighteen cents left in his cigar box, and we crossed the street and headed down the block to our building. Jesse asked if I was going in for lunch and I told him that my mom was still mad about last night and didn't want me around the apartment until dinnertime.

"Well, that's kinda good, anyway," he said, "We can go back and check the paper machines about then and get the cat food at the Junior Mart."

"How much you think cat food costs anyway?" I asked him. "We got a buck twenty-five."

Jesse didn't know how much the cat food would cost, but we figured we could get a bag for a couple of bucks. Jesse had thirty-seven cents in his money jar and he told me he would bring it down with some sandwiches.

"Two Jesse specials comin' up," he said and I sat on the hood of Mom's station wagon while he ran up to his apartment to make us a couple double PB&J sandwiches, his famous specialty.

Jesse made his peanut butter and jellies with peanut butter spread thick on both slices of bread and the jelly smooshed in between. He said it maximized the flavor and kept the jelly from squishing out the edges of the bread. They were good sandwiches but a kid could choke on that much peanut butter and Wonder bread if he didn't have something to wash it down.

While I waited in the parking lot for Jesse to come back down, our apartment door opened and Ben stepped out and sat in his chair on the porch. He had a coffee cup in one hand and he lit a cigarette and puffed smoke out through his nose. He looked at me and squinted and I stared back at him. I was afraid of him, but not as much as I had been because no matter how mean and squinty he made his eyes, I'd seen him the night before, jumping out of his chair, his eyes wide with fright, and I'd heard him holler that scared foghorn "whoop!"

I saw Jesse pop out of the stairwell. He stopped on his toes for a moment when he noticed Ben, who turned his head to look at Jesse for a second then, instead of looking back at me, stared down into his coffee mug. Jesse skirted around Ben and came off the porch, a brown paper sack in one hand and a thermos in the other.

He brought something to wash the sandwiches down. We won't choke to death, after all.

I slid off the hood of the Country Squire and fell in step beside Jesse.

"I see El Creepo Grande survived getting his butt blown off," he said and handed me the thermos, dug in his pocket and slapped a quarter, a dime and two pennies into the palm of my hand. "That's a dollar sixty-two now. I bet we get enough from the paper machines to get the cat food and we can look for bottles down around the bog after we eat."

We hit the alley, climbed on top of one of Tommy's beloved garbage dumpsters and hopped the fence to go have our lunch in the woods by the pond. As we laughed and joked our way down the path to the bog, we heard kids screaming and shrieking in terror or horror or pain and someone cried out at the top of their lungs, "Help! Help me! Somebody help meeeeeeeeee!"

"That's Tommy!" I said and we took off at a run through the woods to find out what was the matter.

As we ran panting down the path, two tanned blurs in cutoff jeans and sneakers, I had the thought that one of us should go back over the fence for home and bring back a grown-up, just in case whatever was happening to Tommy and the rest of the kids was as terrible as it sounded. I made a quick mental list of the adults who were most likely to be around, though, and decided against it. Jesse and I were both fast runners and one of us could get help quickly enough if it was needed. We left the path, skidded down the muddy slope to the pond and we stopped just short of the slimy green water.

What the heck?

In the mud around the bog and in the brown grass and shrubs on the opposite slope, the bodies of kids from the neighborhood lay crumpled on the ground.

It's a massacre!

I heard Tommy shrieking again and he burst out of the woods, covered in mud, running for his life. Behind him, Louis Moretti came bounding through the trees, surprisingly fast for a chubby kid, waving a big, bloodstained knife in the air behind my little brother's head.

It's rubber. Just a rubber knife.

Louis caught up with Tommy on the bank of the pond, stabbed him high in the back with the fake costume-store knife and hopped around gleefully as Tommy fell flat on his belly, playing dead in the sticky sludge. The other 'dead' kids all stirred and sat up where they had fallen, calling "You're 'it', Tommy! Tommy's 'it'!"

"What in the heck are you guys doin?" I asked and Tommy pushed himself up to his knees, smiled at me through the mud that covered his face and told me they were playing Hide and Go Kill.

Jesse laughed and said, "Hide and Go Kill? What the heck kinda dumb game is that supposed to be?"

"A fun one!" the formerly dead Burt Hodges told us and his recently resurrected brother Ross said, "It's just like Hide and Go Seek except when you find someone hiding, you gotta kill 'em before they get back to the safe tree."

Jesse and I laughed and he said, "That's a dumb game."

"What's so dumb about it?" Tommy asked.

"Well, it's dumb 'cause you'll prob'ly get in trouble when you go home covered in mud," I told him. "And you'll prob'ly have nightmares, too."

"I ain't gonna have nightmares," Tommy argued, embarrassed in front of the other kids, but Tommy was afraid of the dark and of the things that go bump in the night and everybody knew it.

"I bet you do," I told him, "You get nightmares from watchin' Scooby-Doo."

"You guys wanna play? Tommy's it," Louis asked us. Jesse and I both shook our heads.

"Nah, you guys go on and play," I said, "we're gonna go up the creek and eat lunch. Me and Jesse got things to talk about." Tommy looked at me curiously and I added, "Private things."

I didn't want to play Hide and Go Kill, but catching the other kids playing the game had given me the beginnings of an idea and I wanted to tell Jesse about it so we could begin to scheme and plot.

Jesse and I headed off around the pond and sloshed away through the bushes along the stream, the other kids screaming behind us as they were flushed from their hiding places and murdered yet again. We sat in a small grassy patch in the warm July sun, eating thick, gooey peanut butter sandwiches, chasing each bite with a swig of Grape Hi-C from Jesse's thermos.

We were far enough up the creek that the sounds of dying kids were distant and low, lost to the breeze and the traffic out on the state route. I told Jesse I had a genius idea for a prank and he leaned in close as I whispered the details. When I was finished telling him what we were going to do, he grinned and said, "Wicked. That's a wicked prank, Richie!"

Six - The Shopkeeper's Daughter

After we ate, we scrounged around the woods and the stream for a few hours and came up with two returnable pop bottles that we would get twenty cents for when we went to Mr. Ratto's Junior Market later in the afternoon to buy the cat food. While we searched the woods, we talked over the details of the plot we had hatched and, when the heat of the afternoon began to weaken and we thought it must be close to five o'clock, we left the woods behind at Grand Avenue and walked the long way around to the strip mall.

Outside the donut shop, I held the empty pop bottles and kept the lookout for the donut lady and for the cops, while Jesse pulled the wads of tissue out of the newspaper machines and collected our stolen coins.

I fidgeted nervously and Jesse muttered "oh, *yeah*" and "*that's* right" as he scooped his fingers into each of the coin slots. I told him to hurry up, but no police cars came screeching up to the curb to haul us off to jail and the grumpy donut lady didn't stick her nosy face out of the shop to run us off. We made a clean getaway down the alley and out the other end at Ratto's Grocery and counted our money. We had two dollars and forty-two cents in coins.

"That's two sixty-two with the bottles," I said. "Not too shabby, Jesse."

As we stepped into the Junior Market, he clapped me on the back and said, "All in a day's work, Richie, my man" and then he let out a low whistle and whispered "hubba, hubba."

Old man Ratto's daughter Antoinette was working behind the counter, smiling at us from over the old-fashion cash register. Antoinette was sixteen or seventeen, and everything about her was long and pretty: her hair, her legs, her eyelashes, her fingers, even her nose. She was one of the prettiest girls in the neighborhood and every boy we knew, from the first grade through to high school, had a crush on her.

"Hello, boys," she said and Jesse tipped an imaginary hat and said "Howdy-do, Ma'am."

I poked Jesse from behind and giggled. Antoinette pretended to blush and then she called us big spenders and asked us what she could do for us today. "Gonna get some candy, Jesse? Soda pop? No, I know… ice cream. It's hot outside."

"Nope," I said. "How much is cat food?"

"Cat food? You got a cat, Richie?"

Jesse looked up at her, tried to wink, and said, "No, Antoinette. Richie doesn't have a cat and I ain't got one, either. There's *no* cat. Got it? We *don't* have a cat."

Antoinette came out from behind the counter, long and pretty in tight bell-bottom jeans, and led us down an aisle to the back of the store to help us with the cat food.

"No cat?" she said, "Two little boys buying cat food but neither one of them has a cat. That's not weird at all."

"It's for an old lady who has a cat," Jesse lied. "We're doin' a good deed on account of she's too old and crippled up to come to the store. "

"Is that so? Well, aren't you the little heroes."

"Yep. Heroes," Jesse said. "That old lady's cat hasn't eaten for about three days."

Antoinette showed us the cat food. There were cans, small bags, and big bags and she showed us the price tags on each of them and told us what the tax would be. We couldn't afford the biggest bag but we got a medium bag and had enough money left over to share a candy bar so we picked up a Hershey's Bar from the candy counter on our way up front to pay.

"Oh how *nice*," Antoinette said, "You got a candy bar for the poor old lady's cat."

We took the shortcut over the wall back to the neighborhood and we snuck back to our building through the alleys and the carports, careful not to be seen with the cat food. I told Jesse we should hide it behind the washing machine in the small laundry room attached to our building and he said, "What if one of our moms finds it there?"

"They never use the laundry room," I told him, "Well, hardly ever. There's only one washer and dryer and my mom says it would take all day to do the wash. That's why she goes to the laundrymat."

Leaving the bag stashed behind the washer, we each took big handfuls of the dry red and brown pellets out behind the building and piled them on the ground near the unscreened opening, where the three-legged momma cat would find them on her way in or out. We rinsed our hands at the sink in the laundry room in case we smelled like cat food, said our goodbyes on the porch and, having fed the cat; we went into our apartments to have our own suppers.

Ben glowered at the dinner table but didn't say much except "pass those potatoes" and "don't use so much salt, Tommy" and Mom stared across the room at the TV while she ate. Gary finished first and went back outside to play ball with the bigger kids and when we were done eating, Tommy and I, both still dirty from the day's adventures, took baths and stayed in for the rest of the night.

Before bed, I made my nightly visit to Gramma's room and rubbed her back with alcohol. When she had kissed me goodnight, I went into my bedroom and Tommy was already in his bed, curled up under a sheet.

I asked him if he had gotten in trouble for coming home so muddy from his killing spree. He told me he had washed most of it off at the hose and only come home wet.

He fell asleep bragging about escaping a spanking, but a few hours later he woke up from a nightmare, crying "Don't kill me, Louis, don't *kill* me!"

I looked over at him in the darkness and said, "I told you so, dummy."

Seven - At the Drive-In

Over the next week, the uneasy quiet around the apartment gave way to the usual noises: Gramma's bedroom TV competing with the big living room set, Mom and Ben mumbling and grumbling at each other in the morning and, later at night, Elvis on the stereo.

Jesse and I hung around the block in the mornings, running through the sprinklers or playing ball with the gang, and in the afternoon we became Old West lawmen, tracking imaginary train robbers along the tracks and down into the woods. We escaped the neighborhood and ditched the gang each day after lunch, but instead of bedrolls and camp gear, we stuffed our knapsacks with the old clothes we would need to carry out our scheme.

One warm evening, Jesse and I came back from the pond, where we had stashed the last of our smuggled t-shirts and pajamas and jeans at the foot of a big tree, and Mom hollered at me from the porch as we came up the walk. "Hurry your ass up, Richie! We're goin' to the drive-in."

Oh, boy!

Going to the drive-in movies was one of the things we did as a family that everyone enjoyed, and when we were all crowded in the car together, munching chips and popcorn and drinking sodas, watching movies on that giant, outdoor screen, everyone got along and, for a few hours, we were all content and happy. We didn't go often, and not at all when Mom didn't have a car, of course, but that night, we would pile into the wagon and drive down the state route to the cheap drive-in (five bucks a car) and we would see three features.

The Starlite drive-in theater was a shady one, in a shady part of town and Mom wouldn't let us out of the car to play on the swings before the movie or to go to the snack bar during the intermissions, unless we all went together, but we went there and watched second-run movies because the other drive-in charged by the person, not the car-load.

"Hurry up and wash up now," Mom said, "And bring the blanket from the hall closet."

"Okay, Mom, I'll hurry, but can I ask you something?"

She looked down at me, shook her head, and put a hand on her hip. "No, Richie," she sighed, "Ben isn't going with us. He's staying home and working on some car with John. That makes you happy, I bet."

Her words made me feel guilty, even though I had been too excited about going to the drive-in to wonder yet if Ben would come along. "I was just gonna ask if Jesse could come with us," I said softly, "It doesn't cost any more for another person to get in."

She sighed and looked back at Jesse. "C'mon then, Jess... hurry up and ask your mom."

Jesse grinned and stomped upstairs to ask his mom and in a flash, he came stomping back down with an open bag of potato chips and a can of cream soda. "I got my own snacks, Miss Frances. My mom says thanks."

It was going to be a great night. The movies that week were all movies I had wanted to see all summer - *The Bad News Bears*, *Eat My Dust* and *Gus*. Ben wasn't going, but Jesse was and when Jesse or another friend went, instead of sitting crowded in the backseat where we couldn't see most of the movie screen, Mom would let us sit on the front bumper of the car.

We got Gramma into the car, left Ben behind in the parking lot with John and drove off down the highway, the oldies station playing on the radio, as the sky darkened grey, then blue, then black. Tommy, Jesse and I chatted about the movies we were going to see and none of us could disguise our anticipation for *The Bad News Bears*. We hadn't seen it yet but word gets around on the block and we all knew that the kids in the movie used foul language like it was going out of style.

We got to the theater after dark and the *Coming Attractions* were already playing on the big screen as we pulled up to the gate to pay admission. A skinny teenage kid with pimples on his face and an Army cap on his head leaned out the window of the little booth, held out his hand and said, "five bucks."

Mom reached into her purse for her wallet and Gramma leaned over in the front seat, crowded Gary up against Mom and told the boy in the booth, "We've got an extra person this time. There's six of us."

The kid stared at her and said, "Um... five bucks per car, ma'am. We don't charge by the person."

"Well, I never knew that," Gramma said. She gave Gary some relief, sat back up in her seat and told my mom, "It's just five dollars for all of us, Fran."

"I know, Ma." Mom handed a five-dollar bill to the kid in the booth. Mom sighed, the kid shook his head and we drove into the gravel lot, dust clouding up in the beams of the station wagon's headlights. Mom drove up and down about seven rows before she found an open space that she liked, and *The Bad News Bears* was just starting as she parked the car on an asphalt hump, pulled the metal speaker from its pole and sealed the car up safe and tight.

Tommy said, "Mom, I thought we could watch from outside when there were too many of us in the back seat," and Mom told us to hurry the hell up then and get our snacks and get out there and watch the damned movie. "And you boys get right back in this car the minute I tell you to."

We spread our chips, popcorn, and sodas out on the rusted hood of the Country Squire and we sat on the cool bumper, Jesse on my left and Tommy on my right, and leaned back against the grill. We laughed and hooted all through *The Bad News Bears* and when the credits started to scroll up the big screen and disappear into the night sky, I called to my mom.

"Mom, we're gonna go to the bathroom. We all gotta pee."

She rolled down her window and leaned her head out. "You wait for Gary," she said and we watched as Gramma's door opened and Gary climbed out over her. Mom looked over at Gramma and I heard her ask, "Ma, do you have to pee?"

Oh, God, please no. We'll miss the whole next movie.

Gramma swallowed a mouthful of popcorn and said, "Do I have to pee?"

Oh, jeez. C'mon, Gramma.

"Yeah, Ma. The boys are goin' to the bathroom. Do you gotta pee or not?" Gramma shook her head.

Whew.

Mom leaned out the window again and said, "Okay, go on, boys. Stay together, and hurry up before the movie starts."

There was a long line to get into the bathroom and we waited while cartoon snacks came alive on the screen above, dancing and singing and telling everyone that tasty treats were available in the snack bar, and when we finally got inside the restroom and crowded at the long stained urinal, Tommy said, "I gotta poop."

"The movie's gonna start," Gary said, "Can't you hold it?"

Tommy shook his head. "For a whole 'nother movie? No way! I'll poop my pants."

Gary told him to hurry up then and waited inside for Tommy to finish and Jesse and I went out and stood by the restroom door, where we could watch the beginning of *Eat My Dust*. My brothers finally came out of the bathroom, Tommy still snapping his jeans and Gary pushing him along. "C'mon, let's get back to the car before Mom gets mad."

We crossed two rows of cars to where our station wagon was parked. Mom was standing at the open driver's side door of the station wagon, waving at us with her hands. "Boys! Boys, come around this way. Right now. Get in this car right now!"

Two men were cursing and shoving each other in the gravel between our car and the big pickup truck parked next to us on Gramma's side. One of the men was bleeding from his nose and the other had a torn shirt. Gramma was staring at them through her window with wide eyes and one hand clasped over her mouth and Jesse said "Wow! A fight!" as Gary herded us around to Mom's side of the car and into the back seat.

He closed the door behind us and Tommy pressed the lock button down as we crowded against the passenger side window to see the fight. Gary climbed in the front and Mom got in right behind him and locked her door, too, as the men shoved and punched each other right outside our car windows.

The man with the bloody nose shoved the other man right up against our car and both Gramma and Mom screamed and Mom started the car, and then all six of us were screaming and hollering when the man pulled a knife out of his back pocket and stuck it in the other man's big beer-belly.

Tommy started to cry and Gramma shouted "Go, Frances!" Mom put her foot on the gas and the car lurched forward. In her panic, Mom had forgotten about the speaker hanging in the window. The window shattered, glass flew into and away from the car, Gramma shouted "Oh Mary, Mother of God!" and I watched through the back window as the speaker whipped around on its cord and clanged against the car parked next to us. Mom flipped on the headlights and kept on going, down the rows, out of the lot and all the way home.

The stabbing at the drive-in was the big talk on our block over the next several days and Jesse and I didn't mind telling our eyewitness accounts a time or two, or ten. Most of the gang were understandably impressed and, for the ones who accused us of making the whole thing up, there was the story in the local paper and the broken window on my mother's station wagon to prove we were telling the truth.

Tommy had bad dreams every night that week and my mother vowed she'd never take us back to that drive-in again, even if they lowered the price to *two* dollars per car, and Gramma told her, "Frances, if you ever do, just leave me at home in bed."

Light – Hiding the Body

That Friday evening, after dinner, while the sky was still light and we could still go outside, Jesse and I met on the porch and snuck off to the pond. We found our stashed supplies, two pillowcases stuffed with old clothes, and carried them down to the pond, where we dumped everything out on the muddy ground and went to work stuffing all the clothes into a single pair of jeans and a long-sleeved flannel shirt until they resembled a pair of legs and a torso. We tucked the shirt down inside of the jeans, joining the two halves of our dummy together, pulled the cuffs of the pants down around a beat-up old pair of sneakers and stood in the twilight, looking down at our creation.

"Looks pretty good," Jesse said, "Except there's no head and no hands."

"That won't matter, Jesse." I was looking around the bog for the perfect spot to stage our dummy. "We'll stick him out there in the middle of the bog in those tall weeds and no one will even notice he doesn't have a head or hands."

The pond was a shallow home to all kinds of slippery things: pollywogs, turtles, snakes, and other things only imagined. Two feet of murky water surrounding mossy humps that rose up from the bottom in search of the sun.

"Gross, Richie. We gotta wade out there to the middle and get that muddy crap all over our shoes and socks?"

Now, Jesse and I had no aversion to getting wet and muddy and we had waded in the pond a time or two before, but he was right when he said it was gross. Still, *that's* where we had to put the dummy if we were going to fool the gang.

"Whatcha wanna do, Jesse? Just dump him right here on the ground where any dummy can see it's just a dummy?"

We laughed at my accidental joke and Jesse relented. "Nah, that'd be lame-o. C'mon, let's get this over with then. We can rinse our shoes and socks in the laundry room when we feed the cat."

We waded out into the greasy water, Jesse carrying the dummy's legs over his shoulder and me lugging the other half over mine, and the sticky goo at the bottom of the pond tried to suck our sneakers straight off of our feet. In the middle of the bog, we reconstructed the dummy, placing it in the weeds and mud so that the lower half was clearly visible and the other half lay shrouded in the leafy muck.

"Whatcha think, Richie?"

I said we would have to look at it from the bank to know for sure and we sloshed back across the bog. The sky was darkening quickly but there was enough light left to see by and we stood on the edge of the pond and admired our handiwork.

"Jeepers creepers! It looks real, Jesse."

Jesse whistled and slapped me on the back. "Oh, man, Richie, if I didn't know we made it, I'd think it was a real kid out there."

We talked over the final details of our plan and made our way up the slippery bank into the woods. The night was falling dark now, but we didn't need light to find the little worn path through the trees and as we wound out of the woods and clambered up the fence, Jesse said, "Man oh man, this is gonna be supreme!"

Back at home, we took off our socks and shoes in the washroom and Jesse rinsed them out in the sink while I scooped a big double-handful of cat food from the hidden bag and carried it out to pile it up for the cat. All week long, we had been feeding the pregnant stray, leaving big piles of food on the ground near the opening in the apartment building's foundation, and every morning every bit of the food was gone. We had no idea how much food a pregnant cat would eat and I worried we weren't leaving her enough, so each night I increased the size of the mound of cat food and still, come morning, there were no leftovers.

I left the cat food on the ground and had a quick look around for the momma cat. I thought I spotted her across the street, but it was another cat, a big dark one with long fur. It skittered under a car when it realized I had seen it.

Jesse and I left our wet socks and shoes out on the porch and parted at the stairwell. When I went into the apartment, Tommy and Gary were on the couch, watching TV, and Mom and Ben were playing cards at the kitchen table. My mom glanced up at me and said, "Cuttin' it close, Richie. Another couple of minutes and you'd have been in trouble."

"Sorry, Mom. Jesse and I got kinda muddy so we stopped to rinse off our shoes."

I changed into my pajama bottoms and went to Gramma's room to rub the alcohol on her back, but she was already asleep, so I pulled the door closed behind me and went to my room to read a comic before bed.

Late that night, I woke up to the sound of a shrieking wail, certain that Tommy was having another nightmare, but when I looked across the room, he was sound asleep on top of the sheet and I realized that the horrible sounds that woke me were coming from outside.

Gary was sitting up in his bed and I said, "What the heck *is* that?"

"Cat fight, dummy." He plunged his head back into his pillow and told me to go back to sleep, but I lay awake in the dark for a few minutes, worried about the Siamese, wondering if she'd been in the fight, maybe with the big grey cat I'd seen sneaking around the tires of the cars parked out on the street. As I drifted back to sleep, I heard my mother's voice drift from her room down the hall.

"God, I hate cats."

Nine - False Alarm

Even in mid-July, when the sounds of kids yelling and laughing rang up and down our block from early morning until the long day faded into the brief, black night, Saturday mornings were the quiet exception. That was the one day of the week almost every kid stayed inside, stayed in their pajamas and stayed glued to their television sets until the marathon of cartoons and kid-shows ended at eleven-thirty and gave way to sports, old movies and news.

Tommy and I were finishing our second late morning bowls of cereal as the last of our Saturday favorites, '*The Krofft Supershow*' was ending, and as we rinsed our bowls and spoons in the kitchen, I sprung the trap.

"Hey, Tommy. Let's get the gang and go down to the bog and play Hide and Go Kill."

Tommy tossed his plastic bowl into the dishrack next to mine and said, "But you said it was a dumb game 'cause it would give me nightmares."

"Well, it's kinda dumb but it sounds kinda fun, too. Besides, it did give you nightmares."

He frowned and dried his hands on the dishtowel that hung from the refrigerator door-handle. "Yeah, but not really bad nightmares," he told me. "Not like the nightmares about that guy at the drive-in. That was real. I peed my bed"

Now, I'd like to tell you that I considered my little brother's fear of all things even a little bit scary, and called the whole thing off. I wish I could tell you now, that I'd had a change of heart and told Tommy we should just go play at the railroad tracks instead, but, of course, I said, "I'll get Jesse and the Hodges, you run down to the corner and get Ray and whoever else is out."

We got dressed, hollered, "We're goin' out!" to my mom and hit the front porch, where Jesse was sitting on the step waiting for us. Tommy raced off down the sidewalk in the direction of Ray's corner building and Jesse and I went up the stairs of the building facing ours to tell Burt and Ross Hodges to come on out and play.

Tommy came back up the block with Ray Laws, his sister Trina and Louis Moretti. We were a noisy bunch of eight crossing the parking lot and the street as we headed for the bog. Redheaded Ricky, the only kid in our gang who didn't live on our street, joined us in the back alley and we were nine when we climbed the fence and hurried single-file down the familiar path.

As we walked, Jesse started singing and the rest of us joined in on the familiar, funny parody that had been making the rounds in our neighborhood all summer long.

We had joy, we had fun
We had seasons in the sun
But the cops had guns
And they shot us in the buns
We had joy, we had fun
We had seasons in the sun...

We skidded down the short slope to the water's edge and Ray said, "Everybody stop in the name of the Laws." Trina laughed, the rest of us groaned and Burt Hodges said, "Okay, everybody, put your right foot in."

We sat in a circle on the muddy bank of Blackberry Bog, our right feet pushed into the center, and Burt started counting around, tapping each of our feet as he went.

"Eenie, meenie, miney, moe..."

Ross looked up from the circle as his brother rhymed his way around our toes and his eyes grew wide and round behind his thick glasses.

"Catch a tiger by the toe..."

Ross's mouth fell open and he stood up from the circle. Jesse and I looked at each other sneakily from the corners of our eyes.

"If he hollers, let him go..."

Burt stopped rhyming, his finger stalling on Tommy's ratty sneaker, and everyone looked up at Ross, who stretched his arm, pointed toward the center of the pond and let out the loudest, longest, most blood-curdling scream any of us had ever heard and probably ever would. Everybody's eyes left Ross' screaming, saucer-eyed face and followed his finger out across the water and Ross was still shrieking when the other kids started jumping to their feet, some of them backing up against the slope and a few of them stepping closer to the water, fascinated.

"It's a *dead* kid!" Ray Laws shouted.

Jesse and I stole triumphant glances at each other as, one by one; the other seven kids realized what they were looking at.

"And his head's gone! His *head* is gone!" Tommy hollered, starting to cry.

I almost laughed as I looked at Jesse and I knew that he was thinking what I was thinking: *so much for no one noticing that.*

All of the kids were pointing and hollering, some of them were crying and, while our attention was on the pond and the calamity we'd created, before Jesse or I could calm him down and tell him it was just a prank, Ross Hodges turned and bolted up the slope and out of sight. He ran toward the neighborhood, faster than I thought any kid could ever run, still screaming as he disappeared into the trees.

Trina and Louis turned tail and took off behind Ross, and Jesse and I exchanged a brief look and a telepathic agreement that we had better just stay quiet about the whole thing. We knew that Ross would be sending back his dad and any other grown-up who happened to notice him running up the block, screaming like a forgotten teakettle.

Just minutes later, we heard the nervous, excited voices of kids and women and men, the sound of a small mob trampling through the brush and Jesse and I climbed to the top of the slope to witness what would have been a comical sight on any other day, under any other circumstances.

A whole crowd of people from the neighborhood was coming down the path, a regular parade of t-shirted men, women in housecoats and kids in shorts or swim-trunks. Mister Hodges and John were leading the procession, and Ross was tucked in right behind them. He had stopped screaming but his face was red and his eyes were still wet from crying. Behind them, in the crowd, I saw Gary and some of the other older kids and, further back at the end of the parade, behind the other parents and kids, my mom was hurrying through the woods with Jesse's mom right at her heels.

I looked at Jesse and he looked back at me and together we slid back down to the bottom of the slope as the neighborhood mob came crashing down to the pond and the wailing, whining sound of sirens rose up in the late morning air, first from the south where the police station was, then from the west where the closest firehouse stood.

"Don't say *anything*," I whispered to Jesse and he looked back at me as if I were the dumbest kid he had ever seen and whispered, "No *shit*, Sherlock Holmes."

Everyone crowded at the edge of the pond to see the dead kid, the men and older boys up front, the women and little kids craning and straining their necks from the rear. Ben took a few steps out into the pond and John said, "Better not go out there, Ben. That's a crime scene." Ben looked at him blankly for a moment and almost slipped and fell on his way back to the bank.

Everybody was chattering (*Oh my God, who do you think it is*) and whispering (*Could it be a murder*) and wondering (*Maybe it was an accident… he coulda fell and drowned*) when the sirens converged into one big wailing sound near the top of the path, whirred down to silence and gave way to the sounds of slamming doors and hustling firefighters and cops rushing through the woods.

When the uniformed men came slipping and sliding down the slope, the moms started shooing all of us kids back from the pond, out of the way, and the men stepped aside to let them through. Two young policemen and a squad of firefighters, sweating in their heavy jackets and boots and helmets, some carrying boxes with latches and handles and a couple of them hoisting a long stretcher, stopped with their toes at the edge of the murky, shallow pond and talked to each other and into big, squawking radios.

One of the cops stepped out into the bog and slowly sloshed his way through the mud and water toward the poor, dead, decapitated kid. Jesse and I were nervous but no one would know we were the ones who had planted the dummy.

Or would they?

The crowd hushed and everyone stared out at the police officer, knee deep in the slimy water, as he bent and reached down to touch the dead boy with his hand. He hooked a finger through one of the belt loops on the muddy jeans and... yanked.

Everyone gasped as he lifted the dead body out of the mud with just one hand and then they gasped again, louder, when the corpse fell apart in his hands, the torso separating from the legs and rolled up t-shirts and wadded pairs of sweatpants tumbling out of both ends and into the muddy bog.

"It's a *dummy!*" someone shouted and the chattering began again.

The young cop in the middle of the pond turned around and looked sourly at his partner and the firemen groaned, sighed, and started climbing back up the slope to load their stretcher and their gear back onto their trucks. I looked at the cop's face as he waded back across the pond. His mouth stretched down in a tight frown, his eyes were angry, and they wandered across the crowd, from the face of one kid to the next. When his eyes settled on *my* face, I hoped my mask of innocence looked a little more convincing than the one Jesse was wearing.

I swallowed hard and snuck another glance at Jesse. He looked nervous, but I reminded myself that nobody knew we had made the dummy and stuck it out there in the middle of the pond to scare a bunch of kids on their summer vacation. Then Tommy pushed his way through the crowd to the edge of the bog and hollered, "Hey, wait a minute... some of those clothes are *mine*!"

With the discovery that the dead kid in the bog had only been a prank, just a dummy stuffed with hand-me-down clothes, and not a tragic drowning or murder, the crowd began to break up and everyone climbed back up the slope and headed down the path. They all disappeared over the fence, the men helping the women and some of the littlest kids get a leg up and over the wooden planks, leaving Jesse and I behind at the head of the path with the firemen, the cops and, worse, our mothers.

The policeman who had waded into the pond and confirmed his professional suspicion that the crumpled form lying still in the mud hadn't been a real kid at all, stood over us. His folded his arms across his chest and his soggy, mud-streaked pants and boots dripped in the dirt. He lectured us about wasting valuable emergency resources and how much it had cost the township to roll out the big firetrucks for no real reason at all and he asked us how we felt about his muddy pants and shoes.

The whole time he talked, Jesse and I had stared up at him sheepishly and our mothers had stood behind him, glaring down at us in embarrassment, shame and anger. The cop reached for his utility belt and I was sure he was going to pull his shiny cuffs from their leather holster, slap them on Jesse and me and haul us downtown to the jail. Instead, he slipped his radio from its strap and called into the station that Patrol 14 was 10-98, and left us to a fate far worse than a judge, a jury or a jail – our mothers.

"Wait 'til I get your ass home, Richie," my mom said as the cop was getting into his patrol car, and Jesse's mom whacked him one across the back of his head as the black-and-white cruiser drove away through the dirt and disappeared down Grand Avenue. There was no getting our moms to struggle back over the fence, and we had to take the long way around, down the main street and then through the whole neighborhood with our moms walking behind us lecturing us and smacking at our butts all the way home, in front of *everyone.*

Ten - Emergency!

Outside our building, Mom stopped to comfort Tommy, who was sitting on the porch steps crying, and I headed straight for my room. Ben was sitting at the kitchen table with a can of beer and a cigarette smoldering in an ashtray, and he smirked at me as I passed into the hall. In the bedroom, I sat on the edge of my bed, waiting for my mother to come and punish me, suffering the muffled sounds of my best friend enduring his own punishment in his room upstairs.

Mom roared in and her eyes were brown fire. Her face was tight with anger, her cheeks flushed, her mouth twisted into that familiar frown I feared so much. In her right hand, she gripped the longest length of the thick leather belt Tommy had scrounged from a garbage can in the early days of the summer.

I felt my lower lip tremble and my eyes filled with tears as she crossed the room, raising the long black strap above her shoulder. I scrambled backward across the bed, up against the wall and drew my knees up against my chest.

"Mom! Mom! It was just a prank!"

"Shut up, Richie!"

She loomed over me (*I have never*) and snapped the belt (*been so embarrassed*) across my arms (*and ashamed*) and my legs (*in all my life*) and my skin burned as if I'd been stung by a thousand wasps. I pulled the sheet up over my body and Mom yanked it off me and swung the belt again... and again. She was breathing heavily and I was howling and crying. I was sure that beating would be the one that sent me to the hospital, but I was saved, tragically, by Gramma.

"Fran! Frances! Come quick!"

Gramma's voice, frightened, scared, and breathless, came calling out from her room and my mother paused, her hand swept back behind her to bring the belt down upon me again, and then Ben was calling "Fran! Your mom is sick! Hurry!"

Mom turned and rushed out of my room and into Gramma's, where Ben and Tommy were standing at the edge of her bed. Gramma was sitting up against her pillows, her face gone so pale, her hand clutched over her chest, panting, "Help...help.

Tommy was crying, Ben was staring uselessly at Gramma and my mom bolted into the room and shoved them both out of the way, then ran for the kitchen and the phone. Ben took Tommy's hand and ran out behind her, leading my little brother out of the apartment, probably to go pound on John's apartment door three buildings up the block to see if his wife Pinky could bring her nurse's bag.

I stood in the open doorway of my bedroom, tears streaming down my cheeks, my skin sizzling where Mom's long leather snake had struck, staring across the hall at Gramma. I was afraid to go to her, afraid to leave my room

She was clutching her chest and sucking air, trying to breathe. Her eyes were wide with panic and pain, staring straight into mine.

My mother's voice bellowed in the kitchen, spitting our address into the phone and I summoned all of my courage and rushed across the hall screaming, "Gramma, don't die! Gramma, don't die!"

For the second time that day, the sound of emergency sirens pierced the still, hot air. Mom sent me out on the porch and she stayed behind, pressing a cool, wet cloth to Gramma's head and patting her hand gently, but Gramma wasn't moaning or moving.

The neighbors had begun to gather outside, drawn from their apartments once again by the promise of mystery and excitement, pulled away from their afternoon television programs by the lure of a true-life drama.

An ambulance came, and a firetruck, too, parking out in the street with their engines still running as the men hurried into the apartment. It was the same squad of firemen who had been dispatched to the pond earlier and one of them gave me a suspicious, sideways glance as he passed me on the porch.

Jesse and his mom came downstairs and I looked at my friend and said, "It's Gramma."

Miss Brenda told us to get off the porch, out of the way, so we gathered with Tommy, Ross and a couple of the other kids, watching from the lawn as the medics wheeled Gramma out on a metal stretcher, a big plastic oxygen mask strapped around her face, and lifted the rolling bed into the back of the ambulance.

One of them climbed in the back with Gramma and pulled the wide door closed, the other ran around and jumped in the driver's seat, and the big ambulance roared away down the block, its siren wailing. All I could think of was Ross Hodges, only an hour or so earlier, running fast through the neighborhood, shrieking at the top of his lungs.

Mom came hurrying out of the apartment, called out "Watch the boys, Brenda" to Jesse's mom and she and Ben ran to the parking lot, got in the station wagon and chased the ambulance down the street as it rushed Gramma to the hospital.

As the siren was fading off down Grand Avenue, Gary came home and dropped his bike on the grass. He looked at me and Jesse, saw our sad faces and shook his head.

"Guess you two are grounded, huh? Man, you dummies, really pulled a stupid one this time. *Everybody's* talkin' about it!"

I told him what had happened to Gramma and Gary hopped back on his bike and pedaled off in the direction of the hospital.

Later that afternoon, Tommy took a nap on the living room carpet and Jesse's mom brewed coffee in our kitchen, sat at the table and smoked cigarettes one after the other. Jesse and I were still sitting out on the stoop when our station wagon rattled around the corner and slipped into our numbered space under the carport. Gary's bicycle was in the back of the wagon and he rode in the seat behind my mom.

They all climbed out of the car and came up the walk and Jesse's mom came out from the kitchen to stand in the doorway of our apartment. Ben walked past us and went inside, probably to get a can of beer, and Mom knelt down in front of me and put her hands on my cheeks.

"Gramma died, Richie."

Tears welled up in her eyes and spilled down her cheeks and she hugged me, but before I could cry with her, Ben came out, a beer can in his hand, and stared at us. I shut my eyes tight and imagined I was a boy made out of stone, a statue of myself that could not cry or bruise.

My mom released me from her embrace, wiped her eyes with a tissue she had been clutching in her fist and reached out with her other hand so Ben could help her stand up.

"Gary, Richie… go inside now. We're all going to go inside. Gramma's gone."

Jesse put his arm around my shoulder and squeezed me tight then followed his mom up the stairs and Gary and I followed our own mom into our apartment. Mom played Elvis records on the stereo while we boys sat in our room and cried for Gramma.

Tommy, awakened from his nap by sad news, lay on my bed in the dim room, crying into my pillow, while I sat on the edge of the mattress and rubbed his back. Gary sat on his own bed in the corner by the closet, his cheeks wet with tears, looking through one of our family photo albums.

Ben and Mom sat in the kitchen and smoked. Some of the neighbor ladies stopped by to hug Mom (*We're oh so sorry, Frances*) and when they had gone and the Elvis record on the turntable had played itself through to the final crackling groove, I heard my mother blow her nose and say, "Richie didn't cry. When I told him she died, he didn't even cry."

I sat there on the edge of my bed, Tommy still sniffling behind me, and stared across the hall into Gramma's silent room. My eyes clouded over and hot tears spilled down my face and I hated God for letting my good Gramma die wide awake and not in her peaceful sleep, like she'd always prayed for, and Gary said, "Come over here, Richie" and I went to his bed and cried in my big brother's arms.

"Gary, is it my fault?" I asked him quietly. "Is it because of me? Did Gramma die 'cause me and Jesse scared everybody and wasted the emergency resources?"

My big brother looked at me with a softness I had never seen in his eyes before and haven't ever seen since and said, "No, Richie. That's dumb. It's not your fault. You waste your smarts doin' things that make Mom mad, but Gramma didn't die because of you."

"Do you promise?" I asked him.

"Yeah. I promise." He sent me back to my own bed and I lay down next to Tommy and fell asleep in the stillness of the saddest July afternoon I had ever known.

Eleven - Life After Death

My mom spent the afternoon and evening on the phone, calling family in townships nearby and talking long-distance to my far-away great uncles. For dinner, we ate a warmed-over taco casserole that Louis' mother had dropped off in a glass dish with tin foil wrapped tight across the top. We didn't talk much around the table and after we ate, we all went to bed early. I fell asleep quickly, but in the middle of the night, I woke up to pee and remembered that I hadn't fed the momma cat.

I didn't flush the toilet because I worried the noise might wake up Ben or my mom, and I crept through the apartment in the dim light cast by the overhead lamp above the stove in the kitchen. I turned the front door-knob ever so slowly and didn't let it go until I had closed the door silently behind me. I stood on the porch in my pajama bottoms and glanced around the dooryard to make sure none of the neighbors were out and about and I snuck into the laundry room and dipped both my hands into the bag of cat food.

I crept around the corner of the building, careful not to drop too much of the food. A black and grey striped cat darted out from under a bush and disappeared into the shadows of the parking lot and another cat, the longhaired grey one I had seen the night before, slunk around the edge of the curb and watched me with low eyes.

In that moment, the obvious reached out and grabbed me and I realized that the cats that had been hanging around and fighting in the alley lately had been coming around to eat the cat food I had been putting out. It hadn't occurred to me until just then that the big mounds of food were always gone in the morning was because the momma cat wasn't the only one eating it, and I wondered if she had been getting enough of it or any at all. Maybe the other cats were running her off and eating it all themselves.

I sat on the ground, with my back against the tree, and waited in the street-lamp's glow, standing guard against the other strays and hoping the Siamese would come out and eat before someone in the apartment woke up and realized I wasn't in my bed.

I thought about Gramma, how much I would miss her talks and her deviled eggs and even rubbing the alcohol on her back and shoulders. I wondered who was going to save me from my mother, now that Gramma was gone, and I was just starting to doze off beneath the tree when the momma cat stuck her head out of the crawlspace, took a look around, stared at me for a moment with glowing eyes, and slunk out to crouch where I'd dumped the food. She crunched the kibble, swishing her tail back and forth. She ate with frequent pauses, lifting her eyes and glancing around, and her back legs looked tense, ready to spring her away at any moment. When she raised herself up to crawl back under the apartment building, I noticed her belly. It wasn't fat and swinging low to the ground anymore. She'd had the kittens!

Oh, boy!

She snuck back under the building and I snuck back into the apartment and stopped in the hall outside of the open door to Gramma's room. I stepped into the room, climbed up onto her bed, and leaned back into the big, soft pillows.

I lay there in the dark, confused and a little guilty, too, wondering how I could be so sad about Gramma dying and so happy about the kittens being born on the very same day, and before I found an answer, I fell fast asleep.

Twelve - The Viewing

The day before Gramma's funeral, my Aunt Toni and Uncle Guy arrived in the morning and Aunt Ellie showed up in the afternoon with my five cousins. Gramma's brothers flew in, Carlo from Florida and Mario from Arizona and Ben picked them up at the airport in the station wagon. Everyone hung around the apartment most of the day, eating the food the neighbors had been dropping off the last few days and reminiscing about Gramma and other dead relatives, some I had known, some I had never even heard of.

That evening we all went to the funeral parlor for the viewing of Gramma's body. I hadn't wanted to go and neither had Tommy, but Aunt Toni took us aside and told us that it would be disrespectful to Gramma's memory if we didn't go and if we couldn't be little men for Gramma's sake, we'd damned sure better be for the sake of our mother. I didn't like the funeral parlor, with its long heavy drapes and thick crimson carpets, fake antique furniture and low yellow lighting. The piped-in music, meant to be soothing, sounded more like the soundtrack to an old scary movie, and the viewing room was somber and tacky and seemed the kind of place where Count Dracula might sleep but where my Gramma never would have spent one night.

Aunt Ellie made us sign the guest book and it seemed such a strange thing to me, a guest book for a dead person, and we sat in hard velvet chairs as Mom and Toni knelt on the carpet beside Gramma's open casket, whispering a prayer and fingering their rosaries. We couldn't see inside the coffin from where we sat, but I knew that Aunt Ellie would make us kneel at the coffin and look at Gramma inside.

I didn't want to see Gramma dead, not because I was afraid of her corpse or of her ghost, but because I was trying hard to remember her the way she had been when she was alive and smiling. It was bad enough to remember the last time I saw her, wide-eyed and frightened in her bed, trying hard to take a breath, clutching her hand to her bosom. It was hard enough to forget that, and I didn't understand how seeing her dead in her coffin could make it any easier.

My mom and Toni got up from the carpet and held each other as they sat in the corner on the hard velvet chairs and sobbed. Ellie took Tommy and me by our hands and led us to the side of the room, where Gramma's inexpensive casket rested against the wall, two big vases of flowers at each end and smaller arrangements in pretty, wrapped pots on the carpet underneath.

We hesitated and Ellie gently pushed us forward. "Don't be afraid, boys. She just looks like she's asleep."

She didn't look like she was sleeping. I knew what my Gramma looked like when she slept, with her wiry gray hair a tangled mess and her head arched back on her big, fluffy pillows, snoring with her mouth wide open and one arm resting across her belly, the other dangling over the edge of the bed. No, she didn't look asleep here in this box in the dreary funeral parlor light, with her hair brushed just so and her lipstick too bright, in a dress from her closet she would have never worn to bed. Here, with her head still and straight on a pillow so small, and a cheap string of pearls against her skin grey and pale, she wasn't asleep and she'd never wake up. She was dead and, to me, that was just exactly how she looked.

Tommy and I stood there beside the casket in silence, looking at Gramma's body, hostages to my Aunt Ellie's misunderstanding of grief and respect. Ellie kneeled between us and began to rub her rosary and pray the Hail Mary and Tommy and I turned our faces from Gramma's and looked at each other over the top of my praying aunt's bowed head. My brother's eyes, the same blue as mine, weren't just sad, shocked, and tired; Tommy's eyes were twin bottomless pits of fear and I found the mercy that I had misplaced a few days earlier when I could have spared him from his fears, but chose to lead him to the pond, and my prank, instead.

"Tommy has nightmares..." I whispered.

Aunt Ellie looked up at me, her rosary beads clutched to her cheek, and quietly said, "What? What is it, Richie?"

"Tommy has nightmares," I repeated. "He's scared of stuff like this. He shouldn't be here."

With a hiss she had meant to be a whisper, she told me that this was absofuckinglutely where Tommy should be, where all of us should be, out of respect for our Gramma, who loved each one of us grandkids more than anything in the world, and was watching over us from Heaven-up-above.

I glanced toward the ceiling and Heaven-up-above and then I looked into the coffin at Gramma and I said, "Gramma *never* woulda made us come *here.*"

Aunt Ellie sighed a grumpy huff and rose from her knees, smoothing her dress with the palms of her fat hands and said, "Well! No one told *me* he was going to have bad dreams. Imagine, a boy afraid of his own gramma."

She leaned over the coffin and kissed Gramma, leaving a trace of red lipstick on her powdered skin.

"C'mon, then, boys, let's go. Kiss your gramma g'bye and come on."

Tommy's eyes widened, blinked when they couldn't get any bigger, and fell on me in horror. I looked up at our aunt in refusal and her eyes, so much like my mom's eyes, measured mine for defiance. I blinked. She did not.

I turned away from Ellie's stubborn stare, wrapped my fingers around the quilted edge of the casket, leaned my face into my Gramma's bed of death and kissed her firmly, briefly, on her breathless lips. Her flesh was stiff and cool, her lips were like soft rubber and, if my kiss was felt in Heaven, it went unanswered here below. No tickled ribs, no crinkly smile; just a cold, one-sided goodbye.

"There," Ellie said softly, "That's how a good boy pays his last respects." She reached down, picked her purse up off the carpet and slung it over her shoulder. "Kiss your gramma, Tommy."

Tommy's bottom lip quivered and he looked at me for only the briefest moment, a look of sad defeat, and stepped up on the platform where Gramma's coffin stood on display.

"No, Tommy," I said. "Don't do it. You don't have to do it."

I watched Ellie's fingers whiten as she clenched the handbag strap in anger. She wouldn't yell or scream at me, not here. No one, not my mother, not her sister, was going to smack me or spank me in the funeral parlor and disturb the solemn peace of Gramma's final rest, but Ellie fixed me with a glare and a telepathic threat and hissed at my brother, "Thomas Joseph Holeman. Kiss. Your. Grandmother!"

"Aunt Eleanor..." I said, reaching out to take my little brother by his hand, turning to walk him up the plush red aisle, past the hard velvet chairs where mourners sat with tears and sniffles, and out the big wooden doors, "Kiss. My. Butt!"

In the parking lot, I sat with Tommy on the hood of our car, waiting for my mother and my fate.

"You're gonna be in trouble, Richie. Aunt Ellie is really pee-oh'd." He slumped his shoulders, sighed, and said, "I shoulda kissed Gramma."

I thought of Gramma's lips, cold and stiff against my kiss, and the way her eyes seemed slammed, not fallen, shut. I remembered how her hands lay clasped across her chest, as if her heart still hurt or to hold her soul inside, and I said, "No, you shouldn't have. Trust me."

"You're gonna get spanked, Richie."

I told him I didn't care, that I was gonna get spanked for something anyway, and Tommy did something he hadn't done since we were both just little kids. He leaned against my shoulder, hugged me around my neck and kissed me on my cheek.

"Thanks, Richie."

Thirteen - In the Dark

On the way home from the funeral parlor, Ben drove with the radio off and Mom sat on the passenger side of the station wagon, crying, staring out the window as the long July sun went down and the streetlamps came on. Tommy fell asleep, his face smashed peacefully against the door-panel, and Gary flipped absently through a stack of baseball cards and listened to his transistor radio, the little white earphone stuffed into one ear. I sat between my brothers in the backseat and snuck a few glances at my mother's reflection in the rearview mirror, searching her face for trouble, looking for anger in her eyes, but all she had was grief and all I saw were tears.

She didn't say a word all the way home, never twisted around in her seat to scream at me or smack me across my face for talking back to my aunt, and when we got home, she carried Tommy in and dumped him on his bed then went into her room with Ben and closed the door. Gary and I watched television in the living room for a couple of hours until Ben came out in his saggy white underwear, stumbled to the kitchen to get a beer from the fridge, and mumbled, "Get your asses in bed, funeral tomorrow" on his way back to the bedroom.

In my bed, I lay awake, waiting for the quiet to hush itself to silence, listening to be sure that everyone had fallen asleep before I crept out from under my sheet and snuck out of the apartment to feed the cat. I tip-toed off the porch and into the laundry room and while I was squeezing behind the washer to reach the half-empty bag of cat food, I heard footsteps behind me and my heart pounded in my chest as I spun around, knowing my Mom had caught me.

"Jesse!" I whispered. He whispered back. "Hey, Richie. You scared me."

"*You* scared *me*," I told him and we giggled quietly in the shadows of the laundry room. "Whatcha doin' out?"

"Same as you, pardner. Feedin' the cat."

I filled my palms with cat food, Jesse shoved the bag back in the dusty place behind the wash machine and we crept around to the back of our building. We sat together on the ground, beneath the tree we had been climbing in and falling out of since we were small, and talked in outlaw whispers while the momma cat ate. We tried to guess how long it would be before the kittens would start to come out of the crawlspace, wondered how long we could keep them a secret from the grown-ups once they did, and reminded each other that we still had to tell Ray that his one-dollar kitten had been born.

I told Jesse what had happened at the funeral parlor, how my Aunt Ellie had forced me to kiss Gramma g'bye and tried to do the same to Tommy until I told her to kiss my butt and took my little brother outside.

"You told her to kiss your *butt*? Jeez, Richie, did you catch a beating?"

I told him that I hadn't gotten in trouble at all, that my aunt had given me a mean look when she came out of the funeral parlor with my cousins to go back to the motel, but that my mom hadn't even said a single word about it, almost as if Gramma really *was* watching over me from Heaven-up-above.

"She *is*, Richie."

I thought about my best friend's words for a long time after we had snuck back into our apartments and our beds, wondering if he was right or if he had only been trying to make me feel better and, to this day, I sometimes wonder still.

Fourteen - A Hole Through Summer

At all the funerals I had seen on television or in the movies, the mourners wore fine clothes; the men and boys in somber dark suits, the women and girls in tasteful black dresses or skirts. My brothers and I didn't own suits, but that morning, hours before the funeral, my great-uncle Carlo came by the apartment, hurried the three of us into his rental car and drove us to the department store, where he bought us identical stiff white shirts, black jeans, shiny shoes and clip-on ties.

"Three places you always want to look sharp, boys," he told us in the store, "Weddings, funerals and court."

Gramma's funeral was what Mom called a graveside service and hearing that made Tommy nervous, but I told him it just meant that the funeral would be outside and that I would sit next to him and everything would be alright. He asked me if the coffin would be open and I told him I didn't know, but we would be sitting down, so we wouldn't be able to see inside the casket even if it *was* open.

"That's good," he said. "I don't wanna have bad dreams about Gramma. I love Gramma."

"I know, Tommy. I'll sit next to you and if you get scared, you go on and hold my hand and I'll let you."

We drove to the funeral in a long line of cars, parading slowly from the mortuary to the cemetery with the headlights on in the bright heat of the afternoon. We followed the hearse through iron gates straight out of an old Hammer horror movie, parked at the curb of a big garden of stones, and everyone piled out of the cars, smoothing their dresses and the creases in their pants.

Gramma's brothers and four of my older second cousins carried the casket to the middle of the lawn and set it down on a small platform beside a dark, empty hole. The flowers from the funeral parlor had been brought to the cemetery and arranged around the grave where Gramma's casket would wait to be spoken over, prayed over and wept over, but all those pretty petals couldn't disguise the bleakness of that fresh, deep hole in the grass. When the talking, the crying, and the praying were done, they would lower her into that hole and shut her bones away forever from the summer sun she had loved so much.

We walked across the grass, careful not to step on any of the graves, and before we'd even reached the rows of folding chairs they'd set up for us to sit in, Tommy placed his left hand in my right and squeezed until he felt me squeezing back. Hand in hand, we walked behind my mother, pretty and sad in a long black dress, and Ben, somehow still sloppy and scruffy, even in the crisp black suit he had borrowed from John.

My aunts and cousins walked with us and, behind us, friends from the neighborhood and some of the ladies who had worked with Gramma when she was a switchboard operator for the telephone company followed in respectful silence. Even The Bicycle Witch was there, at the very back of the procession, wearing a long black dress and a wide purple hat. I wondered if she had come to the cemetery in one of the cars or if she had rode her blue bike all the way from town.

Mom led us to the front row and we took our seats and as the priest stepped from the graveside to shake our hands and soothe our souls, Aunt Ellie sat down in the chair right beside me and whispered, "Someone's got to make sure you two behave, today of *all* days."

I turned in my chair, looked over my shoulder, and found Jesse and his mom, standing behind the last row of chairs with the other neighbors who had come to see Gramma laid to rest. Jesse looked at me and winked and nodded his head (*You got this, Richie*) and I nodded back at him (*No sweat, pardner*) and then Ellie hissed, "Turn around and sit up straight" as the priest began to pray.

I sat up straight and I held Tommy's hand and I tried to pay attention to the priest, but his voice seemed far away and his words, meant to comfort us and assure us that Heaven was near, only made me feel lost and far, far from God. I kept myself from fidgeting, but I couldn't keep my eyes from the dark, open grave and I imagined a bottomless hole that would take Gramma in and then swallow the world and the sky right behind her.

"Richie! Pay attention!"

Aunt Ellie hissed in my ear, wrapped her fingers around my wrist and dug her fingernails into my skin.

The priest was finishing another prayer and all of my family and most of our neighbors were crying. Tommy was sniffling beside me, his hand still clasped in mine, and next to him, Gary cried with his head bowed, his long bangs hanging over his eyes. I realized that the funeral was over and that Gramma's casket was being lowered ever so gently into the ground, while people were standing and forming a line to pass by her grave and pay one last respect.

G'bye, Gramma. I love you forever.

Everyone was crying, but I didn't shed one tear, not with Ben rising from his chair at the end of the row and his eyes prowling over my face as he passed me and stepped toward the grave. I wanted to cry and my eyes ached from trying, but I held to my vow and I flooded my heart with the tears I refused to let loose. Behind Ben came my weeping mother and she reached down and took Tommy's hand from mine and tugged him up out of his chair and he fell in step at her side. Gary came next and I stood up beside him and Mom looked down at me, her wet eyes staring into my dry eyes, burning briefly for a moment before she raised her chin and turned her back to me to follow Ben past Gramma's grave.

As each person passed the grave, they stooped and took up a handful of dirt and tossed it into the hole. I watched Tommy take just a tiny bit, scatter it into the dark and then wipe his palm on the seat of his pants and then it was my turn and I filled my fist with the cemetery dirt, tossed some of it over Gramma's coffin and shoved what remained into the pocket of my brand new black jeans.

On the way back to the cars, walking carefully among the headstones, I saw The Bicycle Witch pushing her Schwinn across the grass. She had come all the way on her bike, after all. I wondered why she'd come to Gramma's funeral and when I stole a peek at her, she was peeking back at me and before I turned away, she winked.

I waited for a baseball or a bolt of lightning, but this time, no magic happened on a day when I needed some most.

After the funeral, everyone gathered at the apartment, eating casseroles in the living room and spilling out onto the porch and the lawn, talking in small groups, remembering Gramma, smoking cigarettes. I went into my room to change my clothes and, with the door closed behind me, I turned out the pocket of my pants, shook the grave dirt onto the top of my dresser and used a Topps baseball card to scoop it into a tiny carton that had once held a Matchbox racer.

I tucked the little box under some socks in my drawer, changed into shorts and a striped tank top and slipped on my sneakers. I grabbed a cold chicken leg from a platter on the kitchen table, wrapped it up in a napkin, and squeezed past my uncles and aunts to go and find Jesse and somewhere to hide. My mother was sitting in Gramma's recliner, drinking iced water and dabbing at her eyes with a tissue. She stopped me with a glance and used just one finger to pull me to her side.

"Vieni qua, Richie." *Come over here.*

She leaned her head next to mine and told me in a very soft voice to go to my room and wait for her there until everyone left.

"But, Mom..."

Her eyes narrowed and she pursed her lips to tell me again, but I turned away and went down the hall and sat on my bed, listening as the crowd began to thin on the other side of the closed bedroom door. I ate the cold fried chicken drumstick, wrapped the bone in the greasy napkin and tossed it into the wastepaper basket in the corner. I was tired but I didn't lie down, afraid I would fall asleep before my mother came in to (*beat me*) talk to me once all her company finally went home or to the airport or back to their motels.

I was still sitting on the edge of my bed two hours later, reading a book about kittens that I'd checked out from the book-mobile a few days earlier, when the bedroom door opened and my mother came into the room, still in her long black dress, and stood over me.

I looked up at her, because I knew she would demand it, and she said, "Your aunt told me what you said to her at the funeral parlor."

"But, Mom, she was gonna make Tommy…"

"I know." She bent forward, closer to me and I found out what I was really in trouble for, what she was *really* angry about. "Richie… why didn't you cry at Gramma's funeral?"

"I couldn't, Ma. I just couldn't cry."

She leaned in closer still and I could feel her breath on my face when she spoke. "Don't you know that you were her favorite?"

I almost raised my hand up to shield my face, a defensive reflex, but I knew it would only make my mother angrier and I let it fall back onto the mattress.

"I… I don't know, Mom."

"You know," she said. "You do know, Richie. You were her favorite grandchild and you couldn't cry for your own Gramma when she died."

I swallowed. My eyes began to sting.

"I *did* cry! I *did* cry when Gramma died," I said. "I just couldn't cry there, Mom. Not at the funeral."

She asked me why and I said I couldn't tell her and she gripped my shoulders and shook me... shook me... shook me. She let go of my shoulders and shoved me backward on the bed and when I sat up again, she spit in my face and screamed at the top of her lungs.

"YOU TELL ME! YOU TELL ME! YOU TELL ME RIGHT FUCKING NOW!"

I wanted to tell her. I wanted to scream right back at her that I would never, ever cry in front of that mean, stupid drunk that *she* let into our apartment, that *she* brought into our lives, that *she* chose over me, but I knew that she would beat me harder if I did and I sat in silence, with my mouth shut tight and my eyes staring wide into hers.

She drew back her hand and, swung it through the air and she smacked me just once, as hard as she could, harder than she had ever slapped me before, and I howled and hot tears spilled down my face.

"There." Just a whisper. "Now you can cry. Now you can sit here and cry for not crying."

She turned on her heels and she stalked out the door, slamming it so hard that one of Gary's Little League trophies tumbled off his shelf and onto his bed, and then I heard her sobbing in the room next to mine.

I wept in the dark and I prayed, not to God, but to Gramma; that she would come back just to take me away.

fifteen - The Cat Riot

That night, it was just me and Tommy in the bedroom and we both slept in my bed, but I made him bring his pillow so his big head wouldn't hog mine. Tommy told me that Gary had gone back to the motel on Route 1 with Aunt Ellie and our cousins, to sleep over on their last night in town.

"They're stayin' at the nice motel," Tommy told me. "That one with the big pool with the slide."

"How come you didn't go? Didn't they ask you to go?"

Tommy rolled onto his side and I could feel his breath on my neck when he spoke. "Sure they asked me, but I didn't wanna go, Richie."

I asked him why, expecting him to answer that he was still mad at Aunt Ellie for trying to make him kiss Gramma's dead body, but instead he said, "I didn't go 'cause you couldn't go."

"Oh."

"The cousins said you should go" Tommy told me, "But Mom said you were in trouble 'cause you didn't cry for Gramma and Aunt Ellie said you had a sassy mouth, too."

I told Tommy that he shouldn't have stayed home because of me and that I wouldn't have went to the motel with crazy Aunt Ellie even if she'd invited me, because she had pinched my wrist at the funeral and I still had red marks where she dug her fake fingernails into my skin. "Richie... how *come* you didn't cry at Gramma's funeral?"

"Because Ben was there. He was right there looking at me."

"So?"

I turned my head on my pillow to face my little brother and I told him that I could never cry in front of Ben. "Never," I whispered, "it's my sacred vow."

"What's a sacred vowel?"

I giggled. "Not a vowel, dummy. A *vow*. It's just when you swear to never do something and you keep your swear."

"But how come, Richie?"

I struggled for a long moment to think of a way to make Tommy understand and finally I said, "You know how you're not supposed to run from a mean dog?"

Mean dogs were on Tommy's list of scary things and he knew what I was talking about. He said, "Because if you run, it will know you're afraid of it and it'll chase after you and bite you."

I nodded in the dark and said, "Yeah. Well, Ben's like a mean dog and if I let him see me cry, he'll know I'm afraid of him."

Tommy sucked in his breath and said, "He is? Richie... I cried in front of him!"

"Don't worry. He doesn't want to bite you, Tommy."

My little brother sighed. "He wants to bite you, though, Richie?"

"I think he wants to kill me."

I made Tommy swear his solemn vow (*vowel*) that he wouldn't tell Mom what I said about Ben and I told him that if he broke his vow, he'd have nightmares every night for a year and we finally fell asleep, together in my bed, Tommy's pillow cast aside and his big head crowding onto mine.

I'm not sure which it was that woke me up some time later, the screeching and yowling screams of the cats fighting outside the open bedroom window or Tommy's hand on my shoulder, shaking me. He was sitting up in the bed, his eyes wide in the dark.

"Richie! Wake up. What's that?"

"Stray cats fightin' outside," I told him, rubbing the back of my hand across my eyes and standing up on the bed to look out the window, "You slept through the last one." I pulled the curtain back and pressed my face against the window, cupping my hands around my eyes, peering out at the patchy lawn behind our building, where the streetlight cast its glow and the shadow of the curbside tree lay dark on the ground.

Tommy stood next to me, leaned his elbows on the windowsill and looked out into the night. "It's scary-sounding, ain't it?"

"Yeah, but it's just cats. You can see 'em out there."

There were four cats outside the building. I could see the momma cat standing on the grass near the curb, her back arched and her tail bushed out and tall, her mouth open to show her teeth, staring at the big, shaggy grey one that I'd first noticed weeks ago. An orange tabby sat on the sidewalk, swishing its tail and I could see a pair of glowing yellow eyes peering out from beneath a car parked along the curb.

"Jeez, Richie... it's a cat *riot*," Tommy whispered.

The momma cat tensed, wailed, and charged across the lawn. She pounced on the big grey tom and they locked together in a rolling, hissing ball of claws and fur. I turned away from the window in a hurry to sneak outside and chase the cats away before they hurt the Siamese, but as I jumped from the bed, the bedroom door flew open, the light flashed on and my mother came into the room, her face angry, her eyes cloudy, wrapping a robe around her shoulders.

"Goddamned cats! Richie, get back in bed." She stalked to the window and pushed the curtain aside, peering out through the screen like Tommy and I had done moments before. "There's three or four of them out there. Tommy, get your ass in your own bed."

She turned to leave the room and as she closed the door behind her, I heard Ben call out from their bedroom, "What is it, Fran? What's going on?"

"Goddamned cats again," she answered, "Tomorrow I'll call the landlord and he'd better get rid of the fucking things."

The next morning, Tommy and I sat at the kitchen table, eating cereal, while Mom put a pot of coffee on so it would be hot and fresh when Ben stumbled out of the bedroom with a cigarette dangling from his lips and one eye scrunched shut like Popeye. She dampened a cloth in the kitchen sink and ran it across the counter where she had spilled some coffee grounds.

"You boys look sleepy," she said, "Those cats kept you up. I've never seen so many stray cats around here before."

Tommy wiped milk from the corner of his lips and said, "I bet they can smell the cat food."

Oh no!

My mom tossed the rag into the dishwater in the sink and looked at Tommy. "Smell the cat food? What cat food?"

"Someone left a whole bag of cat food in the laundry room."

We followed Mom outside and stood on the porch as she disappeared into the laundry room, came back out a moment later with the bag of cat food under one arm and carried it across the parking lot to throw it in the big garbage dumpster. I looked at my little brother.

"Tommy, what were you doing poking around behind the washing machine?"

He shrugged his shoulders. "Sheesh, I dunno. Just scroungin' around for junk."

Sixteen - Freedom Train

All summer long, there'd been a poster tacked up over the checkout table on the bookmobile, blue construction paper with big hand-printed block letters announcing that the American Freedom Train would be passing through our township on July 23rd, in the late morning.

Miss Winters had taught us about the Freedom Train during the last weeks of school and I had paid particularly close attention because I was pretty sure I liked freedom and I was absolutely sure I liked trains. The American Freedom Train was a long train, painted in patriotic red, white and blue, and powered by a real steam engine. It was traveling the country, carrying displays of American treasures in its cars and making station stops in some of the towns and cities along the rails. It wouldn't be stopping in our neighborhood, or even in our township, but we could stand out in the dust along the tracks and watch it steam by on its way to Morristown.

That morning after breakfast, we headed for the tracks, Jesse, Tommy and me. Before we climbed the fence, we sent Tommy diving into a dumpster to scavenge a couple of cardboard boxes from the trash and we tore them into flat pieces that we could use to slide down the steep dirt embankment under the Grand Avenue overpass. We boosted Tommy up, over the fence, dropped down behind him, and walked up the tracks to the shade beneath the overpass.

Within an hour, the Hodges brothers and Ray Laws appeared over the fence and jogged up the tracks to take turns climbing the embankment and taking a bumpy ride to the bottom on our cardboard sleds. As the morning stretched on, people from the neighborhood, mostly kids but some of the grown-ups, too, climbed the fence, or came the long way around from Grand Avenue, and lined both sides of the tracks, some standing in the dirt, others sitting on folding lawn chairs they'd carried from the apartment complex. Some of the littlest kids rode high on the shoulders of their dads or big brothers.

"It's like a party," Tommy said and Jesse said, "Yeah, for five whole minutes while the train passes by."

Gary and a couple of his friends, Bobby Boyd and Mike Renfro, came slouching up the tracks, grabbed the sheets of cardboard away from us and left us standing at the bottom of the embankment as they climbed to the top and raced back down to the bottom.

From down the tracks, a train whistle wailed and the crowd along the rails began to murmur and stir.

"The Freedom Train's coming!" Burt shouted.

Gary tossed aside the piece of cardboard he had stolen from me, and he and his friends began to scoop up rocks from the ground along the tracks. "Bombardment!" Gary hollered, "Let's bomb it!"

"Bomb the Freedom Train?" I said.

"It's just a train, Richie. We bomb 'em all the time."

We *did* bomb trains all the time. We would stuff our pockets with rocks and climb the embankment to Grand Avenue, where we'd stand on the sidewalk, leaning over the railing to hurl our stones at trains passing underneath.

"Yeah... I know... but... the *Freedom Train*?"

He told me I didn't have to bomb the train if I didn't want to, that I could stay down here with the little kids and the old ladies and salute the train when it went by. His friends laughed and that settled it and I bent to the ground and began to shove rocks into the pockets of my cut-offs. The rest of our gang gathered up their own stashes of rocks and we all scrambled up the hill and over the rail to the sidewalk as the Freedom Train appeared far down the tracks, a flash of red, white and blue and silver, a long plume of smoke billowing up and trailing behind it.

Up on the bridge, we lined up along the railing and Tommy hollered, "I'm the lookout!" He was always the lookout when we bombed trains, because he was too short to reach over the railing and throw stones. He would stand on the curb, watch the passing traffic, and shout out an alarm if he saw a police car coming up Grand Avenue.

The train was approaching, steaming hard and slow up the tracks, and I wished that it were making a stop in our town, that I could climb up the iron steps and see the historical documents and movie props and Olympic medals on display in glass cases in the red, white and blue cars, instead of standing on the Grand Avenue bridge with my pockets full of warm stones.

As the big steam engine passed into the shadow of the overpass, Gary hollered "BOMBS AWAAAAAAY!" and we all began hurling rocks down on the tops of the train cars passing beneath us. The rocks banged onto the cars, bounced off, and rolled in the dirt and the people gathered along the tracks looked up at us and pointed and some of the men hollered.

"Cops! Cops!" Tommy shouted and we all stopped chucking rocks and turned to look up the street. There wasn't a police car in sight, just an Animal Control truck idling at the red light at the bottom of the bridge.

"That's a dog-catcher, Tommy," Gary said, "Not the police."

"But he can call the police on his radio," Tommy argued.

"Don't be a dummy, Tommy." Gary laughed and leaned back over the railing, digging in his pocket for another rock, and we all began to bombard the train again.

A few minutes later, our stockpile of rocks nearly spent, the last few cars of the train crawling under the bridge, Tommy shouted again (*Cops! Cops!*) and we all turned to see a black and white police cruiser rolling up Grand Avenue. Its siren wasn't wailing, but the lights mounted on top were flashing red and blue.

"Run!" Gary shouted and we dropped our rocks and jumped over the railing, scrambled down the embankment and over the fence. We didn't look back as we ran, but I imagined the cop leaping out of his car and hurrying behind us, the people along the tracks pointing and hollering, "There they go! That way!"

We ran through the neighborhood, laughing and shouting, an unruly mob of boys beating a path along the sidewalk in worn-out sneakers, and burst around the corner of our building, collapsing in a panting heap on the lawn. Ben was sitting in his chair on the porch, drinking coffee and smoking. Mom was standing behind him, one hand on his shoulder, the other holding her own coffee mug.

"What the hell kind of trouble are you boys gettin' into?" Ben sneered and then my mother stepped off the porch and said, "And where the hell is your brother?"

I looked at Gary, he looked at me, and we both looked around us, where the other kids lay strewn across the grass, catching their breath. Tommy wasn't among them.

We're dead!

"Where in the hell is Tommy?" Mom shouted, "Where did you leave your little brother?"

She was looking at Gary and I felt a fleeting relief that he would bear most of her anger this time, being the oldest, the one who should have been watching out for Tommy, but I also knew that both of us would catch a beating for leaving our little brother behind in whatever trouble we had started.

Gary stared up at her, but before he could answer, a police car pulled up to the curb and all heads turned to watch the tall policeman climb out and come around to the curb.

"Oh, shit..." Ross Hodges whispered.

The cop came around the car and opened the back door and Tommy climbed out and stood beside him on the curb. He looked at Mom and then he looked at Gary, put his hands on his hips and shouted, "Guess who called the cops, dummy! The goshdanged *dog-catcher*!"

After the tall policeman had folded himself back into his black and white patrol car and drove away down the block and around the corner and Jesse and the Hodges brothers had been marched up to their apartments by their mothers, my mom ran the other kids off with a glare and ordered my brothers and me into our bedroom.

She snatched the longest strip of leather from the wall and followed us to our room, screaming at us about throwing rocks at trains (*The Goddamned American Freedom Train*) and getting in trouble with the cops (*If you end up in juvenile hall, I'll let you rot there*) and leaving our little brother behind (*How goddamned stupid are you two*) while she swatted at the back of Gary's head with the belt and Tommy and I dove for the cover of our bedsheets.

Gary didn't cower on his bed, didn't try to disappear into the wall and he didn't cry while Mom strapped his butt and legs and screamed at him. He stood at the edge of his bed, his feet planted firmly in the carpet, and he took his beating, but his eyes brimmed with tears and he had to clench his jaw to keep from hollering out.

From my own bed, I watched Mom strap Gary with the belt that Tommy had brought home and I felt sorry for him and I wanted her to stop, but I couldn't look away and I knew that when she did stop, when she was done with him, she would cross the room and come for me.

Gary's defiance finally crumbled and she smacked him one last time, hard across his thigh, as he retreated to his bed and crumpled on his mattress, crying at last. My mother turned from him, her fiery eyes darted from me to Tommy and back to me and she descended on me with the belt. Her rage and her resolve had been spent on Gary and she only strapped me a few times, hard across my back and butt, and then she stood in the center of the room, the belt dangling at her side, her face red and sweaty and her eyes hard and mean.

"You boys are grounded for life! And if you ever leave your little brother behind again, I'll beat you until they call the cops on *me*." She walked to the edge of Tommy's bed and smacked him across the cheek with the palm of her hand. "And you! When your brothers say run, you run; you don't stand around like a little idiot!"

"Yes, Momma." Whimpers.

She left us in our room the rest of the afternoon and when we crept out to the kitchen at dinnertime, she ate in the living room with Ben and sent us straight to bed as soon as we'd finished our macaroni and cheese.

We lay in our beds and talked in low voices and Gary asked Tommy why he hadn't run away behind us when the cop had come and Tommy told him, "I just wanted to ride in the police car. He wouldn't put me in the handcuffs, though."

Seventeen - Fire!

After three solid days of confinement to our room, worn down by Gary's constant pleas to be allowed to go outside, Mom commuted our life sentence and said we weren't grounded anymore, but we'd better not get into any trouble the rest of the summer or she'd throw us right back into our room. We rushed out of the apartment and into the last week of July, three precious days of summer lost to us forever.

We played out in the street and across the fence in the woods and I spent almost every waking moment with Jesse, neither of us mentioning the swiftness of time going by, but both of us painfully aware that the summer was burning away toward the day when we would say goodbye and Jesse would move away with his mother, leaving me behind, alone in the place that belonged to us both.

On the last Saturday of the month, when it got dark and Mom came out on the porch to call us in from the street, I asked her if Jesse could sleepover at our apartment and she said yes, he could, if it was okay with his mother. Jesse ran upstairs to ask his mom and before he came back down with his sleeping bag tucked under one arm and his pillow tucked under the other, my mother looked down at me, took my chin in her hand the way Gramma used to do, and said, "Jesse's a good friend, Richie. I'm sorry he's moving away."

"He's the *best* friend, Mom. I'm gonna miss him bad."

"I know, honey," she said and she knelt down and kissed me on my forehead and I hugged her and told her I loved her and I almost cried, but Ben appeared in the doorway. I wiped my damp eyes on the shoulder of my mother's blouse and slid from her arms as she stood up and went to the porch to sit with him.

Jesse came stomping down the stairs and we went into our apartment and played board games and when everyone else was going to bed, Mom said Jesse and I could sit up awhile and watch TV in the living room.

We ate Cap'n Crunch on the sofa and watched *Creature Features* on channel 12, giggling in the dark and teasing each other about who was more afraid of *The Creature from the Black Lagoon* and just as the slimy swamp monster was emerging from the dark pool of water in the moonlight, we heard some kind of a commotion outside and a loud BANGBANGBANG on the front door that scared both of us off of the couch and onto our feet.

We recognized John's booming voice, calling out from the other side of the door, hollering "Fran! Frances! Your car's on fire!" and my mom and Ben rushed groggily out from the hallway, my brothers following right behind them. Mom slid the chain from its latch, twisted the dead bolt and yanked the door open. The courtyard was aglow with an orange light that flickered and splashed on the apartment building walls. John was standing on the porch in pajama pants, his thick black hair sticking up on his head in messy clumps, waving for my mom to come outside and the familiar wail of sirens filled the night, echoing down the alley between our building and the carport.

We stood on the courtyard lawn and watched the Country Squire burn, bright flames rising up from the station wagon to lick the wooden beams of the carport, smoke filling the alleyway. Mom stood in silence, the flames reflected in the lenses of her glasses, her eyes dark and stormy and I remembered Gramma telling me that there was bound to be more than a hundred dollars' worth of trouble over the car.

The firemen swarmed off their trucks, connected their big canvas hoses, and sprayed the fire with water until the car was a smoldering heap of metal, steaming in the carport.

"Well, there goes our trip to Wildwood," I said, and Mom spun around and her hand whipped out and slapped me across my mouth. I felt warm blood trickle from my lip and hot tears fill my eyes and I turned and fled barefoot down the block, across Bloomfield Street and into the night.

I could hear footsteps falling fast behind me and I knew that Jesse was chasing after me through the neighborhood. I climbed the fence, lowered myself carefully to the dirt on the other side and made my way down the path to the pond. I sat on the edge of the water and cried and Jesse came and sat beside me and put his arm around my shoulder.

"You okay, Richie?"

I wiped my eyes and looked out across the water, into the shadows of the trees beyond, listening to the sounds of the cars and big trucks out on the highway.

"I can't take it, Jesse. She hits me and hits me and hits me," I whispered. "Everything isn't my fault, Jesse."

"I know, Richie," he said and, because he probably didn't know what else to say, he drew me closer into his brotherly embrace.

"She didn't *used* to hit me," I whispered, "Not like she does now. Something happened and she got meaner, Jess."

He sighed and looked thoughtful. "What do you think happened to her, Richie?"

I shrugged my shoulders and wiped my tears. "I dunno, Jess. It doesn't matter, anyway. It's too late to fix it now."

I stared into the dark woods and wondered if I just got up right that moment and walked into the trees, out past the highway and never came back, would I find my place to hide or would my mother find me first.

"Maybe you're lucky, Jesse. You're gonna move to Ohio and your mom will have a job and maybe you'll get to live in a better neighborhood, where the grown-ups are... grown up."

Jesse looked at me, straight into my eyes.

"This is the best neighborhood, Richie," he told me, "There's nicer neighborhoods, like the big houses over by the river, but they're not better. Nope. This is the best neighborhood."

"Why, Jesse? Everything is so crummy here."

"Because..." he sighed and he looked up at the stars and I waited while he struggled to find the words to tell me something he felt, but didn't know how to say. "Because, *we* were here, Richie. This is *our* place."

We sat in the darkness, on the bank of the pond where we had spent summer days playing cowboys and pirates, listening to the night sounds of frogs and birds and the summer wind in the trees. We sat with our arms slung across each other's shoulders, and I realized that when the sun came up, July would be gone and August would begin to fall like a curtain over the last days of summer.

Soon, Jesse would be gone, too, far, far away to goshdanged Ohio.

Part Three
August Moon

One - Heat Wave

August smothered the neighborhood with a heat wave, as if summer had saved up all its hottest days, stacked them in a sweltering row and dropped them on us all at once. I spent that first hot, humid week of the month in my room, grounded for my selfish outburst and for running off into the woods the night of the car fire, while the dog days of summer panted just outside my window-screen. In the day, I would lay on my bed or on the floor, reading comics or writing stories beneath the whirring fan that stirred the air in the room, but didn't seem to cool it at all, and in the evening, between dinner and dark, Jesse would appear on the lawn behind our building and we'd gossip quietly through the open window while he tossed scraps into the grass for the momma cat.

One night at the end of the week, he told me he could hear the kittens meowing and that it probably wouldn't be much longer before they started coming out from under the building.

"When are you gettin' off groundation, Richie?"

"Tomorrow's my last day. I can come out on Saturday."

"Well, don't mess it up and get in trouble again, Richie. It's been dullsville around here."

"Don't worry. I won't." All week, I had been careful not to upset Mom so she wouldn't add any more days to my punishment. I didn't talk back to her, make any messes, or fight with my brothers and I stayed in my room most of the time, avoiding Ben as much as I could in our small apartment. "Hey, I heard Bobby is back."

Bobby Bozart and his sisters went to Pennsylvania every summer to visit their dad for a month and they had been gone since the end of June. Two nights before, lying awake in my bed, I had overheard Ben tell my mom that he was going to the train station in the morning to help his sister Cathy collect the kids.

"Yeah, he's back. Helen is stayin' at their dad's the rest of the summer, but Bobby and Cheryl are home," Jesse said, grinning, "Betcha can't wait to see Cheryl, huh, Richie?"

"Sheesh, Jesse."

"You gonna smooch her, Richie?" he teased, squeezing his lips together and making wet kissing noises. "You gonna tell her what a lonely ol' summer it's been?" He wiped the back of his hand across his forehead in an exaggerated sweep and pretended to shake sweat from the end of his fingers.

"C'mon, Jesse," I whispered. My cheeks felt warm and I knew I was blushing. "Knock it off already."

"Okay, okay," Jesse giggled and a big, goofy grin briefly split his face in half. "Well, Bobby wants to build a fort in the bog," he said, "I told him we had to wait 'til you could come out to start building, but we already scrapped some boards and nails and stuff from that construction site over on Grand Avenue."

"Sounds like a plan, Stan," I said. "Tell Bobby we'll all meet down at the bog Saturday after cartoons. I'll see you later, Jesse."

"See ya, Richie." He turned to go back upstairs to his apartment, but before I let the curtain close over the open window, he looked back and smiled. "Should I tell Cheryl to be there, too, Romeo?"

"Sheesh, Jesse!"

I left the window and lay in my bed, hands folded behind me on the pillow, thinking about the fort we would build in the woods. I made a mental list of the tools I would have to dig out of the closet and from under my bed and, much to my own surprise and the ruination of my practical thoughts, I found myself wondering if Cheryl Bozart's hair had gotten even more blonde and even curlier after a month in the Pennsylvania sunshine.

When I woke up the next morning, I moved cautiously and quietly around the apartment, determined not to get in trouble on the last day of my groundation. It was nearly the second week of August, the summer was almost over and in just two weeks, Jesse would be moving away. I couldn't spend even one more day of the summer vacation locked up in the apartment, a hostage to my mother's sudden temper, not with autumn's fuse already burning.

Mom was on the couch, reading the National Enquirer. She glanced up at me for a moment when I came out of the hall, but her eyes fell back to the magazine and she only mumbled when I told her good morning. I went into the kitchen and poured a bowl of cereal, careful with the milk, not to use too much or to spill, and at the table I hid behind the Froot Loops box while Ben sat across from me with his coffee and his cigarette.

I ate fast and rinsed my bowl and spoon in the sink and on my way back to the bedroom, Mom stopped me.

"Richie."

I came back, stood at the end of the hall, and looked at her. "Huh, Mom?"

She looked up from the tabloid stories about two-headed alien babies and Hollywood affairs and said, "I want you to clean your room today. You've been cooped up in there and you've got your comics and toys all over the floor."

"Okay, Mom. I'll do it right now."

I went into the bedroom and she called out, "And don't just shove everything under your goddamned bed!"

"I won't, Ma."

I stacked up all my comic books and put them in my night table and I picked up all the toys, even the ones Tommy had left on the floor and on his bed, and put them in the big cardboard carton in the closet. I gathered up a few pairs of socks and underwear I had left on the floor and stuffed them into the hamper, then I knelt down on the carpet and looked under my bed.

Sheeshomighty.

The dark space beneath my bed was cluttered with more comics, toys and stray socks and I was stretched out on the floor, halfway under the bed, when I heard a knock on the apartment door and then my mother's voice when she opened it to see who was there.

"G'morning, Ray," she said. "Richie can't come out until tomorrow. He's grounded."

I lay still beneath my bed, listening.

"Okay, Missus Frances," I heard Ray say. "Could you tell him to come and get me tomorrow when he can come out? So he can show me the kittens."

Oh, no!

"Ray... what are you talking about?" Mom's voice had changed its tone. "*What* kittens?"

No! Ray, shut up! Stop in the name of the Laws!

Ray told my mom about the momma cat under the building and that I had promised him the pick of the litter because he had given me a dollar to buy cat food. Mom told him to go on home, slammed the apartment door and, before I could crawl all the way under my bed, she was in the room, her hands around my ankles, pulling me out to face her.

I rolled over on my back and put my hand up in front of my face, but she got a good smack in and screamed, "*You* put that cat food in the laundry room?"

Smack!

"You've been feeding the damned strays, Richie?" she hollered. "All those goddamned cats screeching and fighting in the middle of the night! Goddammit, Richie!'

Smack!

I couldn't get up off the floor. She was crouched over me, her lips twisted and thin and her eyes blazing and dark, smacking my face and the side of my head. The skin on my belly stung from being dragged across the carpet and my cheek burned beneath the palm of her hand, but I couldn't cry because Ben was looming in the bedroom doorway, gawking over Mom's shoulder while she hit me.

Mom exhausted her rage, stood up straight and let me climb up on to my bed. "You're grounded, Richie. For the rest of the goddamned summer!"

She turned to leave me and I pulled the sheet up over my legs and said, "Mom! Wait!" She turned around to look at me, fierce fire in her eyes. "Mom... please. I'll miss all my time with Jesse."

I braced myself for another smack, but she didn't raise her hand or scream at me and the warning in her eyes dimmed just a little.

"Richie." She sounded exhausted. "What the hell were you thinking?"

I told her that I had felt sorry for the Siamese cat because it was pregnant and only had three legs. "It was living under the building anyway, Mom," I said, "I just wanted to feed her until she had her kittens."

Mom frowned. "Richie, those kittens are going to grow fast and then there will be a whole mess of stray cats living under our apartment. I'll have to call the landlord or the animal control."

I told her the kittens had been born almost a month ago, the night that gramma had died, and that they'd probably start coming out from under the building soon. "When they come out," I told her, "Me and Jesse are gonna catch them up and set them free down by the pond. They won't be around here, Mom. They don't have to go to the pound."

In the doorway, Ben grunted and said, "I'll crawl under the building and get the damned things out of here, Fran."

"No. Leave them be." My mom looked at Ben. "Let Richie and Jesse have this. They won't be together very much longer."

I almost jumped out of my bed to hug her. "Thanks, Mom! Really?"

She looked at me again and that warning, dim but dangerous, was back in her eyes. "If you boys can't round them up when they come out, I'm calling the landlord to get rid of them," she said. "And don't you feed them anymore. I mean it, Richie."

"I won't, Mom."

You threw the cat food in the dumpster.

She told me to finish cleaning my room and as she followed Ben down the hall, I heard him say, "Those boys aren't gonna be able to catch those fucking kittens, Fran."

"They might," she said. "Richie's good with animals. Always has been."

Two - No Girls Allowed

After being confined to the house for an entire week, I skipped the traditional Saturday morning yawn of pajamas, cartoons and cereal, dug my hammer and saw out of the closet and burst out onto the block to round up the gang.

Every summer, we built a fort in the woods and by fall, the older kids would claim it. They would trash it by winter and by the time spring came around, there would be nothing left of our clubhouse but a few odd boards with nails sticking out of them. If you stepped on one of those nails, it would poke right through the sole of your sneaker and your mom would drag you down to the emergency room for a tetanus shot. Every kid knew that if you stepped on a nail and didn't get a tetanus shot, you'd end up with the lockjaw and would have to eat your dinner through a straw for the rest of your life.

This fort wouldn't last any longer than all the ones we had built before it. We would build it and then the big kids would wreck it, but for the last remaining weeks of summer, it would belong to us. The real fun was always in the planning and building, anyway.

Upstairs in apartment 3, I dragged Jesse away from 'The Bugs Bunny/Road Runner Hour' and rummaged through his toy-box for his tool-belt and his tape measure while he put on his jeans and sneakers.

"Hey, Jess... you remember the first fort we ever built together?"

He scrunched up his forehead. "The one in the tree out back? Your mom made us tear it down as soon as we finished it."

I laughed at the memory and Jesse laughed, too. "Well, no," I told him, "Before that even. Right here in your room, when I first moved into the building. Remember we used to build blanket forts on rainy days?"

He nodded and smiled, but his smile took a grinning twist. "Richie... you're so cute when you go all memory lane."

"Sheesh, Jesse!"

In the courtyard, we met up with Tommy and the Hodges brothers and sent them to round up Ray and Louis while we went up the block to get Bobby Bozart. Bobby came out with his hammer and an old coffee can filled with nails, nuts and bolts and the three of us hung out on the porch in front of his apartment, waiting for the others.

Bobby told us about his trip to his dad's in Pennsylvania (*guys, seriously... it was so boring*) and said they had gone camping (*guys, honestly... I got poison ivy*) and went to the carnival (*guys, I swear... Helen threw up all over me*) and then he said, "How is it, Richie?"

"How's what?"

"I mean... living with my uncle," he said. "How is it?"

Jesse glanced at me and looked down at the sidewalk. I looked at Bobby, called him by the nickname he pretended to hate and told him the truth. "Well, Bozo... it ain't so great."

Bobby sat down beside me on the porch step and clunked his can of nails down on the concrete between his feet. "I know," he said. "Ben was talkin' to my mom about you when they came to pick us up from the train."

"What did he say?"

Bobby clapped me on the shoulder. "Just stupid stuff, Rich. He's my uncle, but I know he's mean and stupid."

"Just tell me what he was sayin' to her, Bozo," I told him. "I gotta know."

"Well..." Bobby sighed. "He said you had a smart mouth and you didn't know when to shut it and that you give your mom a hard time. He said he'd spank your ass good except your mom would throw him out if he did."

"What a dummy!" Jesse said. "I mean... sorry, Bobby, but your uncle is one stupid hombre."

"Yeah," I said. "If he thinks he can spank me better than my mom does, I'd like to see him try it."

We heard the guys coming up the block and when we met them on the sidewalk Ray Laws was complaining about missing the end of *Jabber Jaw* and Louis Moretti was telling him it wasn't a very good episode anyway and Burt Hodges told them both that building a fort was way better than sitting inside watching cartoons all morning.

"What took you guys so long?" Jesse asked them.

"I had to get my stuff," Tommy said. He had a hammer stuck through a belt-loop, a big monkey-wrench poking out of his pocket and a length of tattered rope looped around his shoulder. He was carrying a cracked cabinet door he had dug out of a garbage dumpster. "I can't find my hard-hat construction helmet, Richie."

Tommy loved that hard hat, but I knew where he had left it and that he wasn't ever going to wear it again.

"I hate to say it, Tommy, but I think it was in the car," I told him.

He gasped. "When it got burned up?"

"Yeah."

"Well, poop!" he said. "I'll never find another one of those again."

We crossed the courtyard in front of Bobby's building, a noisy construction crew of seven with five hammers between us and not one hard-hat construction helmet, already beginning to argue about what kind of fort we should build, when Bobby's sister Cheryl came out of their apartment. She was with a brown-haired girl I had never seen before.

"Hey, Richie!" Cheryl called. "Hey, guys! Whatcha doin?"

Burt Hodges said, "We're goin' to the bog, to build a fort."

Cheryl looked at her brother, then at me and Jesse. "Can we come? We'll help."

Tommy shrugged his shoulders and Louis moaned and Ray Laws said, "You can't come, dummy. You guys are girls!"

The brown-haired girl giggled and said, "What's *that* got to do with anything?" and Cheryl said, "Yeah... what's that got to do with anything?"

Ray looked around at the rest of us in disbelief then he looked back at the girls. "Are you kidding me?" he said, "We're building a *clubhouse*! No girls allowed!"

Cheryl stepped down off the porch. "That's a stupid rule," she told Ray. "Richie, is it really no girls allowed?"

"Well, we never *said* that was a rule," I told her. I glanced at Jesse and he shrugged his shoulders.

"Of course it's a rule," Ray said. "It's like a code or an unwritten law."

Bobby said, "Guys, really... it's my sister," and Ross Hodges said, "Yeah, it's his sister." Ray threw up his hands in defeat when I said, "Yeah, they can come."

We cut through the parking lot and crossed Bloomfield Street and when we climbed the fence and started down the path to the pond, Ray said, "Girls! In the clubhouse! I can't even believe this is happening."

Jesse sighed and said, "Ray... shut up already." He leaned in to Bobby's ear. "Hey, Bozo... who's that new girl?"

"That's Brenda...um...Clark, or something. Why? You like her?"

Jesse blushed. "No way, Jose! She has the same name as my mom!"

Jesse and Bobby had swiped a lot of boards and beams and plywood from the construction site on Grand Avenue and stashed them in a big pile in the woods, under a tree, and covered it with branches.

"Jeez!" Louis exclaimed. "You guys really cleaned out the construction site."

We sat on the ground, debating what kind of fort to build and discussing the ones we had built in summers before. The Hodges wanted a tree fort and Tommy thought we should dig an underground cave, but Ray told him, "We can't dig a cave, dummy. We don't even have a shovel."

I scowled at Ray and said, "Don't call my brother a dummy," and Louis said, "My dad has a shovel."

"Yeah, Mister Moretti has a shovel," Jesse said, winking at me. "Remember he whacked Tubbs with it?"

That was a mean thing for Jesse to say, but it shut Ray up and we all fell back to arguing over tree houses and cave hideouts It was the new girl, Brenda who came up with the genius idea to build a pond fort. "We can build it up on stilts," she said, "Right on the bank and out over the water."

"Wicked," Jesse said.

Over the next two days, the woods around the pond were noisy with the banging of our hammers, our shouting and our laughter. We rolled our jeans up and waded into the mucky water to sink beams into the muddy bottom and we shored them up with big round stones we dug up in the woods. We sawed lengths of boards, pulled bent nails from the plywood and built a platform on the muddy bank that hung out over the pond. Tommy beamed with pride when we placed his scavenged cabinet door over an opening in the floor and nailed the hinges down.

"Yay!" he hollered. "It's a secret hatch!"

It took us three days to build the fort and when we finished, Tommy and Burt went scavenging in the dumpsters and brought back a wobbly chair and a stained couch cushion. The girls hung an old tablecloth in the window for a curtain and we stood on the slippery bank and admired our work.

The clubhouse only had three walls, it leaned a little to the left, and Ray said it would probably collapse and send us all tumbling into the pond, but Jesse and Bobby jumped up and down on the platform to prove him wrong.

"It's a great fort," Ross Hodges said and his brother looked at Ray and said, "Yeah. And a *girl* thought of it."

We hung around the pond for the rest of the day, playing tag and catching tadpoles and frogs and even Ray got over his aversion to girls long enough to have a good time. When we tired of chasing each other through the woods and chasing frogs through the silty mud at the bottom of the bog, we lounged in the grass beneath the small trees at the top of the slope and talked.

Bobby told everybody about his sister Helen throwing up on him at the carnival in Pennsylvania and we told him about the dummy Jesse and I had made to scare the other kids, and how Ross had run home and brought back the whole neighborhood, the cops and the fire department, too.

Louis mentioned that it was getting close to dinnertime and we all got up from the slope and brushed the dirt and grass from our pants. Shoes were found and put back on and when we started up the path to leave, Jesse stopped and looked back at the fort we had built.

"It's a really cool clubhouse," he said. He looked at the new girl. "That was a genius idea, Brenda. Building it up on the beams like that."

"Yeah," Ross agreed. "It's like a jungle house out of National Geographic or something."

Brenda smiled and on the walk back to the apartment complex, she told us that she and her mom had moved into the apartment above the Bozarts just the week before. She said they used to live in a big house in Plainfield, but her father had died two years ago and her mom couldn't find a job. When they couldn't afford the house anymore, they had packed all their stuff into a hired truck and moved to the neighborhood.

"Well, it ain't so bad around here," Burt Hodges told her and Brenda said, "I know. At least, I have friends now."

We left Louis and Ray on the corner of our block and the rest of us walked up the sidewalk and stopped in front of our building. Burt and Ross cut across the courtyard and disappeared up the stairs to their apartment. The rest of us stood around on the sidewalk for a few minutes, making plans to get enough lumber from the construction site to finish the clubhouse with a fourth wall.

"If we make another wall, we gotta make a door," Tommy said and Jesse told him we would figure that out.

Brenda asked if we were coming back out after dinner and Tommy told her that in the summertime our mom let us stay out until it got dark. She smiled and said, "Well, there's a full moon tonight so it won't hardly get dark at all."

We all agreed to come back out and play after we ate our dinner and Bobby and the girls walked away up the sidewalk and, as we turned to cross the courtyard and go inside, Tommy said, "Hey! Look!"

Across the lawn, in the dirt patch near the apartment building wall, the three-legged Siamese cat lay swishing her tail and four kittens crawled and bounced around her in the dust. Tommy took two steps toward the cats and I grabbed a handful of his t-shirt, yanked him back and said, "Wait. You'll scare 'em off."

We stood beneath the tree, quietly, almost breathlessly, and watched the kittens play in the dirt at their mother's feet. Two of the kittens were black, one was grey and one of them looked just like the momma cat. Sometimes they climbed right up on top of her and every once in a while the momma cat would touch each of her kittens, licking their faces and touching her nose to their heads, almost as if she were counting them.

"They're out," I said. "Jesse, look at 'em!"

Jesse lay his arm across my shoulder and I looked at him, expecting to see his face-splitting smile, but his bottom lip was trembling and tears brimmed in his eyes.

"Hey, man," I said. "What's the matter, Jess?"

"I dunno, Richie," he said softly, "It's just... summer's almost over."

"Yeah...I know. Goshdanged Ohio."

Jesse's mom hollered down from a window, calling him in for supper, and the kittens scrambled under the building. The momma cat gave us a low-eyed glance, swished her tail and followed behind her babies into the dark crawlspace.

Three - Tommy the Acrobat

That evening, we played in the street under the big silver moon. Ray and Louis came up from their end of the block and Redheaded Ricky wandered over from Bloomfield Street. We boys chose up sides for kickball while Cheryl and Brenda played hopscotch, giggling and stomping on their shadows as they hopped from square to square. Gary and Mike Renfro were leaning against the streetlight, too cool for kickball, making wisecracks and teasing the girls.

Jesse pitched the big red rubber ball and Ross kicked it high in the air and started running around the bases (we used our t-shirts, wadded up on the blacktop), chasing Ray off second and both of them heading for home. We all watched the ball, a dark circle in the bright summer night, arc and fall. It was coming down right over Tommy's head and all he had to do was raise his hands above his head and grab it. There was no way he could miss it.

"You got it, Tommy!" I hollered. "Easy out!"

The ball descended, but instead of catching it, Tommy turned away and it hit the street with a springy thump, bounced a few times and rolled under a parked car.

Ray and Ross ran across home base and Ray shouted, "Four to three! Four to three! We're winning."

"Yeah, yeah," Jesse said. He turned around and hollered, "Hey, Tommy! Whatcha doin' out there, kid? Go get the ball!"

Tommy pointed at the streetlight and said, "Look at Gary! What's he doing?"

Gary was shinnying up the lamppost. He got halfway up the tall metal pole and slid back down to the bottom, the soles of his high-top sneakers smacking the street. Mike slapped him on the shoulder and said, "Pretty good. My turn!" He wrapped his arms and legs around the pole and scooted up and up, almost as high as Gary had gone, before he slid back down and fell on his butt at the bottom.

We wandered over to the streetlamp, the game and the ball left behind, and gathered around on the sidewalk. "What are you guys, doin'?" Ross Hodges said and his brother Burt said, "Yeah... whatcha doin'?"

Gary looked at the Hodges and said, "What's it look like we're doing? We're seeing who can climb the highest up the light-pole."

"I can do that!" Tommy said. "I can go all the way up to the light!"

We all looked at him, eyes and mouths wide open, and Gary said, "You can't shinny to the top, Tommy. You're too little."

Tommy's eyes followed the pole up and up and he looked at the big yellow light at the top then looked at our big brother.

"Bull-pucky!" he said. "I climb the poles at school and I climbed to the top of that big tree in the bog."

"He *did* climb that tree," Jesse said, looking around, nodding his head. "He was only like six years old then, too!"

"Lemme try!" Tommy said. He spit in the palms of his hands and rubbed them together, wrapped his arms and legs around the pole and used his elbows and knees to pull himself up off the ground. "Here I go! To the top!"

I looked up at the shining top of the pole, so high above the street, and glanced at our apartment door. Tommy was about six feet up the pole and I said, "Tommy, don't do it. You're gonna fall and break your neck."

He paused, clinging to the pole, and looked down at me, his cheeks stretched out by a silly smile. "Don't worry, Richie. I won't fall."

He inched his way up the pole, higher and higher, and we all stood around in a circle on the street, our heads tilted up to the light, watching him and chattering. We were a divided audience and some of us whispered worry (*He's gonna fall for sure*) and some of us cheered him on (*You can do it, Tommy*) and Ray Laws said, "He's like a monkey!"

The girls gave up their hopscotch game and joined us at the bottom of the lamppost. They looked up at Tommy, more than halfway up the pole and still climbing, and Cheryl said, "What in the world is Tommy doing?"

He's climbing to the top of the street-light," Ray said. "He's like a monkey."

Cheryl smacked me on my shoulder. "You let him climb up there, Richie?" she scolded me. "He's gonna fall and get hurt bad."

I couldn't take my eyes off Tommy. None of us could. I was about to tell Cheryl that I'd tried to stop him, that I'd told him not to do it, but before I could say anything Tommy pulled himself up onto the wide, flat top of the pole and lay there on his belly with his arms and legs wrapped tightly around the lamp.

"I did it! Look at me!" he hollered. "*Jeez*, there's lots of bugs up here!"

Gary cupped his hands around his mouth and shouted, "Okay, Tommy! Come down now! And be careful!"

Tommy stared down at us, but he didn't move. "I can't come down!" he hollered. "I'm too scared."

Gary frowned. His eyes looked just like Mom's when he frowned. "You weren't scared goin' up!"

he yelled. "Just come down. We'll catch you if you fall!"

Brenda looked at Gary, shook her head and said, "Are you an idiot? We can't catch him!" and Tommy shouted, "I *heard* that!"

I looked at my big brother. "Sheeshomighty, Gary! How are we gonna get him down?" He looked at me and shrugged his shoulders and before he could answer, my mother's voice pierced the summer night.

"Thomas Joseph Holeman!" she shrieked, "You come down from there *right now*!"

She came rushing off the porch and hurrying down the sidewalk, cinching the belt of her robe, her slippers swishing on the concrete, her face tilted up and her eyes wide with worry and anger. She smacked Gary across the back of his head, scorched me with a glance and hollered up at my little brother again.

"Tommy! Get your little ass down from there!"

Tommy stared down at her and shouted, "I can't, Momma! I'm stuck!"

My mom looked around at us and Cheryl said, "He's scared to come down, Miss Fran."

Mom told Gary to run down the block and bring back Ben and John and she rushed back up the sidewalk, hollering back at me over her shoulder. "You stay right there, Richie!"

"But, what are we gonna do, Mom?"

She looked back at me, almost tripped going up the porch steps and shouted, "I'm calling the goddamned fire department!"

The crowd gathering around the bottom of the streetlight grew as neighbors came out of their apartments up and down the block, drawn by our shouts up to Tommy and his shouts back down to us. Mom came back out of the apartment, ran down the sidewalk and stared up at the top of the pole. Gary came running up the street with Ben and John stumbling along behind him as the sound of sirens echoed through the neighborhood and the fire trucks rolled around the corner, lighting up the block with flashes of red and white.

The grown-ups waved the kids out of the way and we all stood on the lawn as the big bucket truck rolled to a noisy stop under the streetlight and the rescue squad pulled up along the curb behind it and the firemen scrambled into action. One of them climbed into the big white bucket on the top of the truck and another pointed the truck's big, bright searchlight up at Tommy.

"I can't believe it," Louis Moretti said. "He's *smiling*! Tommy's *smiling* up there!"

My mom rushed up alongside the truck and cried "That's my baby up there!" and the fire captain said "Don't worry, ma'am, we'll get him down." The fireman in the bucket twisted a knob and pulled some levers and the boom started to rise up from the top of the truck.

A police car rolled up the street and two cops climbed out and one of them told my mom to move back from the scene and wait on the lawn with the rest of us. My mom glared at him, stood right where she was and said, "I'm not moving until they get my son down from there!"

The crowd hushed and the firetruck huffed as the bucket rose up and up and the fireman guided it to the top of the light-pole. He wrapped a big canvas strap under Tommy's belly, buckled it to his own safety-harness, grabbed Tommy up in his arms and pulled him off the streetlight. Tommy disappeared inside the bucket, everyone down on the street cheered and clapped their hands, and the fireman looked down from the bucket, stuck out his hand and turned his thumb up.

The bucket eased away from the lamppost and slowly descended until it was folded up on top of the big red truck, and the fireman lifted Tommy up out of the bucket. The crowd moved closer and circled the truck, some of the neighbors still cheering, and Tommy raised his arms above his head and shouted, "I did it!"

The fireman unbuckled the strap and handed Tommy down from the top of the truck and when my little brother was safely back on the ground, smiling and slapping high-fives with the Hodges brothers, my mom came up behind him and swatted him hard on his butt. She grabbed his t-shirt and dragged him up the sidewalk, shouting, "You are in so much trouble! So! Much! Trouble!"

The firemen got back in their trucks and drove away and the cops told the neighbors to go on home ("Okay, folks, the show's over") and I stood on the lawn with my friends, all of us chattering about Tommy's amazing climb and the exciting rescue. Gary and Mike climbed on their bikes and started to pedal away, but my mom stuck her head out of the apartment door and hollered, "Gary! Richard! Get in here right now!"

Sheesh!

I told my friends I would see them tomorrow, if my mom didn't ground me, and turned to go inside, but Cheryl Bozart said, "Richie, wait."

I stopped and looked at her. *Huh?*

"Thanks for letting us help with the clubhouse," she said and she leaned her face into mine, bumped me on the nose with her glasses and kissed me right on the lips.

"Holy *moly!*" Jesse exclaimed as Cheryl ran away up the sidewalk and I ran across the courtyard into our apartment, my heart racing in my chest and my cheeks blushing warm and red.

Mom didn't ground us, but she gave Tommy a hard spanking and she hollered at Gary and me for standing by and letting our little brother climb to the top of the light-pole. "He could've gotten killed!" she screamed. "Do you even realize that?"

"But I knew I wouldn't fall, Mom," Tommy said, wiping tears from his eyes with the cuff of his pajama shirt, and Mom leaned right down in his face and hollered, "SHUT UP, TOMMY!"

She turned out the light and before she closed the door, she said, "Go to sleep. All three of you. In the morning, we're cleaning out Gramma's room."

She shut the bedroom door and we lay there in the dark, Tommy still sniffling and crying a little, and Gary said, "I'm getting my own room again."

Four - Gramma's Surprise

In the morning, Mom sent Gary and me around to the back of Ratto's Junior Market to collect empty cartons and we brought home three big boxes. Ben and Gary carried the furniture from Mom's room out to the dumpster because she wanted Gramma's bedroom set, while she, Tommy, and I went through the closet and drawers in Gramma's room, stuffing all the clothes, papers, and junk into the cartons.

I was sitting on the floor, with the nightstand drawer pulled open in front of me, going through all the papers and envelopes that Gramma had saved over the years. Mom told me to look at everything and to save any letters and cards and throw away all the receipts, bills and advertisements. I picked up a stack of papers, pulled a faded K-Mart receipt off the top and found an envelope with one word written across the back in Gramma's familiar scrawl.

Wildwood

The envelope wasn't sealed and I lifted the flap and peeked inside. *Oh, wow!* There was money in the envelope, a neat, thin stack, and the one on top was a hundred-dollar bill.

"Mom! Mom!"

She was kneeling on the floor of the closet, sorting through all of Gramma's shoes and rainboots and slippers, and she turned her head and looked at me. There was the beginning of a scowl in her eyes and in the lines on her forehead, but her expression brightened and her hand shot out for the envelope when I held it up and said, "Money! I found *money*!"

As if I had spoken a magic word, Ben and Gary appeared in the bedroom doorway and Tommy turned away from the stack of romance novels he'd been stuffing into a brown paper grocery bag and stared at Mom. She slipped the money out of the envelope and counted the bills.

"Six hundred dollars," she said, staring at the money in her hands. She looked at Ben. "There's six hundred dollars here, Ben. We can get a car."

A car?

Ben grinned, nodded his head, and said, "Shit fire and save a match! Good ol' Anna!"

"But, Mom…" She looked at me and her eyebrows sharpened and I knew I was about to talk myself into a beating, but Gramma had written 'Wildwood' on that envelope and she had promised me, months ago when the summer was young, that she would make sure we all went to the boardwalk. "Mom! Look at the back of the envelope. Gramma saved all that money for Wildwood."

Mom turned the wrinkled envelope over in her hands and I saw tears sneaking down her cheeks. She tucked the money back inside the envelope and said, "Richie... listen..."

Ben interrupted her. "Your grandma didn't know that crazy bitch Linda was gonna burn up your mom's car, Richie," he growled, "Don't be so goddamned selfish!"

"Ben, shut up," my mom said softly, "Leave him alone."

Ben grunted and stalked off down the hallway and called Gary after him. Mom folded the envelope in half and tucked it in the pocket of her robe. She looked at me and her eyes held neither the anger, nor the sadness I expected, only a strange, clear calm.

"Richie, let's just put this money away for now," she said. "Give Mom a little time to think of what to do, okay?"

Her calm tone and her obvious struggle surprised me and I leaned against her and hugged her. "Okay, Mom."

We went back to work packing away the last of Gramma's things. Mom taped up the boxes and

Tommy said, "I didn't even know Gramma was rich."

Mom laughed and that got me laughing so Tommy shrugged his shoulders and joined in, too. Gramma would have laughed right along with us, if she had been there.

By early afternoon, the cartons had been stored in the cabinet above our parking space in the carport, Gary's things had been moved into Gramma's room and Tommy and I had pushed our beds and dressers around in our room until we were both satisfied with the bigger space.

"We have lots more room now, Richie," he said, "We can set up your slot car track in here now."

Five - Buried Treasures

After a sandwich and a glass of milk, I went outside and found Jesse behind our building, sitting on the ground, his back leaning against the tree. He was eating a *Lik-M-Aid*, dipping the white candy stick into the pouch of colored, sweet powder and he stuck his purple tongue out at me as I sat down beside him.

"Want some?" he held out the paper pouch and I licked my finger, dipped it into the candy, and stuck it in my mouth.

"Were the kittens out?" I asked him.

"Yeah, I saw 'em," he said. He told me he had tried to get close to them but the momma cat had noticed him crawling slowly across the lawn and nudged the kittens back into the crawlspace. "That momma cat won't let us get near 'em, Richie. What if we can't catch them? Jeez, what if we can't give Ray his kitten?"

I took another dip from his *Lik-M-Aid* pouch and shrugged my shoulders. "They prob'ly just gotta get used to kids," I said. "I bet in a couple of weeks we'll be able to pet 'em and pick 'em up."

"I hope it's before I move away," Jesse said and we sat together beneath the tree for a few quiet moments then I stood up, brushed the dirt from the seat of my pants and said, "So, whatcha wanna do today?"

Jesse stood up, too, and said, "I had a genius idea. Let's bury a time capsule."

"A time capsule?"

"Yeah, a time capsule," he said, "I got that metal box with the lock. The one I got at the flea market. We can put stuff in it that reminds us of our friendship and bury it in the woods. In the future, like in ten or twenty years, we can come back and dig it up. Or some other kids might find it and it will be a big mystery to them."

I told Jesse it *was* a genius idea and we went into our apartments to find the treasures we wanted to bury in the time capsule. In my room, I stuffed my pockets with toys and tokens and tore a sheet of paper from my notebook, wrote on it with a marker and folded it in half. Mom was in the kitchen when I left the apartment and I hollered at her as I went out the door.

"Goin' to the bog with Jesse!"

Outside, Jesse was waiting in the courtyard, talking with Burt Hodges. He was holding the slim metal lock-box in his hand and his army-surplus field shovel was tucked under his belt. He waved the grey box at me as I jumped off the porch and said, "I already put my stuff in. I'll show you at the bog."

"Whatcha gonna do at the bog?" Burt said. "Can I come with you guys?"

Jesse rested one hand on Burt's shoulder and said, "Just me and Richie this time, pal. We just gotta do something. You know... best friend stuff."

Burt shrugged his shoulders and said, "Yeah, sure, Jess. I understand if it's best friend stuff and all."

I told Burt we would all hang out the next day at the clubhouse and Jesse and I took off running through the carport, sprinting down the alley, racing over the fence. "Last one there's a rotten egg!" Jesse hollered as he shot ahead of me down the path and into the trees.

I was the rotten egg and I threw myself down next to Jesse in the grass at the top of the slope, both of us breathing hard and holding our sides. We rested in the shade beneath the trees, listening to the bugs, the birds, and the breeze, and I asked Jesse where we should bury the time capsule.

"Well, not too close to the pond," he said. "It floods over in the winter. The box could get washed away."

"Yeah," I agreed. "Let's bury it in the woods, by a tree so we can find it again if we ever come back here."

I followed Jesse around the pond and into the woods and he said, "Do you think we ever will,

Richie? Come back here, I mean? When we're grown up?"

I shrugged my shoulders and clapped my best friend on the back. "I dunno, Jesse. Sometimes I think I'll just go away one day, when I'm bigger, and never come back here again and sometimes I think I'll never ever leave here at all."

Jesse pointed to a big, thick tree and said, "That looks like a good spot." We knelt in the patch of weeds and dirt beneath the big, shady branches and Jesse pulled his field shovel out of his belt and started digging in the soft ground.

"You *will* go away one day, Richie. You're gonna ride a motorcycle to Ohio and we're gonna ride away wherever we want to go. Remember?"

I told him that I remembered, and while he dug the shallow hole, I flipped open the lock-box and looked at the things he'd stashed inside of it; a kid's sentimental tokens and trinkets, friendship's treasures cast in plastic and copper and tin. I took them out of the box, held them in my hands, and remembered the days our lives had attached to each one.

He had chosen to bury the cheap pocketknife that I had given him on his eighth birthday. It had two thin blades and the smaller one had broken in half before the birthday party was even over, but Jesse had carried it in his pocket for two years and found almost any excuse to pull it out and use it or just show it off. There was also the thin copper wafer that had once been a penny we'd placed on the hot railroad tracks the year before, flattened by the steel wheels of a long freight train. A cheap tin star (*Sheriff*) that he pinned to his shirt when we played cowboys, the pinewood and leather necklace from our summer at Three Links Camp and a flat triangular stone that we had thought was an Indian arrowhead when we were six and found it in the creek. These were the things that Jesse had held on to, the things that he loved enough to let go.

"Real good stuff, Jess," I said softly. I could have cried just then, but I forced a grin, emptied my pockets, and showed Jesse the things that I had brought to bury. Into the box I put a green plastic army man, one of one hundred that had come in a bag, wrapped clumsily by Jesse as a Christmas present for me, and a Matchbox hot-rod that I'd won from Jesse one time when we'd raced 'for keeps.' Jesse laughed when he saw that I'd brought my own Three Links Camp necklace (*No way, man!*) and when I showed him the plastic vampire fangs I'd saved from the party his mom let him have the year before at Halloween, but when I pulled out the photograph, his laughter shrunk to a fragile smile and he softly said, "Lemme see that, Richie."

I handed him a black and white picture of the two of us, taken in a photo-booth at the county fair when I was seven and Jesse was six. We had our arms around each other's shoulders and our faces pressed close together, two goofy kids frozen in time. I wore a *Gunsmoke* t-shirt and had a bad haircut and Jesse's smile was broken by the gap where his front teeth should have been. Our faces were sunburned. Jesse held it between his fingers and he looked at me and said, "Can I keep this, Richie?"

"Yeah, you can keep it," I said, and I started to cry. I took the sheet of notebook paper from my pocket, unfolded it and showed Jesse what I had written on it. He read it out loud (*Richie Holeman & Jesse Gwinn. 1976. We ruled!*) and he cried a little, too, and said, "You're the best friend I ever had in my life, Richie."

"I know, Jess," I told him. "You're my best friend, too. I won't ever forget you."

"You better not," he whispered and he closed the metal box, locked it and handed me the little silver key. "You keep the key, Richie," he said and I stuck it deep in my pocket. We put the box in the hole and covered it up and Jesse used his shovel to pat down the loose dirt.

On our way back up the path, Jesse smiled and said, "We *did* rule this summer, Richie."

"Yeah!" I said. "And it ain't over *yet*, pardner."

Six - The Bicycle Thieves

Walking home, we took the long way, following the railroad tracks around to Grand Avenue instead of climbing the fence at the top of the path. Neither one of us was in a hurry to trade the quiet, private sadness of burying our shared treasures for the rest of our gang and all the late summer noise back on the block. We walked on the slick silver rails, Jesse on one and me on the other, balancing ourselves with exaggerated drama like circus acrobats up on the high wire, teasing each other about who would be the first to slip off.

"Who's that?" Jesse said.

Up ahead, there were two bigger boys standing on the edge of the tracks. I couldn't see their faces at that distance, but one of them was Mike Renfro. He was the only boy in our neighborhood with really long hair, like a rock star, and he was always flipping it over his shoulder, out of his face. I knew him but I couldn't see his face at that distance. I recognized him by the way he was tossing his hair back.

The other boy was someone we had never seen around the neighborhood before, a big kid with a crew cut and freckles who looked like he could eat Jesse for lunch and save me for a snack. He was leaning on a bicycle and as we drew closer, our sneakers abandoning the rails for solid ground, we both recognized the big blue Schwinn. There was only one like it in the whole town; a grown-up's bike with a little kid's bell mounted on the handlebar and a big white basket hanging off the front, and we both knew who it belonged to.

"Hey! What are you guys doin' with that bike?"

We were standing just above them on the greasy tracks. I had hollered at Mike Renfro, but it was the freckle-faced boy who answered back.

"What's it to you?" he scowled, "Why don't you go on and mind your own business, kid?"

I glanced at Jesse, he looked back at me with firm eyes, and I knew that he was with me. He was *always* with me.

The boy with the freckles pressed the bicycle bell with his thumb (*riiiiiiinnng, briiiiiiing)* and smiled like a wolf. He had a chipped tooth right up front. He probably broke it gnawing on the bones of the last smart-mouthed ten year old who hollered at him.

"That's not your bike," I said, "It belongs to The Bicycle Witch. You know that, Mike Renfro. Heck, *everybody* knows."

The other boy held on to the stolen bike with one hand and with the other, he cocked his thumb against his chest. "Not me," he said, "I don't know *anything.*"

"*That's* obvious," Jesse whispered close at my side.

"I told you already," I said, "That bike belongs to The Bicycle Witch."

He wriggled his fingers in front of his face and made an exaggerated, frightened face. "Oooooooh, a witch!' he said, "Dang, Mikey, I hope she doesn't turn us into a couple of warty toads."

"Looks like she already did," Jesse grinned, and Mike Renfro almost laughed, but his laughter squeaked away into a frown when the bigger boy gave his shoulder a little shove.

WOOOOO! WOOO-WOOOOO!

There was a train coming down the track, its big air horn blasting as it chugged toward the Grand Avenue crossing.

CLANG-CLANG! CLANG-CLANG-CLANG!

Jesse and I scrambled down the railroad track embankment, skidding on loose stones, and we stood together near the fence, far from the tracks.

All of the kids in our gang, even the girls, played on the railroad tracks, but each of us had a fearful respect of moving trains that ran the spectrum from healthy to phobic. Mike stepped farther from the tracks, too, but the freckle-faced bully didn't budge. He just stood at the edge of the crossties, leaning on The Witch's bike.

The train was crossing Grand Avenue, hauling fast up the track, a long, swaying freighter pounding north, and the engineer was leaning out the window and blasting away on the diesel's horn.

"Better get out of the way, kid!" Jesse hollered. The tracks were humming now and the sound of the train grew louder and louder until it was rolling thunder all around us, and Mike Renfro cupped his hands around his mouth and shouted, "C'mon, get off the tracks, man."

The new bully looked at me and smiled his snaggle-toothed grin and I knew exactly what he was going to do. I started up the embankment with my little hands balled into tight fists, but Jesse reached out and grabbed my elbow gently, stopping me in my tracks.

"No, Richie." He nodded toward the train, so close now. Too close now.

The train was a giant grey monster eating up the rails and freckle-face picked up the big blue Schwinn in his meaty hands, tossed it in front of the locomotive and hurried away from the tracks in a great leap. He ran for the fence, with Mike Renfro hot on his heels, and they scrambled up and over the fence, escaping into the neighborhood, just as the train hit the bike.

The big horn wailed again and the flat nose of the diesel engine smacked into The Bicycle Witch's Schwinn with a clanging sound that was nearly lost in all the noise of the train. The bike crumpled and sailed through the air, bits and pieces of it flying off in every direction. The basket caught air and tumbled across the nose of the train and out of sight, the silver bell spun silently into the bushes along the fence and a pedal nearly hit Jesse on his head. The bike, twisted and ruined, landed hard in the gravel at the bottom of the embankment and the train engineer pulled hard on the horn and scowled down at us as the freight muscled past.

"Holy cow!" I hollered and Jesse whistled sharp and said, "Man, oh *man!*"

We hunkered down to examine the dead bike. The handlebars were hanging limp, the front wheel was bent and there were loose spokes poking every which way they could. The seat had spun around sideways, the crossbar was crimped and the cracked lens of the bike's lone reflector glared up at us like an accusing eye.

"Sheeshomighty, Jesse," I said, "What a catastrophe."

We were so intent on studying the ruined Schwinn that we didn't notice the police car cruising up from Grand Avenue until its tires were crunching the gravel right behind us and a policeman climbed out and blocked out the sky, his long shadow falling over us in the late afternoon sun.

We recognized the cop from the day we had put the dummy in the bog *and* from the night Tommy had gotten himself stuck up on the light pole. I squinted up at him and Jesse smiled and said, "Howdy, lawman" and the big cop put his hands on his hips, panned his glare from Jesse's face to mine and said, "You two, huh? Just what in the world are you boys doing throwing a bicycle on the railroad tracks."

My mouth fell open and Jesse hollered, "We're innocent!"

The cop shook his head, muttered something about the bike being stolen and held the back door of his cruiser open as we climbed in. He told us to watch our heads, just like they do on the television shows, but his grim face told me he wouldn't mind if a couple of bike rustlers like us banged our heads getting arrested. No, he wouldn't mind it very much at all.

Jesse and I sat straight up in the back of the cop car, stared at each other with wide eyes and the cop slid into the front seat and started up the motor. He glanced at us in the rearview mirror and said something into the microphone of the patrol car's radio as he swung the big black and white Ford left onto Grand Avenue.

"Hey!" I said, "You shoulda turned right. We live back the other way."

The cop glanced in the mirror again and shook his head. "I'm not taking you home, fellas. Gotta take you down to the station house for this one."

The station house!

I slouched low in the seat with a long sigh and Jesse leaned forward and told the cop, "We've been framed!"

Seven - Hard Time

At the police station, they didn't lock us up behind bars with a bunch of greasy criminals or shine a bright light in our faces and grill us about the stolen bicycle. They just sat us down on a hardwood bench and the policeman who brought us downtown left out the same door he had brought us in through, back to his patrol. Another cop, one who knew our first names without even asking, wrote down our telephone numbers in a little black notepad and asked us if we wanted a soda. We did.

"I don't trust that cop," Jesse whispered after the policeman had gone into the next room, either to get our sodas or call our mothers, or both. "He's up to something."

"He is? " I whispered back, "What's he up to?"

Jesse shrugged his shoulders and frowned. "I don't know, Richie," he sighed, "But you ever see any of them suspects on the cop shows get a soda? Have you?"

I thought it over. I had seen about a million cop shows in my life, but Jesse was right; I'd never seen the cops fetch a nice cold soda for a bad guy and, like it or not, for the moment that's what we were: bad guys.

I looked at Jesse. "Cigarettes," I said, "They always ask the bad guy if he wants a cigarette."

"Yeah," Jesse said, "To soften 'em up so they can crack 'em. They can't give cigarettes to kids, though, so they're giving us sodas."

I wasn't so sure. "To crack us?"

Jesse sighed. "That's right, pardner. Oldest trick of the lawman's trade. They call it good cop/bad cop."

"But doesn't there have to be *two* cops for that, Jess. A good one *and* a bad one."

Jesse grinned like the devil and whispered, "Not if he's *both* of them."

I was about to ask Jesse what the heck he was talking about, but the cop came back into the room, with a can of Pepsi in each hand and passed them down to me and Jesse. I said "thanks, officer," but Jesse must have decided he was gonna be a hard one to crack because he just nodded his head at the cop and sipped his soda. The policeman smiled and said, "Just sit tight, boys. I've gotta give your folks a call."

He turned to go make two dreaded phone calls, took three steps and turned back around.

"You fellas want a cigarette?"

Jesse's mouth opened in wise surprise and mine must have fallen open, too, because there was Pepsi-Cola bubbling down my chin and dribbling onto my t-shirt.

The policeman laughed big and booming as he walked across the room to a grey metal desk and found the telephone in a clutter of yellow folders, loose papers and carryout coffee cups. He was still chuckling a little when he started talking into the phone and I knew he had called *my* mother first because I could hear her shouting through the telephone all the way across the big police station squad room.

Jesse had demanded an attorney, but we got our mothers instead and they burst into the station house fifteen minutes after the policeman had called to inform them that their sons were being held downtown on charges of bicycle thievery and destruction of property. My mom, of course, was first through the door and she was hollering at the cop before he even looked up to notice her.

"Where's my son? I want to see my child *right now*!"

Jesse's mom came in right on my mother's heels, her hair all rolled up in curlers and covered with a stretchy plastic cap, but wasn't saying anything, probably because *no one* could say anything while my mom was shouting.

The cop got up from his desk and opened a paneled gate to let our moms in to see us. "Just calm down, will you, lady," he said to my mom, "They're right over here."

My mom was so furious that I wondered if she might get herself arrested before she managed to get me and Jesse out of the mess we were in; a mess that, for once, we hadn't made ourselves. She barged through the gate and into the squad room with her chin jutting out and her eyes all ablaze, and the cop took two steps back when she whirled on him and pointed a finger in his boyish face.

"Don't you tell me when to calm down!" she hollered, "I'll calm down when I've got my son and you idiots drop this whole ridiculous thing!"

She saw me and hurried over to bend down and hug me and Jesse's mom sat down beside him on the bench and wrapped her arm around his shoulders. My mom stood up, turned back to the cop and said, "You should be ashamed; arresting little boys on their summer break."

The cop sighed and said, "They haven't actually been arrested, ma'am. There'll be an investigation and the juvenile court will contact you both. For now, they're being released to your custody."

Jesse and I both exhaled in dramatic relief, but the news that we were being freed wasn't enough to satisfy my mother's temper. "An investigation?" she said, "An *investigation*? Here's your first clue, detective..."

"It's 'patrolman' actually," the cop interrupted her, "I'm not a detective, ma'am"

"Well, that's pretty damned obvious," my mother hissed, "But I'm sure you're bright enough to figure out the answer to this one; do you honestly believe these boys would steal a bicycle from a *witch*?"

I could tell by her satisfied smirk and the way she crossed her arms very slowly across her chest that my mother thought she had just settled the case, but the policeman looked at her with one eyebrow arched and answered her question with one of his own.

"Ma'am, you do realize she isn't *really* a witch, right?"

My mother's arms unfolded from her chest and her hands slid down to her hips. "Of course I know she isn't a witch," she said low and slow, "But *the boys* don't know she isn't a witch."

The cop blushed a little picked up some papers from his desk and handed some to my mom and the rest to Jesse's mom.

"Ma'am, everything will be worked out with the juvenile court. If you'll both just sign these release forms, you can take your boys home. Like I said, the court will contact you."

Our mothers signed the papers, collected us up, and put us in the backseat of Brenda Gwinn's old sedan. On the ride back to the neighborhood, we took turns telling them what had happened at the railroad tracks, how we'd come across Mike Renfro and the other boy after they'd stolen the bike and been left behind at the scene of the crime when the police showed up.

My mom looked over her shoulder at me and said, "We believe you boys. We know you didn't steal that old witch's bike."

Mom's faith in our innocence tamed all of my wild worries over the bicycle and the police. If my mother believed we hadn't stolen The Bicycle Witch's Schwinn and thrown it in front of a freight train, then there was no way on earth we were going to get in trouble for something we didn't do. She wouldn't allow it.

Eight - First Boy on the Moon

By the time we got home, it was late in the day, nearly evening, and our mothers took us in for supper. Over macaroni and cheese with hot dogs, I told my brothers everything that had happened, while Ben sat silently behind his plate, scowling, huffing and sighing through my entire story. Gary laughed when I told how Jesse had been suspicious of the cop and the Pepsi and Tommy was jealous that we had been hauled downtown to the police station.

"Dang it, Richie," he sighed, "Why didn't you take me with you to the bog? I coulda got hauled downtown, too."

Gary said he would tell Mike Renfro he had to admit to the cops that he'd stolen the bike, not me and Jesse, and that he knew who the kid was who tossed it on the railroad tracks, and my mom said, "You tell Mike Renfro that he'd better talk to the police before he has to talk to *me*!"

"Yeah, you better tell him that, Gary," I said, grinning at my mom, "I'm not going to juvenile hall for something I didn't do!"

My mom agreed. "No, you're *not*," she said, but then her absolute defense of me crumbled just a little bit, "But I should ground you just for being there when it happened!"

"Mom? What? I didn't do anything wrong. Neither did Jess."

She looked at me and there was just a hint of anger in her eyes, not enough to make me afraid, but enough to make me feel sad and disappointed that she had found a way to put at least some of the blame for this mess right on me.

"Maybe if you weren't always playing in the alleys and fooling around by those filthy railroad tracks, you wouldn't always end up in the wrong place at the wrong time. Have you ever considered that, Richie?"

Ben, who hadn't said a word all through supper, put his fork down on his empty plate, pushed his chair back from the table hard enough that it squealed across the linoleum, and said, "What about it, Richie? You ever consider *that*?"

I didn't look at him and I answered the question my mother had asked me, not Ben's echo. "But, mom...where else *is there* to play in this neighborhood?'

She had been wiping the table with a damp cloth, but she stopped and stared hard into my disappointed eyes and, though I hadn't realized I'd even done it, she said, "Don't you *dare* try to blame this on me."

She didn't say anything more and Ben couldn't seem to come up with a smart remark on his own, so I pushed my chair back from the table and followed Tommy out the door, into the kind of still, blue evening that only happens in the late summer under an August moon.

Our gang was out on the block, most of them anyway, and Jesse had already told them all about our run-in with the law, so there was nothing left for me to tell, except that being innocent doesn't always mean you're not in trouble. We played around at tag for a little while, chasing each other and sometimes our own shadows between the apartment buildings and up and down the block, streetlight to streetlight, but the night was so still that soon it stilled us, too.

We sat together on the lawn, a loose circle of seven: five boys and two girls, all more closely connected to each other's hearts and lives than any of us fully understood at the time. We talked and laughed together about the things that children wonder, while fireflies flickered across the lawn and the moon shone softly above us like a big blue lamp.

When I was a kid, I thought the best of times were the games we played, running and hollering up and down the block or over the fences, into the fields. I lived for the cap gun shootouts; the high-stakes games of marbles; bike rides through our town, exploring all the same old places we already knew by heart. Those memories were magic, even when they were fresh, and they remain magical to me even now, but when I think back on it all, I understand that it was those rambling summer night discussions, those infrequent evenings when we were all together, gathered in our stillest voices, that mattered most of all. Those are the memories of our gang that mean the most to me now, and *those* were the best times of all.

That night we debated the Beatles and Beach Boys and decided that we liked the Beach Boys better because they sang about California and *all* of us wanted to go to California. Ray Laws pulled the fall preview issue of TV Guide from his back pocket and we talked about our favorite programs and which new shows we wanted to watch, and the only new series all seven of us could agree to get excited about was Charlie's Angels. Cheryl pointed into the summer sky and named the constellations and we boys sighed and pretended to be bored while Brenda Clark improvised a poem about the stars. It was a pretty good poem, though, and I knew the other guys thought so, too, because none of them made any jokes about it when she finished with a rhyme about Orion's belt and the sky like black felt.

We didn't talk about school because it still seemed so far away, and we didn't talk about Ohio because it *was* so far away, but Tommy asked a question that all of us other kids knew the answer to, even if we had never really thought about it before.

"Guys...how come the ice cream truck doesn't come every single day?"

I sighed and looked at my little brother. "Tommy, could you *buy* an ice cream every single day?"

He frowned. "Well, no, I guess not. But other kids might."

Bobby Bozart snorted and said, "Not around here, Tommy. Not in *this* neighborhood."

"Why not?" Tommy said. He clapped his hands in front of his face and a passing firefly barely escaped death. "What's wrong with *our* neighborhood?"

For a moment, none of us answered. It's not that we were shy of talking about how poor we all were, not in our neighborhood, among our own gang of friends. We were kids who had been poor long enough that we had learned to wear our hand-me down shame like a mark of honor. We were the tough ones, we were the brave and clever ones, and the rich kids who called us welfare brats; we called them soft and spoiled and said they didn't deserve it.

"It's not that there's anything wrong with our neighborhood," Cheryl said and Bobby said, "Yeah, Tommy, we just don't have money around here for ice cream every day."

Jesse nodded his head. "Yep. The ice cream man knows that, so he doesn't come around every day except at the first and the middle of the month. He's up and down the block twice a day then."

Before Tommy could ask why, Ray said, "That's when the welfare checks come out."

Tommy crossed his legs Indian-style and rested his chin in his hands. "Well, when I grow up, I'm gonna have enough money for ice cream every day if I want it."

That led to a recurring topic of discussion among us kids and Brenda said, "Hey...what do you guys want to be when you grow up?"

Ray Laws groaned and said, "Aw, man, we *always* talk about that. That is *so* boring."

Jesse shook his head. "Yeah, Ray, we talk about it all the time and every time we do, you say you wanna be something different"

Cheryl giggled and said, "We *all* do. We always change our minds. So it's not boring."

They were right and Ray knew it. A few months ago, he wanted to grow up to be an airline pilot and a few months before that, he wanted to be a double secret agent.

"Besides, Ray," I said quietly, "Brenda's new on the block. She ain't ever talked about this with us before."

Ray sighed and said, "That's true, Richie. Okay! Can I go first though? C'mon, guys, can I go first?"

"Yeah, go on," Jesse giggled, "What you wanna be this time, Ray? The Kool-Aid King of New Jersey?"

It was a funny joke and we all laughed, even Ray, but this time he said he wanted to be bionic, like Steve Austin, The Six-Million Dollar Man. "I'll have bionic arms and legs and a bionic eye, just like on the show. That'd be awesome!"

Jesse pointed out that, before he could have those awesome bionic limbs he wanted, Ray would have to lose the arms and legs he already had in some kind of terrible accident. Ray thought it would be worth it and the conversation went around the group like that; one of us saying what they wanted to be when they grew up and the rest of us debating the wisdom of their choice.

To this day, I still remember what each of us said we wanted to be when we were grown up and gone. I remember who wanted to be a race car driver and which of the girls wanted to be the first woman President and that both Bobby and Jesse said they would grow up to be firemen.

When the question came around to me, I had no idea what my answer should be. This game had always been such an easy one, but in that moment I couldn't imagine myself ever being any older than I was right then and, for the first time in my life, I wished I would never grow up at all. I only knew that if I did have to grow up, I wanted to go someplace far away and free and live alone and I blurted out, "I'm gonna be the first boy on the moon!"

"Richie," Ray Laws said, "That is *so* dumb."

"No, it isn't," Jesse said, "That's not so dumb."

Ray smacked his forehead. "Are you kidding me? There's already been a first man on the moon, and a whole bunch of other guys, too."

"I didn't say *man*," I told him, "I said first *boy* on the moon."

"Well, that's even dumber," Ray snorted.

Cheryl Bozart twirled a finger through her curls and smiled at me. "It's not dumb, Richie," she said, "It's just that you can't grow up to be the first boy on the moon because you won't be a boy when you're all grown up."

"Yes, I will."

Cheryl sighed and Ray snorted for the third time, but Jesse looked at me and said softly, "I get it, Richie."

I knew he did. Jesse always got it.

It was getting late. Cathy Bozart hollered from up the block for Bobby and Cheryl to come home and we knew that would start our mothers calling us in, too. We got up from the grass and the Bozarts headed up the block with Brenda Clark, but she stopped and turned around and called out to me.

"I get it, too, Richie," she said, "About the moon."

I believed her. She was the one who made a poem out of the stars.

Nine - Pick of the Litter

The next afternoon, the kittens were out and I sent Tommy down to the corner to bring back Ray Laws so he could choose his pick of the litter. "Make sure you tell Ray not to spaz out when he gets up here," I told Tommy and he lit out down the block, his bare feet slapping the hot sidewalk and his long hair (*Mom didn't waste money on haircuts when school was out*) waving as he ran.

I sat in the grass under the tree and watched the kittens. They came out a few times each day, mostly in the morning and the afternoon, always with their momma nearby to watch over them. If one of us kids crept too close, they would all disappear into the shadows under the building, but if we kept our distance, if we just sat quietly and didn't bother them, the momma cat would relax and lie down. The kittens would roll around, hop on each other, and explore just a little bit farther from the unscreened opening that was the doorway to their crawlspace home.

I saw Ray sprinting up the block with Tommy running behind him, his arms and legs pumping hard to catch up, shouting "Ray! Slow down! Richie said don't be a spaz!"

Jeez Louise!

Ray came running up the sidewalk and he didn't stop in the name of the Laws until he was halfway across the back lawn. He clapped his hands and hopped up and down and the momma cat arched her back. Her fur bristled and she chased her kittens into the crawlspace.

"Ray," I said, "Are you totally mental or what?"

"I just got excited, Richie."

Tommy sat down on the sidewalk and squinted up at Ray with the sun in his eyes. "I told you not to be a spaz," he said to Ray. "I told him that, Richie."

"I didn't even get a good look at them," Ray complained. "I can't pick one if I can't get a good look at them, Richie. And they sure are scared of people."

I frowned and stood up. I put my face close to his. "Well, jeez, Ray! Whatta you *expect*?" I shouted at him. "You come stompin' around and clapping your hands like some kinda moron!"

"Sheesh, Richie!" he said. "Say it, don't spray it! We want the news, not the weather!"

I balled up my fists. "Seriously, Ray! You're a *complete* mental case!"

A window slid open and I saw my mom looking out through the screen. "Richie!" she hollered, "Who are you shouting at out there?"

"Aw, Mom...it's just Ray Laws! He's a spaz!"

"Okay."

"Can I punch him in the belly?"

"No, Richie!" Mom hollered and slammed the window shut.

Ray sat down in the grass and Jesse came around the corner of the building and sat down next to me under the tree. "Man, Richie! I could hear you hollerin' all the way upstairs."

I told Ray to just sit still and be quiet and maybe the kittens would come back out. We waited in the shade under the tree for a half hour or so, but the kittens stayed hidden in the dark and Ray said he had to go home. I told him we would come get him when they were out again, but he had to be calm and not come hauling ass up the sidewalk like a freak.

"I will, Richie," he said. "I just got a little hyper over picking out my kitten."

He walked off down the sidewalk with one hand jammed in his pocket and the other one up his nose. Well, probably not his whole hand, but at least one finger.

Jesse sighed and said, "That kid has a major malfunction."

"Yeah," Tommy said. "Ray Laws is really, *really* weird."

"Seriously," I sighed. "He's a total spaz."

Ray disappeared down the sidewalk and as soon as he was out of sight, four pairs of glowing green eyes appeared in the crawlspace, looking out from the darkness just inside the opening.

Tommy said, "Don't worry, kitties...the weirdo is gone" and we all burst out laughing, and then Jesse's mom called down to him from the upstairs window.

"Jesse! Jesse!" She hollered. "Get back up here and finish packing up your room!"

I looked at Jesse and my frown found its twin. He stood up, brushed dirt and grass off the seat of his jeans and hollered "Yeah, Mom... I'm comin' up right now."

Summer was ending. Ohio was waiting.

Ten - A Dog and Pony Show

On Saturday morning, Tommy and I were sprawled on the living room carpet watching *Speed Buggy* and I heard Jessie stomping down the steps. I jumped up and opened the door before he could bang on it and wake up Mom and Ben. I put a finger to my lips, stepped out on the porch and pulled the apartment door shut behind me. Tommy's face appeared in the living room window, peeking out from the corner of the drapes.

"Holy cow, Jess," I said, "My mom and Ben are still in bed."

Jesse caught his breath and said, "Yeah... sorry, sorry." He shoved a newspaper advertisement into my face and said, "Read that, Richie!"

It was a big colorful ad for a carnival. There were big block letters promising *FUN!FUN!FUN!* and a picture of a carousel and another of a clown. A banner at the bottom of the page guaranteed games, rides and attractions. In the middle of the ad, there was a creepy voodoo eyeball and underneath it a long, coiled snake with a tattoo on its skin that said *FREAKSHOW – 50 CENTS!*

"They're set up in the big field over by the river," Jesse said. "Today and tomorrow only. We're goin' to the carnival, Richie! My mom said she'll take us. You, Tommy and me. Gary, too, if he wants to come."

Oh, boy!

"Really? Your mom's gonna pay for *all* of us?" Jesse nodded and I told him I would ask my mom as soon as she woke up. "She should be up pretty soon, Jess."

"Tell her she can come, too. My mom said to tell your mom to come with us."

Jesse ran back up the stairs and I went back inside the apartment and told Tommy that Jesse's mom was going to take us to the carnival and before I could tell him to be quiet, his whooping and hollering dragged Mom and Ben out of bed.

Mom went into the kitchen to brew the coffee and Ben came out of the bedroom in just his underwear and sat at the table, his messy hair hanging in his messy face, mumbling about noisy brats and thin walls while he smoked and waited for Mom to bring him his 'cuppa joe'.

"Tell her, Richie," Tommy whispered. "Are you gonna tell her?"

I could hear Mom in the kitchen, pouring coffee into two cups, and she called out, "Tell me what, Richie." I heard her sigh. "I swear, you better not be waking me up to trouble."

I squinted one eye at my little brother. *Thanks, Tommy.* "It's not bad, Mom. It's good," I said. "I was just gonna wait until you drank some coffee. You always say not to bother you in the morning until..."

"Oh, for God's sake, Richie... just tell me already!"

She carried two steaming cups to the table, set one in front of Ben and poured milk and sugar into her own. I got up off the carpet and went in the kitchen and Tommy followed me. Ben lit another cigarette and took a noisy gulp of his coffee and Mom lifted hers to her lips with both hands and took a sip. She looked at me over the rim of the cup, the steam from the coffee fogging up her glasses.

"Well?"

"There's a carnival in town! Over by the river," I told her. "Jesse's mom wants to take us. She's gonna pay for *all* of us, Mom."

Mom set her cup down on the table and shook a cigarette out of Ben's pack. She blew smoke up at the ceiling fan and tapped the tip of the cigarette on the ashtray. "Brenda said she can pay for all of you?"

"Yeah, Mom. She wants you to come, too."

Mom said we could go and that she'd go upstairs and talk to Jesse's mother after she made breakfast for Ben and she shooed us out of the kitchen. "Go watch cartoons or go outside and play."

We went back to the couch and watched *The Krofft Supershow* while Mom fried potatoes and eggs for Ben. When he finished eating, Ben got dressed, combed his greasy hair, and went outside and Mom went upstairs to talk to Jesse's mother. When she came back down, she told us we would leave at four o'clock and she banged on Gary's (*Gramma's*) bedroom door and asked him if he wanted to go to the carnival with us.

"That cheap-o carnival at the river?" he hollered from behind the closed door. "Do I gotta go, Mom? I was gonna play ball."

Mom told Gary he didn't have to go with us and she went into her room to get dressed. Gary came out of his room, went to the kitchen for a bowl of cereal and squeezed Tommy and I to the ends of the couch. "Don't you guys gotta get dressed or something?" Gary said through a mouthful of Froot Loops. Milk dripped from the corners of his lips. "I wanna turn this baby show off and watch somethin' else."

"C'mon, Tommy." We gave Gary the couch and the TV and got up to go get dressed and Tommy said, "Don'tcha wanna go to the carnival, Gary?"

"That rinky-dink carnival ain't any good," Gary said, "But it's okay for a bunch of little kids like you."

Tommy nodded. "Well, I'll try and win you something at the dime pitch."

In the late afternoon, we drove across town in Brenda Gwinn's big sedan, us three boys giggling and chatting excitedly in the back seat, our moms up in front smoking and listening to the country music station on the radio. We pulled into the bumpy dirt lot that had been roped off for parking and before Jesse's mom had even turned off the motor, Jesse, Tommy and I were bounding out of the back seat and running for the midway.

"You boys wait!" My mom hollered and the three of us skidded in the dirt, full stop, and turned around to wait for our mothers.

When they caught up to us, Mom said, "You boys stay together on the midway. You can go off on your own without us, but you stay together and, Richie, you keep an eye on your brother." She opened her purse, pulled out a crumpled tissue and spat in it. She wiped a smudge off Tommy's cheek and when she shoved the tissue back in her pocketbook, she pulled out three ten dollar bills and handed one to each of us.

"Wow!" Jesse and Tommy said in stereo.

"Ten dollars!" I shouted. I couldn't remember the last time I had held a ten-dollar bill in my hands that was my own to spend on whatever I wanted. "Mom? Really?"

She bent over, kissed my forehead, and said softly in my ear, "It's just a little bit from Gramma's money. Just in case we can't go to Wildwood. I want you to have a good time with Jesse."

I hugged her and said, "Okay, Mom. Thanks, Mom!"

On the midway, Miss Brenda bought a big book of ride tickets and handed it to Jesse ("Don't lose these") and he shoved them into his back pocket, reconsidered, then took them out and shoved them into his front pocket, where they'd be safer. My mom wagged her finger at us and said, "Remember what I told you. Stay together. And meet us right back here in three hours to check in and eat some dinner."

"Okay, Mom. We will," I said and we ran off down the midway and Mom hollered after us, "And watch out for the Carnies!"

It was just a small traveling carnival, the kind Gramma used to call a dog and pony show and Gary called rinky-dink, but the half-dozen rides and the rows of rigged games and the trailers selling salty and sugary treats were a world of rare opportunity for a kid on his summer vacation with a ten dollar bill in his pocket.

We rode the bumper cars first because they were Tommy's favorite and we ate big slices of pizza and guzzled large lemon-lime sodas. At the shooting gallery, Jesse and I won prizes, but Tommy didn't shoot down enough targets and he blamed his rifle and said he would rather throw darts and pitch dimes anyway.

There was a kiddie coaster and we rode it twice in a row, shouting and throwing our hands up in the air as the short, colorful train bumped and rolled around the track. Our fingertips turned blue and sticky as we walked among the tents and booths, pulling puffs of cotton candy from big clouds on paper cones. Tommy bought a plastic shrunken head and we all got fake tattoos and rolled our shirtsleeves up to our shoulders to show off the black-eyed skulls on our skinny arms.

At the far end of the midway, on the green bank of the river, there was a wooden pen and a sign that said *Petting Zoo*. We walked up to the rails of the wooden fence and looked inside and I smiled when I saw the baby goats, piglets, and chickens. There was a pony tied to a post and ducks floating in a plastic blue kiddie pool.

"Uh-oh," Jesse said. "Animals. We just lost Richie Doolittle."

Tommy giggled and said, "Yeah...Richie Doolittle"

I asked the lady at the gate how much it cost to pet the animals. She had a round, happy face and she wore a bonnet on her head and a long country dress with a checkered apron. She smiled at me and said, "You can pet 'em for free all day long, kiddo, but if you wanna feed 'em, the pellets are fifteen cents a cup."

We spent half an hour in the pen and I petted all of the animals and spent over two dollars buying paper cups of food. It was my favorite part of the day. I loved the way it tickled when the baby goats nuzzled my palm for the green pellets of food and how they butted their heads against me when my hand was empty. I rubbed my hand along the pony's side. His hair was coarse and thick and when I scratched under his chin, he chuffed warm breath in my face. I fed him a handful of straw and a whole cup of feed, kissed him on his wet nose and smiled into his brown eyes.

After the petting zoo, Jesse asked a cop what time it was and on the way to meet our moms we stopped at a red and white wagon and bought bags of hot roasted peanuts. We found our mothers near the ticket booth, sitting at a round table with a big umbrella popped open above it. They were drinking lemonade and laughing.
They made us go wash our hands and faces and when we came back, Jesse's mom asked us what we wanted to eat for dinner and all three of us said we weren't even hungry at all.

"Didn't you boys save any room for dinner?" she asked and we told her we hadn't eaten that much junk and my mom cocked one eyebrow at us and said, "Not that much junk, huh?"

"Jeez, Mom, it's a carnival," Jesse said. "We checked in like you wanted us to. Can't we just go ride some more rides and play some games and just eat a hot dog or something?"

"Two more hours," my mom said. She looked at Jesse's mom and they both nodded. "Two hours," she repeated, "It'll start getting dark by then."

We hurried off toward the rides and when we were standing in line to ride the Scrambler, I heard a girl's voice calling out my name and saw Cheryl and Brenda walking toward us across the midway, waving their hands. "Hey, you guys! Hey!"

"Here comes Richie's girlfriend," Jesse whispered and Tommy giggled and said, "Richie's got cooties."

I felt my face warming up to turn red and I hushed Jesse and Tommy. "C'mon, guys, knock it off. They're coming over here."

The girls were eating candied apples, their lips were shiny and red, and they stood outside the railing and chatted with us while we moved through the line. Jesse asked them if they were going to ride the Scrambler and Brenda said they would just wait for us until we got off the ride, if we wanted to hang out with them.

"Neat-o!" Tommy said and we climbed up the riveted steps and strapped ourselves into one of the gondolas. A carny came around and checked the lap bar and as the ride started to spin, Jesse said, "Well, looks like we got dates, Romeo."

Sheesh!

"I ain't got no *date*!" Tommy said and the ride spun faster and faster and when it stopped, we climbed down, dizzy and laughing. Cheryl and Brenda were sitting on a bench, finishing their candied apples, and they smiled and waved as we came off the Scrambler's iron deck.

"Don't be nervous, pardner," Jesse teased me. "You ain't gotta worry unless she asks you to ride the Ferris wheel."

Tommy giggled and I looked at him and said, "If she does, *you're* sitting in between us!"

We popped balloons with darts and all of us won mirrors with cartoon characters painted on them, but at the milk-jug booth, all of us lost. We bought hot dogs, fries, and big cups of lemonade and we laughed our way through the funhouse, and then waited at the exit for fifteen minutes while Tommy banged and bumped his way through the mirror maze. We threw our money away at the dime pitch tent, but Tommy won an ashtray (*I'll give it to Mom*) and a purple goblet for Gary to keep on his shelf.

"We only got an hour left," Jesse said. "What you guys wanna do now?"

I remembered the big voodoo eyeball and the tattooed snake from the newspaper ad, and I looked around at my brother and my friends and said, "Freak Show!"

We stood outside the big Freak Show tent and gawked at the panels of colorful posters on both sides of the entrance. *SEE THE BEARDED LADY! WORLD'S SMALLEST MAN! LIVE TWO-HEADED*

SNAKE! THE MUMMY BABY OF EGYPT! ODDITIES, ABNORMALITIES & FREAKS OF NATURE!

"I don't wanna go in there," Tommy said. "I don't wanna see no scary freaks of nature."

"Don't worry, Tommy... it's all fake or just people with birth defects," I told him. "Besides, you can't wait out here by yourself."

Tommy looked at me and said. "You got a birth defect, Richie. I don't think you're a freak."

I smiled at my brother and Jesse winked at me and said, "Oh, you're pretty freaky, alright."

We lined up at the entrance and each of us handed two quarters to the skinny man at the curtain. He smiled at us and his teeth were yellow and broken and he looked down at Tommy and said, "Gonna getcher freak on, huh, kid?"

Tommy grabbed my hand and looked up at the skinny man with the jack-o-lantern smile and said, "We ain't supposed to talk to carnies, mister."

The man took Tommy's fifty cents, shrugged his shoulders, and said, "Yeah, well, I ain't supposed to talk to kids, but I gotta make a buck."

Jesse whispered in my ear (*creepy*) and we passed through the curtain and into the dim Freak Show tent, huddled close together, Tommy still clutching my hand in his.

"Step this way, step this way," The Bearded Lady called. "Be my guest, then see the rest." She was sitting on a big plush chair with a high back, smoking a cigarette through a skinny white tube. There was a little table next to her chair with a lamp and a book on it and she absently stroked the fur of a little dog that slept on her lap. She looked like any lady you might see around the neighborhood, but she had sideburns like Elvis and a scraggly beard.

"Is that a real beard?" Jesse whispered, but she heard him and said, "Come get a kiss, handsome, and find out for yourself."

Jesse blushed and the girls giggled as we hurried away down the carpeted path that led to the next freakish display and Jesse called over his shoulder, "My pal Richie does all the smoochin' around here, mister ma'am."

The two-headed snake was real, but it wasn't alive. It lay stiff and still in a big glass case and there was a hand-printed sign taped to the glass that said *'Sorry. It just died last week.'*

"What a rip-off!" I said and Jesse snorted and said, "Ray Laws is freakier than everything in this tent."

We all laughed as we walked through the tent and we mocked the Mummy Baby of Egypt ("That's a doll wrapped in bandages"), doubted the Space Alien Skeleton "(Um… that looks like a monkey") and debunked each display as a fake and a fraud. At the exit, we met The World's Smallest Man, a fancy dresser in a top hat and tails, and we stared at him in disbelief. He was an inch taller than Tommy.

We burst through the curtain and onto the midway and Tommy said, "You guys! Hey, you guys! Oh, my gosh!"

All of us looked at him and Brenda Clark said, "What's the matter?"

Tommy smiled and put his hands on his hips and said, "*I'm* the world's smallest man!"

It was almost time to go home. We walked up the midway with our prizes in our hands, and the scent of fresh, hot dough lured us to a purple and pink wagon where each of us traded a dollar for a giant soft pretzel, sprinkled with big shards of salt. We sat on the grass behind the Milk-Bottle Toss and ate our salty pretzels with mustard squeezed on them. Cheryl looked up and smiled, colored lights reflected in her glasses, spinning slowly round and round.

"C'mon!" she said. "Let's go on the Ferris wheel!"

She ran off toward the big wheel, we all chased behind her, and when we lined up for the ride, she said, "Richie, will you ride with me?"

Gulp!

I jammed my hands deep in my pockets, twisted nervously on my toes and said, "Sure, I'll ride with you, but Tommy has to ride with us and he has to sit in the middle 'cause he's scared of heights.

"I ain't scared of no heights!" Tommy argued and Brenda Clark said, "He climbed to the top of the light-pole!"

Oops!

The man at the gate scowled down at us and said, "You kids getting' on or what? You're holdin' up the line."

Jesse and Brenda handed him their tickets and climbed into a shiny red gondola. Another man pulled a lever that brought the next car around. The three of us gave up our tickets and piled in, my brother and I at each end and Cheryl Bozart squeezed in between us.

The cart lurched and stopped, lurched and stopped, but when all of the gondolas were filled with riders, the wheel turned smooth and fast. We rose and fell in the August sky on a circle of flashing light, and when we stopped at the top, Cheryl squeezed my hand with hers and my tummy felt ticklish.

Tommy rocked the cart back and forth and hollered, "I can see the neighborhood from up here! I can see the *whole* neighborhood!"

When we got off the Ferris wheel and came down the steps, Jesse poked me with his elbow and said, "You okay, Richie? You look a little pale, pardner."

"I just ate too much junk, that's all. I got a stomach ache."

We had to hurry to meet our moms and we were out of breath when we found them near the ticket booth, both of them holding big stuffed animals and smoking cigarettes. They smiled at the girls and Jesse's mom said, "Do you girls need a ride home?"

Cheryl shook her head and Brenda Clark said, "Thanks, but my mom is picking us up."

We said goodbye to the girls and followed our moms toward the gate, past a yellow Arabian tent with bright red trim and a sign shaped like a hand that said 'Madam Isabella, Fortunes Told.'

Jesse looked over his shoulder and said, "Mom, can me and Richie get our fortunes told?"

Our mothers stopped and looked back at the tent and Jesse's mom said, "I'm tired, Jess. You've had all night. Let's just go home."

"But the tent's right here. It will only take a few minutes."

My mom frowned, sighed, looked at Jesse's mom, and said, "It's up to you, Brenda. I don't mind if you don't."

"Go on then, boys. Hurry up."

Tommy said he wanted his fortune told, too, but Mom told him he could get his palm read the next time.

"Let Richie and Jess have this to themselves."

We stepped through silky drapes into the spooky tent. It was dimly lit with candles and it smelled of spices and incense. There were drapes on the inside, too, hanging from the ceiling, and there was a short round table cluttered with beads and a big dusty book, a strange deck of cards and a sparkling crystal ball. Madam Isabella sat on a big tasseled pillow on the other side of the table. She wore a long black robe and a veil across her face and her eyes were lost in shadow cast by the glow of the magic orb. She held one hand over the crystal ball. With the other, she waved us closer.

I looked at Jesse and his eyes were as wide and round as my own must have been. We sat down on a wide, soft cushion and the Madam said, "Ah... two boys. Not brothers, but you come to see me together."

"Yeah, we're *blood* brothers," Jesse said. "Best friends."

Madam Isabella nodded. "Of course you are," she said. "Adventurous boys. I can tell. Show me the palms of your hands."

We held our hands out over the table, palms up, and the Madam lit a candle then blew it right out. She looked at Jesse's hands and then she looked at mine and she took them in her own and rubbed her fingertips over the puckered skin where my thumb should have been.

"You're a troubled boy," she said and she traced the lines in my palms with her fingers and then she took Jesse's hands and read his palms, too.

"You boys are connected. A very strong bond." She looked into the crystal ball and said, "But one of you will go away."

She's a real fortuneteller!

She pointed her finger at me and said, "You will travel far."

I shook my head. "No. Not me," I said. "Jesse. He's moving away to Ohio."

Madam Isabella looked into the glass again and said, "Yes. Your friend will go to Ohio, but you will travel far."

Jesse leaned over the table and said, "But will we ever see each other again? When we're older?"

"Of course, you will. You're best friends."

She picked up a little silver bell, rang it, and said, "That is all the spirits have to say tonight. That'll be two dollars, sweeties."

Eleven - In the Name of the Laws

The third week of August broke even hotter than the week before, the mercury in the cheap dime-store thermometer that hung on a nail next to our apartment door hit 90 by mid-morning and at night, the heatwave lingered and it was hard to sleep. It was too hot for bike riding or for chasing each other through the bog and we stayed on the block, cooling ourselves in the sprinklers or splashing in the crowded community swimming pool, and when the sun went down, we played ball in the street or tag on the lawn.

Coming back from the pool that Wednesday afternoon, towels slung around our necks, our swimming trunks still dripping but drying fast, Jesse and I crossed Bloomfield Street at the corner of our block. We had only three days left together before Jesse and his mom would leave the neighborhood forever and we were talking quietly about days gone by and days that would never come and as we passed Ray's building, we heard him call out to us.

"Hey, guys! Stop in the name of the Laws."

Ray Laws was looking at us from his open bedroom window, his face pressed up against the screen, his hands cupped around his eyes. Jesse and I looked at each other, shrugged our shoulders and walked across the brown grass in our bare feet.

"Whatcha want, Ray?" I asked, looking up at him. He had a dark smudge on the tip of his nose from pressing it against the dusty screen.

"You guys been at the pool, huh? My mom won't let me come out."

Jesse smirked. "Why not? Your mom catch you eatin' your boogers at the dinner table or something?"

I giggled, but Ray frowned. "Boy, that's *real* funny," he said. "You're a real laugh riot, Jesse. I ain't in trouble. I can't come outside 'cause my mom says it's too hot and I'll get a heatstroke."

Ray's mom had a seasonal list of reasons to keep Ray and his sister inside on days when the other kids in the neighborhood braved the weather in the name of fun and went home at night alive and well. In the spring, it was the dreaded hay fever and the fall brought the threat of pneumonia. On the coldest days of winter, especially if it snowed, Ray's mother worried about frostbite and on sweltering summer days like those blistered days of August, it was sunburn and heatstroke that had Ray bound to his room.

"Ray," I said, "I'll bet you it's hotter in that apartment than it is out here. Your mom's nuts."

Ray sighed, shook his head and lowered his voice. "Anyway, what about the kittens? Can I come up tonight when it's cool out and pick my kitten?"

"Seriously, Ray? You're actually *whispering*?" I said. "You already blabbed to my mom about the kittens and the whole neighborhood knows about them, but you're whispering?"

Ray looked over his shoulder. "Well, yeah," he said, "I still want it to be a surprise for my mom and Trina. So what about it? Do they come out at night?"

I told Ray that the kittens mostly came out in the morning and the late afternoon, and it occurred to me that I hadn't seen the kittens or the momma cat since before we'd left for the carnival Saturday afternoon. "Why don'tcha try to come in the morning before it gets too hot out?"

"Yeah," Jesse said, "but don't get a heatstroke on our lawn."

Ray said he would ask his mom in the morning and Jesse and I headed back up the block. When we got to our building, I asked Jesse if he had seen the kittens in the last couple of days. He shook his head and shrugged his shoulders.

"It's prob'ly on account of the heatwave," he said, "I bet that momma cat is keepin' them under the building 'cause it's too hot outside."

"Yeah," I agreed. "Maybe she's worried about a heatstroke, like Ray's mom."

Jesse giggled at my joke and went upstairs. "I'll see you after dinner, Richie," he called down from the top, "I gotta help my mom finish packing."

I looked out at the curb where a long, rented trailer sat hitched to the back of Brenda Gwinn's car, sighed up at the cloudless sky and went into the apartment.

At supper, I didn't have an appetite and I pushed my food around on the end of my fork and only drank half my milk. Ben told me to stop playing with my food and eat it and Mom felt my forehead with the back of her hand and asked me if I was feeling alright.

"What's the matter, Richie?" she said, "You get too much sun today or are you upset about Jess and Brenda moving away?"

"He's brokenhearted 'cause his boyfriend is movin' away!" Gary said. Ben laughed behind his beer can (*coward*), but mom glared at Gary and told him to shut his mouth before she popped him one.

"I'm just worried 'bout the kittens," I said. "They haven't been out since Saturday."

Mom told me the same thing that Jesse had said, that it was probably just too hot for them and Ben said, "The momma cat prob'ly took 'em and moved 'em somewhere else."

I looked at him, though I could hardly stand to. "Why would she move them?"

He looked at me as if I was the dumbest kid in the world and said, "Every damn kid on the block has been comin' around lookin' at those kittens. That idiot friend of yours, Ray, just scared the hell out of 'em a couple days ago. That cat prob'ly moved those kittens far away from here, that's for sure."

I looked at my mom and asked her if she thought the cat took the kittens away and she shrugged her shoulders. "She might have, Richie," she said, "but if she did, don't be too sad about it. You were gonna have to get rid of them anyway."

Twelve - Last Night on Earth

Overnight, the heatwave lifted and the following day was cooler than it had been for weeks. In the morning, we helped Jesse and his mom load the moving trailer. Ben, John and Gary carried the couch, the mattresses, and other heavy things down the stairs and Tommy, Jesse and I lumped smaller boxes to the curb where our moms were supervising the loading.

When we finished packing up the trailer, we kids cooled off in the sprinklers and Ben and John sat on the lawn in folding chairs, drinking beer and smoking cigarettes. Our shouts and giggles drew the other kids out of their apartments.

The Hodges brothers came out, Bobby and Ray came up from their ends of the block and we started up a game of Wiffle ball in the parking lot. Gary took the Hodges on one team and the rest of us made up the other, but Tommy didn't want to play.

"I'm gonna check the dumpsters," he said, "I haven't found anything good in a long time."

He walked up the alley, climbed up on one of the big garbage dumpsters and leaned into the opening. His legs stuck up out of the opening for a moment, waggling back and forth, and then he slid inside the dumpster and disappeared from sight.

"Seriously, guys..." Bobby Bozart said, shaking his head. "One of these days, Tommy's gonna end up in the back of the garbage truck."

Our team was losing the Wiffle ball game by three runs and it was my turn up at bat. Jesse was on second base, Gary was winding up the pitch and Tommy's head popped up out of the dumpster and he shouted, "Richie! Richie, come quick!"

Gary took advantage of the distraction and pitched the perforated plastic ball right past me for a strike and I smacked the asphalt with the yellow plastic bat and hollered, "Sheesh, Tommy! Whatta you want? I'm playin' ball over here!"

Tommy tossed a plastic garbage bag over the side of the dumpster (*thud*) and jumped down after it. I was about to holler at him that I didn't want to see any stupid junk he found in the garbage, but I realized that he was crying and I jogged toward him, dragging the Wiffle ball bat behind me across the blacktop.

"Jeez, Tommy...what's the matter?" I said. The other kids had followed me across the parking lot and we stood around the dumpster, looking down at the plastic garbage bag. Tommy's eyes were wide and wet and tears streamed down his cheeks. Gary knelt down and tore the plastic bag open and in a collective moment of shocked horror, all of us realized what we were looking at and all of us gasped at once.

No!

In a matted, fuzzy pile, the three-legged Siamese cat and her four kittens lay dead at the bottom of the garbage bag, their bodies stiff and their necks twisted. Maggots squirmed in their fur and the thick putrid smell rising out of the bag drove everyone back except me. I leaned over the dead cats, staring down at them through burning eyes, gripping the plastic bat tight in my sweaty hands.

I looked up and found Jesse's eyes. He was crying. "He did this," I whispered, "he killed them!"

I turned and ran toward our building, my eyes filling up with hot tears, and I couldn't tell if the pounding in my ears was the raging of my own heart or the sound of the other kids chasing behind me across the parking lot. I rounded the corner of the building, ran across the lawn and raised the bat above my head.

"You killed them!" I shouted and I swung the plastic bat so hard that it crumpled and bent across the side of Ben's head. He tumbled out of the lawn-chair, stumbled to his feet and balled up a fist that struck me in the cheek and knocked me on the ground. He loomed over me, yanked the bat from my grip and raised it waggling over his shoulder.

The right side of his face was bright red where I had smacked him with the bat and his mouth was open in a silent snarl. He stood over me and blocked out the sun, staring down at me with the bat poised to strike and in that moment, I forgot my sacred vow and burst into tears.

He sees you! He sees you now!

I raised my hands up in front of my face and cowered on the lawn, waiting for Ben to strike, certain he would kill me with my own Wiffle ball bat. His flabby muscles tensed and the bat waggled and just as he was about to bring the toy bat crashing down to beat me, Jesse stepped in between us, his arms held out to protect me, his skinny chest puffed out in impossible bravery, his chin turned up in defiance.

"Go on! Hit me!" Jesse shouted, "See how fast *my mom* calls the cops, you asshole!"

Briefly, time stood still and in that eternal, furious moment, our mothers rushed out of our apartment and stood on the porch, their mouths open wide in surprise, their eyes open wider in shock.

Gary knelt behind me and put his hands on my shoulders and my friends gathered around us in a frightened mob. Tommy ran for the porch and for mom, screaming, "Ben killed the kittens! Ben killed the kittens!" and my best friend stood his ground until big, greasy John finally stood up, cocked back his huge fist and punched Ben across his jaw.

CRACK!

Ben's head swung around, his dingy hair fell in his eyes, and he stumbled backward and fell on the ground, blood trickling from the corner of his mouth. John leaned over him, grabbed the front of his t-shirt in one fist and hit him again with the other.

"You don't ever hit these boys!" John growled. "You hear me? You don't ever, ever hit these kids!"

Jesse and Gary helped me up off the lawn and Brenda Gwinn rushed off the porch and took me in her arms. My mom turned and ran into our apartment, then came back out on the porch with her arms full of jeans and t-shirts and socks and threw all the clothes on the ground. Her face was red and raging, her eyes were dark and threatening, and she ran across the courtyard to the lawn where Ben lay cowering beneath John's fist.

She kicked Ben in his ribs and I heard the air rush out of his lungs (*oof*!) and she smacked him hard across his face and screamed, "You get out! You get your shit and you get the fuck out of here!"

Ben raised his hands in front of his face, scooted backward across the grass, and said, "Fran... Frances, wait."

John tugged Ben up off the ground and shoved him hard. "You better do what she says, Ben, or you're gonna wish she'd called the cops."

Ben wiped the back of his hand across his bloody lips, pushed his fingers through his greasy hair and stumbled across the yard. He bent and picked up his clothes and mumbled at his nephew, "Bobby, get over here and help me pick this shit up."

My mom took me in her arms and held me against her side and I buried my face against her belly and cried every tear I'd denied myself since June.

That night, Mom didn't cook dinner. She ordered delivery pizza and sat at the kitchen table, chain-smoking cigarettes while my brothers and I devoured the pie in front of the television set. We left two slices in the box for Mom and by the time the sitcoms were over, the apartment had dimmed and filled with smoke. Mom turned on the light above the table, told Gary to close the front door and then called us in to the kitchen. My brothers and I sat around the table, fidgeting nervously, while Mom lit another cigarette and blew the smoke out on a sigh.

"It's been a hard summer," she said softly, looking at each of us in turn around the table. "We lost Gramma. We're losing Jesse. The car."

"The kittens," Tommy whispered and Gary shushed him, but Mom didn't scold him for interrupting her.

She took another deep drag on her cigarette, breathed another smoky sigh and when she spoke again, she was talking to all three of us, but she was looking straight into my eyes.

"I never mean to hurt you boys," she said and she began to cry. Tears pooled behind her glasses, then trickled under the lenses and down her cheeks. "I never do. I love you and you're all I have. You're all I'll ever have."

She sucked on the cigarette again, but she choked on the smoke and her chest began to heave and she hung her head and sobbed. Her shoulders shook, her lips trembled and she sobbed through clenched teeth and I realized in that moment that I looked as much like her as I did my father. I'd never seen her weep like that before, none of us had, and I sat frozen in that wobbly chair, unsure of what to say or do, afraid of what might lurk behind her sorrow, and Gary stood up and went to her and hugged her. She pulled him close to her shoulder and pressed her face against his chest and Tommy left his chair and threw his arms around her neck and then I knew just what to do. I went to her and wrapped my arms around her, too.

There was a rap at the door, Brenda Gwinn opened it up and peeked in, and Jesse poked his head around her hip and peeked in, too. Brenda came into the kitchen, sent us off to bed with hugs, and shooed Jesse back upstairs.

"Go to bed, Jess. Big day tomorrow. I'll be up in a little while to tuck you in."

Big day tomorrow. The biggest of them all.

I lay in my bed, the palm of my hand pressed softly against the black-and-blue side of my face, falling asleep against my will, listening to my mother crying in the kitchen, and I heard her softly say to Jesse's mom, "I'm so lonely. I'm so lonely all the time."

I cried for her in the dark, cried into my pillow so she wouldn't hear me, and I wasn't sure if I dreamed it or if I was still awake, but I heard her tell Brenda Gwinn, "I'm gonna take the boys to Wildwood. They deserve it, especially Richie."

Thirteen - So Long Pardner

In the morning, I woke up to a banging on our apartment door, the frantic sound of Brenda Gwinn's voice and my mother shouting at me before the sun was even up.

"Richie! Richie, get out here! Hurry up!"

I hurried out of bed, saw Tommy sitting up in his bed, wiping sleep out of his eyes, and said, "C'mon. Wake up. Something's wrong!"

Tommy climbed out of bed and followed me into the hall. Gary came out of his room and stood behind us and I said, "Mom, what happened?"

Brenda Gwinn burst into tears and my mom looked at me and said, "Jesse's gone! He ran away! Richard, did you know?"

He ran away without me?

I shook my head and came out of the hallway. "I didn't know, Mom. He didn't tell me. I swear."

My mom put her arm around Brenda's shoulder, put her in a chair at the kitchen table and reached for the phone hanging on the wall.

"Mom, wait," I said, "Don't call the cops on Jesse. I bet I know where he is."

Jesse's mom looked at me and said, "Where?"

I lowered my eyes from hers and said, "Jeez, I don't wanna tattle on him, Miss Brenda." In the years that we had been friends, in a neighborhood full of ratfinks and tattle-tails, Jesse and I had been true to our friendship's childish code. I'd never tattled on Jesse, he'd never tattled on me, and I couldn't (*wouldn't*) betray that trust on a day when we would be forced into goodbyes.

I felt my mother's eyes, lifted mine and met her gaze, not in defiance, but frightening trust. "Just let me go get him," I said, "Just let me go get him and tell him he has to come back."

"It's four in the goddamned morning, Richie," my mother said, but she didn't sound angry and she didn't look mean. "Take Gary with you."

I could just *feel* my big brother puffing out his chest behind me and I said, "No, Ma. I don't need Gary. Just me. Please?"

Mom waved her hand and I ran to my room for my sneakers and ran out the door, up the block without a shirt, over the fence without a splinter, down the path without a light, and found Jesse asleep in the clubhouse, curled up on the wooden floor without a pillow.

He sat up, rubbed his eyes, and blinked at me in the moonlight. "Hey, pardner."

"You were gonna run away without me?"

He leaned against the clubhouse wall and drew his knees up to his chest, wrapped his arms around his legs. His face disappeared in shadow. "No, man... no way. I didn't wanna wake up your mom, Richie. I knew you'd find me if I waited here."

His lips quivered and sagged and he hung his head and cried and I sat down beside him and wrapped my arm around his shoulder and, because his pain was my pain, I cried with him in the dark and remembered what the fortune-teller had said about us.

Two boys. Not brothers. A very strong bond.

"Well, the jig is up, pal," I said, still crying a little, wiping the back of my hand under my nose, "Everyone knows you're gone. Your mom came down to our place havin' a conniption fit! We gotta go back, Jess, or my mom's gonna call the cops."

Jesse laughed through a frown and said, "Some outlaw I turned out to be. I didn't even make it outta the neighborhood."

"You coulda made it," I told him. "You coulda made it, but you waited for me."

He smiled then, but it was brief, and his frown returned and flattened his face with sadness.

"I don't wanna move to Ohio," he said, "I don't wanna go away."

"I know. I don't want you to go. I wish and wish you wouldn't go." I sighed, held my breath, and felt my tears subside. "But we can't stop it, Jesse. We're *just* kids."

We stood up and I took his daypack from the clubhouse floor and handed it to him. It was light. "Whatcha pack to run away on anyway?" I asked him.

"Socks and jeans and t-shirts," he said as we climbed the slope and took our last walk up the path our feet had worn through the woods over the years since we were small. "My toothbrush. And four peanut butter and jelly sandwiches."

"Jesse specials?"

"Of course."

We climbed the fence together and sat for a moment at the top, looking back over our shoulders at the shadowy stand of woods. It was quiet in the early morning dark, just the faint rumble of the trucks out on the highway and the frogs and birds and bugs waking up down in the bog, and when Jesse spoke again, he whispered softly in my ear.

"I love you like my brother, Richie."

"I love you just like mine."

We slid over the fence, slipped down a dumpster and snuck through the alley. On the corner at Bloomfield Street, Jesse clapped me on the back and said, "At least you'll still have Ray Laws."

We laughed at that the best we could and walked up the block with our arms slung across each other's shoulders, blood brothers to the end. When we got to our building, Tommy was standing on the porch and he pointed at us and hollered, "He found him! Richie found Jesse!"

Jesse didn't get in trouble. He got breakfast and hugs and we sat at the table and ate with my brothers, big stacks of pancakes slathered with margarine and syrup, and our mothers sat on the porch, sipping coffee, smoking, and saying goodbye.

The sun was up when Jesse's mom told him it was time to go and we all stood on the sidewalk as they stuffed the last of their things into the trunk of the car. Bobby Bozart and his sisters came down the block to say goodbye to Jesse and Cheryl slipped a folded piece of paper into the palm of my hand. I shoved it in my pocket and Jesse's mom hugged us all and kissed me on my cheek.

"I'm sorry we have to move away, Richie," she whispered in my ear. "I really, really am. Your mom has our address. You write to Jesse."

"I will."

Brenda hugged my mom and got into the car and Jesse said goodbye to everyone and slipped the palm of his hand into mine. We shook the secret handshake we had created long ago and we didn't burst into tears because we'd had ours in the woods. The car engine rumbled and Jesse climbed in next to his mother. I stared at him through the window, but he looked straight ahead as his mom slipped the car into gear and they pulled away from the curb.

The brake lights flashed, the trailer lurched and then the car rolled away down the block. I took a single step off the curb and stopped, looked back at my mother and found no forbidding in her eyes, and I ran off down the block, chasing my friend out of town in the early morning heat.

I ran behind the car all the way down Bloomfield Street, wondering if they could see me in the mirrors, and I caught them at the corner when they slowed to make the turn onto Grand Avenue. Jesse turned his head and saw me and as they left me behind and sped off toward the highway, toward Ohio, he stuck his head out the open window and shouted, "Don't forget me, pardner!"

Don't worry, Jesse. I never, ever will.

I stood on the corner until their car crossed the bridge and shimmered down the highway out of sight and, though I knew Jesse couldn't see me, even if he were still looking back, I raised my hand and waved him goodbye.

Fourteen - Dog Days

In the days after Jesse moved away, I moped around the apartment until my mom got tired of me and sent me outside, where I moped around the neighborhood until I got tired of the other kids trying to cheer me up and went off alone to mope around the bog.

I chased frogs around the pond, but didn't try to catch them and I trampled through the woods, wandering and whistling, and on a late afternoon in the middle of the week, I found myself beneath the tree where Jesse and I had buried our time capsule. I sat beside the soft mound of dirt like a mourner at a newly covered grave.

For a moment, I thought of digging up the lockbox, taking it home and hiding it away in a drawer, where I could keep the tokens of our friendship safe and close, but we'd buried those treasures together, in memory of ourselves, and I left them in the ground, where the dark would keep them safe and time would turn them sacred.

I heard footsteps crashing in the woods, sneakers scuffling in the brush, and I imagined it was Jesse, come back from Ohio to finish growing up with me, but, of course, I knew it wasn't him. Jesse's footsteps never would have been so clumsy and confused and before I even looked, I had a feeling I knew who it was. I turned and looked behind me, to see who'd found me crying in the woods, and Ray Laws burst through the bushes, running with his mouth wide open, his face wet from tears and sweat, his clothes streaked with mud and slime.

"Richie! Richie!" He tumbled to his knees in the dirt beneath the tree. His t-shirt was torn and there were angry red scratches on his neck. He was huffing and puffing to catch his breath. "Richie! Oh, man, Richie!"

"Jeez, Ray, don't have a fit!" I told him. "What the heck is the matter?"

"Big kids!" Ray moaned. "They threw me out of the clubhouse, Richie, and they pushed me right into the pond!"

I helped Ray up from the ground. There was a commotion of crackling twigs and frightened birds and Mike Renfro sprinted from the tree line, hollering over his shoulder and the big freckle-faced kid I had only ever seen once before, the same mean boy who had thrown The Bicycle Witch's Schwinn in front of a train, burst clumsily into the sunshine.

They drew up on us, breathing hard and spitting mad and Ray backed up against the tree, his hands over his mouth, whimpering through his fingers. Mike stared at us with his mouth hanging open and the freckle-face pushed past me and poked Ray hard in his chest.

"Hey!" I shouted at him, "Go pick on someone your own size, why don'tcha!"

He looked at me and said, "I remember you."

"I remember *you*, too," I told him, "You're a bike thief."

He squinted at me with his lip curled up and he shoved Ray against the rough bark of the tree trunk. Ray yelped and burst into tears and I shoved the bully from behind and balled up my fists in front of my face. He turned and showed me his broken-toothed grin and raised his own fat fists.

"You little shrimp," he said. "I'm gonna pound you!"

I glanced over my fists at Mike Renfro and he finally closed his mouth. He clapped his mean friend on the back and told him to lay off me. "You can't beat him up," he said, "He's my friend's brother."

The big boy sighed and lowered his hands, but he didn't open his fists. "Alright, alright." He looked at Ray. "What about him? We still gonna beat *him* up?"

"Nah, you already roughed him up enough and scared him plenty," Mike said. "C'mon, Kenny, let's go mess around at the railroad tracks or something."

Now I knew the second bike thief's name.

Kenny poked Ray in the chest one last time and stalked off into the trees and Mike Renfro grinned at us, shrugged his shoulders and followed after him.

As they slunk off into the woods, I hollered after them as loud as I could. "You guys better tell the cops it wasn't me and Jesse who stole the Witch's bicycle!"

Ray pulled his t-shirt up over his face, blotted his tears, and peeled himself off the tree trunk.

"Jeez Louise, Richie! You saved my life!"

I frowned at him. "They weren't gonna *kill* you, Ray. They were just razzin' you."

Ray shook his head. "Uh-uh... not that new kid," he said. "Maybe Mike wouldn't beat me up, but that freckle-faced kid is a bully! Seriously, Richie... thank you!"

"Well, sheesh, you don't gotta make a big deal out of everything, Ray. C'mon, let's go home."

"Okay, Richie, but thanks for stickin' up for me. I owe you one. Big time."

We walked through the woods and climbed over the fence and at the corner, we stopped in front of Ray's building. I told him I hoped he didn't get in trouble for coming home with his shirt torn. "I'll see you later, Ray. I gotta get home."

"Hey, Richie…"

I sighed, irritated, thinking he was going to thank me again for saving him from the snaggle-toothed bully.

"Well…" he said, "I was wondering when you could pay me back the dollar I gave you for the kitten."

What?

"I mean, on account of I ain't gonna get any kitten out of the deal."

Sheeshomighty!

You'd think saving a kid's life would settle a one-dollar debt.

I balled up my fist and I slugged Ray Laws in the gut. He let out a whooshing breath and I left him crying on the corner of our block, bent over with his hands clasped over his belly, and I stomped up the block toward my building.

Cheryl and Brenda were sitting on the sidewalk playing jacks (*onesies… twosies… threesies…*) and Tommy, Red-Headed Ricky and the Hodges brothers were playing kickball in the street. The girls looked up, saw me coming, and giggled and Ricky waved his arms and hollered at me.

"Hey, Richie! Come play some kickball!"

I looked over my shoulder at him and kept on walking. "Maybe later. You got even teams anyway."

Ricky sighed and bounced the ratty ball off the blacktop. "Aw, *c'mon*, Richie," he shouted, "You can pitch for both teams. C'mon, and play some ball!"

I cut across the lawn and the courtyard and just as I stepped up onto the porch, I heard Cheryl call out to me.

"Richie! Wait!"

She got up from her game, smoothed out the pleats of her skirt, skipped across the courtyard and hopped up onto the first porch step. Brenda Clark was watching us from the sidewalk, giggling behind her hand.

"Hi, Richie." Cheryl smiled at me and twirled a finger in her curls. "Did you read my note? You didn't send it back to me."

Oops.

"Jeez, Cheryl," I said. I stuffed my hands in the pockets of my shorts. "I forgot it in my pants pocket."

Cheryl frowned at me. "You forgot it?"

Her frown spread up her cheeks, misted her eyes and crinkled her forehead.

"You know something, Richie Holeman?" She wagged her finger in my face. "If someone writes you a nice note, even if you don't write one back, well, the least you could do is *read* the darned thing!"

She spun on the tip of one buckled shoe and ran back to Brenda, who looked at me and shook her head. They picked up their ball and jacks and ran off together up the sidewalk.

"I'll read the darned thing right now!" I hollered after them. "But I'm not writing one back!"

I stomped into the apartment and Mom was sitting at the kitchen table, the phone pressed to her ear, listening but not talking. I headed for the kitchen to make a peanut butter sandwich, but Mom hung the phone up hard and stopped me in my tracks with a glare that threatened to melt the lenses of her glasses.

Oh, no! Now what?

"Goddammit, Richie!" she hollered. "I thought I told you not to punch Raymond Laws in the belly!"

"You did, Mom. But that was like a week ago or something," I said. "I punched him in the belly today, but he wasn't being very..."

She burst up out of her chair and crossed the kitchen. "Don't you smart-mouth me, Richie!" she screamed, "You think I like getting' a call from Carol Laws and listening to that hypochondriac shout at me about you knocking the wind out of her pansy son?"

I didn't know what a hypochondriac was, but if my mom was saying it when she was mad, it probably wasn't a very nice thing to call someone. I backed up a step, bumped into the wall and held my hand up to the bruise that covered the left side of my face.

"Please, Mom...smack me on the *other* side."

Her hand wavered above my face and her eyes looked even angrier with tears boiling up in them. She lowered her hand, swatted me on my butt, and told me to go to my goddamned room. I closed the bedroom door behind me, but I could still hear her shouting at me.

"You can't take it out on the world just because Jesse moved away!"

I'm not taking it out on the world. Just the neighborhood.

In my room, I dug through the dirty clothes hamper and the closet for the jeans I had been wearing the morning Jesse had left and found them under my bed. I searched the pockets and found the folded, crumpled slip of paper that I had tucked away and forgotten. I unfolded it at the creases and read the note that Cheryl Bozart had written on a sheet of girls' stationery with hearts in the margins.

It was the kind of note that kids passed around in class; simple and to the point and usually closing with a pair of neatly drawn checkboxes so you could easily answer whatever question the note contained. Those questions were mostly of the romantic variety. I'd passed notes like Cheryl's between rows in class, but I'd never gotten one myself, not a note like this from a girl and, as brief as it was, I read it three times and still didn't know what I should do.

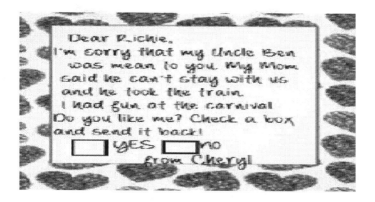

I stared at the note for a moment, folded it up and stuck it under my pillow, but then I took it out again and smoothed it out on the bed. I found a marker in the nightstand drawer, drew a big black X in the box next to yes, and folded it up again.

Later, when Tommy came in to dig his roller skates out of the closet, I handed him the note and told him to give it to Cheryl, but not in front of any of the guys.

"How come the guys can't see me give it to her?" he asked.

"Because it's private, okay?" I frowned at him. "And you better not open it up and read it, Tommy."

He blinked at me. "Jeez, Richie, I won't. I don't want you to punch me in the belly like you did to Ray."

fifteen - Ice Cream, Ice Cream

That night over supper, Mom asked me why I had punched Ray Laws in the belly. I told her what had happened in the woods that afternoon and why, afterward, I had gotten angry with Ray.

"They were gonna beat him up, Mom," I told her. "He was all scratched up and everything! I took up for him and then, even after I basically saved his life, he told me I had to pay him back the dollar that he gave me for the kitten!"

Mom frowned, but I knew she wasn't getting mad at me because her eyes didn't flash and she didn't yell. "Listen to me, Richie," she said, "I know Ray Laws is a royal pain in the ass..."

My brothers and I giggled and Gary said, "He's a pain in the ass, alright."

"He sure is," I laughed, taking advantage of an apparent temporary license to say curse words at the table, "He's a *huge* pain in the ass!"

"A *royal* one!" Tommy said, "He's Prince Pain In The Ass!"

We were all laughing, even mom, and I looked around the table at my family and I knew that, no matter how I felt most of the time, in my heart, I was glad to be a part of them. It wasn't always that way at supper; the four of us laughing together over our favorite Hamburger Helper, none of us boys worrying that we'd get a smack if our giggles caused us to spill a little milk on the table, but when it *was* that way, those were the nights when being called in for supper felt like a welcome home.

I wished it were that way every single day, but I knew it was a silly wish to make, so I settled for the moments that were real and felt thankful for my mom and my brothers and the half gallon of strawberry ice cream I knew was waiting in the freezer.

"Okay, boys, that's enough now," Mom said, "Ray is a pain in the ass, but he's still your friend, Richie, and he *did* pay you a dollar for a kitten that he didn't get."

"But, Mom, the kittens are dead," I sighed and I was careful not to add that they were dead because her boyfriend had killed them all.

Mom got up to get the ice cream from the freezer and Gary helped her with the bowls and spoons. "I know they're dead, Richie, and I'm sorry about that," she said and she looked at me from across the kitchen as she dug Gramma's old tarnished ice cream scooper into the carton. I could tell by her eyes and the way the corners of her mouth gently turned down, that she really *was* sorry. "You shouldn't have sold Ray a kitten that wasn't really yours to sell, Richie, especially if you couldn't hand him over the kitten when he gave you the money."

She brought two bowls of ice cream to the table and Gary brought the other two and when Mom set my bowl on the placemat in front of me, she tousled my hair and said, "You're gonna have to pay Ray that dollar, kiddo."

"Alright, Mom, I will."

I wasn't happy about having to give Ray a dollar for a kitten I didn't kill, but it's hard to stay unhappy with a spoonful of creamy strawberry ice cream melting in your mouth and I reminded myself that it was a good night and I found my smile again.

When our ice cream was gone, Mom looked around at our empty bowls and asked us who wanted more?

We all did, of course, and this time we all crowded at the kitchen counter and took turns scooping. I couldn't remember ever getting a *second* dish of ice cream after dinner and I suppose Tommy couldn't, either, because he said, "How come we get two bowls of ice cream?"

Mom smiled and said, "Because we're celebrating."

Celebrating?

Mom smiled and her brown eyes sparkled the way they did when she felt particularly happy or proud of herself and she said, "We're goin' down the shore, boys. We're going to Wildwood!"

My brothers and I looked at each other, and then we all looked at mom.

She was beaming.

"This Saturday," she said, "We're going this Saturday and we're gonna have a wonderful time."

She told us that we couldn't afford to go for three days like she had planned back at the beginning of the summer, but that she would use half of the money we'd found in Gramma's nightstand to take us for one day. We would take a taxi downtown, ride the bus to Wildwood and get a hotel room. We would spend the day on the beach and in the evening, we would go to the boardwalk, ride the rides, and play the games. Then we would sleep in the hotel and take the bus home on Sunday morning.

"I have to use the other half of the money to get a car. We need a car, boys. School's just around the corner."

Even the summer's first mention of the coming school year couldn't shrink the smile on my face or ruin a night of happy news and ice cream. We laughed and chattered about how much fun we were going to have down the shore and Mom said she was gonna buy a whole roll of dimes to toss at the dime pitch. That was her favorite thing to do on the boardwalk and she treasured every tacky piece of glass any of us had ever won. Tommy was excited about riding on a big bus all the way to Wildwood and Gary asked if we could get a room at the Sandpiper motel (*they got a pool that stays open all night*) and I wondered, to myself, if I was finally tall enough to ride the *Jackrabbit* roller coaster by myself.

"How 'bout you, Richie?" Mom said, "Whatcha wanna do most when we get there?"

I smiled back at her and I said, "It's a secret,"

Mom looked surprised. Usually she didn't like secrets, but she smiled around a spoonful of ice cream and said, "Ooh, a secret? I wonder what it is."

We finished our ice cream, rinsed our bowls in the sink and went in the living room to watch television. Later, when we went to bed, Mom came in and leaned over me. She pressed the palm of her hand gently, softly against the fading bruise on my left cheek and kissed me on my forehead.

"I know it's only one day, Richie," she whispered. "It's the best Momma can do, okay?"

I sat up in bed and hugged her tight. "It's great, Mom. It's really, really great."

Tommy was already asleep, but she kissed him anyway before she left the room and when she had pulled the door closed behind her, I closed my eyes and whispered in the dark.

"Thank you, Gramma."

Sixteen - Blind Love

The rest of the week, waiting to go to Wildwood might have been a torturous test of patience if I hadn't gotten myself tangled up in a romantic mess that reminded me of the melodramatic stories Gramma had loved to watch on her television soap operas. I hadn't seen Cheryl Bozart since I'd checked a box on her note and sent Tommy as a messenger to deliver it back to her. I'd been wondering how things might change, if they even changed at all, now that Cheryl and I had shared a kiss, a Ferris wheel ride and a love letter.

I spent Tuesday morning in the bog, playing army with the guys. They had wanted to play cowboys when they invited me out, but I didn't have the heart to be a cowboy without my pardner Jesse, and the gang understood and settled for being soldiers. When it came down to it, they were good friends. Besides, they didn't *really* care what game we played as long as it involved guns and shooting your buddies until they were dead.

Coming back from the war, I ditched the guys halfway down the block and ran over to where Cheryl and Brenda were playing hopscotch on the sidewalk. Brenda smiled and gave a small wave `hello', but Cheryl must have been really concentrating on her hopscotching because she didn't seem to even notice me at all.

I stood on the curb and fidgeted, shoved my hands into the pockets of my shorts and, because I felt shy and didn't know what else to do, when Cheryl stooped to pick up her marker on the fly, I clapped my hands and gave her a standing ovation of one.

Brenda giggled and Cheryl turned toward me with a sour frown on her face and the sunlight glaring in the lenses of her pretty glasses. "Richie," she said, "Why in the world are you clapping?"

Hmmmmmm.

I didn't know much about girls and I knew even less about romance, but Cheryl didn't seem to be acting like a girl who had just received a true confession of love in a box marked "yes."

I shrugged and blushed. "Sheesh, I dunno, Cheryl. I just think you hopscotch good, that's all."

I knew a sassy tilt of the head when I saw one and I knew what it meant when any woman of any age put one hand on her hip and pointed at you with the other one. I was in trouble.

"Richie, you haven't ever watched me hopscotch before in your entire life so don't start *now*!"

That wasn't entirely true. Of course, I avoided hopscotch, like all of the guys in our gang did, not because it didn't look like a fun game, but because there were two things you just didn't do on our block, if you were a boy: you didn't hopscotch and you didn't jump rope.

Cheryl was right that I had never watched her play hopscotch; at least, not ever in a way she or the gang might have noticed, but she didn't know that I had stolen plenty enough glances at her, skipping and hopping along the sidewalk in her pleated skirts and buckled shoes.

Well, I wasn't going to tell her *that* and I was getting more and more fidgety the longer she frowned at me and I stared down at the boxes and numbers she'd drawn on the sidewalk in purple chalk.

"That's a nice hopscotch court."

Cheryl sighed and now she had *both* hands on her hips and she said, "Richie Holeman. Why don't you go on and leave me alone? I don't even like you as much as I thought I liked you."

What?

I left the girls on the sidewalk with their hopscotch game and their mysterious moods and sulked off to find Tommy. Maybe he knew something about why Cheryl was acting so mad with me, since he was the one who had delivered the note.

I found Tommy in the alley, laying on top of a garbage dumpster, flat on his belly, poking down into the trash with the casual end of an old mop. He was peering into the dumpster, trying to fish out some discarded treasure without having to climb down into this particularly smelly pile of trash, and he didn't notice me until I climbed up onto the dumpster and sat beside him.

He looked up from his treasure hunting expedition and smiled at me. "Hey, Richie! I think I see something good, but it's extra stinky in there."

I could have leaned over the open end of the dumpster and looked for myself, but regular garbage smells bad enough; no way was I gonna get my nose any closer to this extra stinky batch.

"Well," I said, "What is it, then?"

Tommy blinked at me. "Sheesh, Richie, I just told you. It's something good...I think."

I drew my legs up against my chest, wrapped my arms around my knees and stared at my feet. My sneakers were tattered and torn, but we would be going shopping for new school clothes pretty soon and I had a few more weeks of barefooting if I wanted it.

"Hey, Tommy...remember when you delivered that note to Cheryl?"

He stopped poking the garbage with the mop, sat up and blinked at me again. "Well...I sorta, kinda remember it."

I shook my head. "You sort of remember?"

Tommy frowned. "Well, don't get mad at me, Richie," he said slowly, "But I didn't give Cheryl the note. I gave it to Brenda Clark."

I smacked my palm against my forehead. "Sheeshomighty, Tommy! Why'd you do that? I told you the note was private, didn't I?"

Tommy frowned again and shrugged his small shoulders. "Gosh, Richie," he said, "I went all around the block lookin' for Cheryl and when I went to knock on her door, I saw Brenda on the sidewalk and she didn't know where Cheryl was either."

He took a deep breath.

"Well, I told Brenda I had to find Cheryl on account of I had an important note from you and she told me just give it to *her* and *she'd* deliver it."

I hopped down from the dumpster and brushed off the seat of my pants. Now, I had to talk to Brenda Clark and ask her if *she* knew why Cheryl was mad at me and I wondered, if she *did* know, would she even tell me?

Tommy had gone back to exploring the dumpster, but he hollered after me as I went around the corner of the apartment building.

"Sorry, Richie!"

I wasted most of the early evening peeking around trees and light poles and watching out the corner of my eye for a chance to talk to Brenda Clark alone, but trying to find her out on the block without Cheryl right beside her was almost impossible. They were closer than sisters, almost like Siamese twins the way they seemed connected and inseparable. I had a friend like that, but he'd gone away and if Jesse were here right now, where he belonged, instead of goshdanged Ohio, he would help me figure out my girl troubles.

I didn't have a chance to talk to Brenda that night or all the next day, but on Tuesday, while the whole Bozart family was out shopping for school clothes, I found Brenda sitting alone on her stoop, playing with an Etch-A-Sketch. She saw me coming up the sidewalk and she showed me her pretty smile and the picture of a house and tree she made on the Etch-A-Sketch.

"Hi, Richie!"

I sat down beside her on the stoop and she shook the Etch-A-Sketch blank and offered it to me. "You wanna draw something, Richie? I'm bored of it."

I shook my head. "No, Brenda," I said quietly, in case any of the neighbors had their apartment windows open, "Can I ask you about something?"

She smoothed out her skirt with her hands.

"Did Cheryl say anything to you when you gave her the note I sent? After she looked at it?"

Brenda blushed and flipped her hair back from her face in a way that made her seem nervous. "Well, Richie..."

Uh-oh.

Cheryl must have said *something* to Brenda about me. I took a deep breath, forced myself not to fidget and said, "Go on, Brenda. You can tell me what she said."

"She didn't say *anything*," Brenda nearly whispered, "I didn't give her the note, Richie."

Jeez.

I now knew one more thing about romance than I did a half-hour before; if you want to send a love note to a girl, especially one with your feelings checked off in bold black magic marker, you're better off delivering it yourself.

I looked at Brenda. "Why not? Why didn't you give it to her?"

Brenda sighed. "Gosh, Richie, don't you even notice *anything*?" she almost hollered. Then she got quiet again and said, "Can't you tell that *I* like you, *too*."

She got up from the stoop and walked a nervous circle around a single square of sidewalk. I felt fluttery in my tummy, the way I did when I got fresh off a carnival ride, the palms of my hands were sweaty and I wished I had a drink of water.

"Sheesh, Brenda," I said, "That's kind of a mean trick to play, ain't it?"

Brenda had tears in her eyes and she turned to go upstairs to her apartment, but she stopped on the first step and looked back. "I know it's a mean trick, Richie, but I wanted to tell you that I like you before Cheryl saw the note."

I was mad at Brenda Clark, but mostly, I was sad. I thought she was Cheryl's best friend, but I knew a thing or two about having a *real* best friend and you just didn't pull a sneaky trick like the one she had pulled on Cheryl.

Brenda sighed. "Oh, Richie, I'm the one who knew what you meant about the moon; not Cheryl."

She *had* understood what I meant when I said I wanted to be the first boy on the moon, and I'd liked her pretty poem about the stars, but I sure didn't like the way I felt just then, standing on that porch wishing I hadn't checked either box on Cheryl's note or even ever read it at all. A boy on the moon would never get a love note, let alone have to send one back.

"You shouldn't have kept that note, Brenda," I said, "That was a mean thing to do."

Brenda balled up her fists at her sides and huffed a long puff of air up from her lips that lifted her bangs away from her forehead. "Dang it, Richie!" she said, "Don't you know love is blind?"

Well, I *had* heard that love is blind, but I didn't know it was deaf and dumb, too.

Brenda twirled a finger through her long brown hair and said, "You gotta at least think about it, Richie; do you wanna go around with Cheryl or do you wanna go around with me?"

"I don't wanna go around with *anybody*," I said, "This love stuff is *way* too complicated for me."

I turned down the sidewalk to go back home and I heard Brenda rushing up the stairs, crying all the way to her apartment door.

Seventeen - All Aboard!

That Friday night, we packed our swimming trunks, toothbrushes and a change of clothes for each of us into one suitcase and Mom sent us to bed early. The taxicab would be picking us up at 4 o'clock in the morning, but we were too excited to sleep. Tommy and I lay awake in our beds for hours, whispering about the beach and the rides and the saltwater taffy, and when my little brother finally dozed off; I stayed awake a little longer, thinking about riding the *Jackrabbit* roller coaster by myself.

Mom woke us up in the middle of the night, she told us to hurry up and get dressed and to eat a bowl of cereal because the taxi would be here soon. Gary took a long time in the bathroom, Tommy and I took a long time getting dressed, and we hadn't even finished our breakfast when a car horn honked twice outside.

"That's the taxi," Mom said. "Gary, get the suitcase. C'mon, boys, we gotta hustle."

She picked up the Styrofoam cooler she had packed our lunch in, herded us out of the apartment, locked the door behind us and Tommy jumped off the porch, singing, "Do the hustle! Bomp boomp bomp buh bomp!"

We rushed down the sidewalk and the taxi cab driver got out of the big yellow car, opened the trunk and helped Gary stow the suitcase. Mom got in the front seat, Tommy climbed in the back, and Gary pushed me from behind, not a mean shove, just a hurrying nudge.

"Get in, Richie!" he said.

I hesitated on the curb, remembering something I had left behind, hidden among the socks and underwear in a top dresser drawer. The cabby got in the taxi and flipped the meter on and my mom looked out at me. "Richie, c'mon," she said and the driver said, "Meter's runnin', lady."

"I forgot something!" I said.

"Maronna mia!" Mom hissed through her teeth, "What the hell did you forget?"

It's a secret.

"I gotta go pee!' I blurted out. "Please, Mom. I'll hurry."

Mom handed me her key-ring (*"Hurry the hell up, Richie!"*) and I ran back up the sidewalk, rushed into the apartment, and when I came back out she hollered, "Don't forget to lock the door!"

On the taxicab ride downtown, the streets were quiet and still, but my brothers and I were noisy, maybe even rowdy by pre-dawn standards. The driver kept glancing in the rearview mirror and frowning while we chattered excitedly about the boardwalk.

The cab pulled up along the curb out in front of the big Greyhound station and we all got out. The grumpy driver got out, too, and helped Mom get our suitcase and ice chest from the trunk. He set the ice chest down on the sidewalk and Mom handed him the money for the fare. I don't think she gave him a tip, because he frowned at the bills in the palm of his hand the way he had frowned at us in the mirror.

Tommy looked up at the taxi driver and said, "We're takin' the bus down the shore. Sorry you can't take us all the way to Wildwood in your taxi, Mister."

The driver shook his head and said, "Believe me, kid, that's *quite* alright by me,"

I liked the bus station. It had a revolving door that spun you around and let you out in a big room with shiny marble walls and fancy wooden stairs. There were four clocks on the wall that showed the time all the way across the whole country, but what I loved the most about the big station was how busy and noisy it was, even at 4:40 in the morning.

People were lined up at the ticket counter and at the boarding doors or sitting in hard plastic chairs and they were all talking at once, but everyone quieted down whenever a loud voice crackled over the PA system, announcing a departure or arrival. Some of the chairs had small televisions mounted on the arm so you could watch a show while you waited for your bus.

There were pinball machines, a newspaper stand and a coffee shop that was open all night and there was a row of old-fashioned stained wood telephone booths against a wall. I decided to check the empty booths for forgotten dimes and went down the row, poking a finger into each coin return slot, coming up empty every time.

In one of the booths, a big round man with an angry red face was yelling into the telephone, cursing a blue streak at somebody named Martha. I had heard curse words all my life and even said a few, but I had never heard some of the words and phrases that man was shouting at Martha. He was a creative curser and I sat on a bench near the phone booths and eavesdropped, giggling softly when he came up with an especially dirty word that made the men back in the neighborhood seem like choirboys.

He was quiet for a moment and Martha must have said something that *really* made the man mad because he shouted "Jesus fucking jumping jacks" and slammed the receiver down in its cradle so hard that it bounced off and swung at the end of its cord as he squeezed his way out of the phone booth in a rush. He grumbled his way toward the coffee shop and I thought of following him to see if he cursed at the waitress, too, but I heard tinkling sounds and saw four or five dimes rolling from the telephone booth onto the black and white tiled floor.

I hurried into the booth and folded the door closed behind me. There were more dimes on the floor, nickels and even some quarters, too. He had broken the payphone. Maybe he'd done it slamming the receiver down so hard or maybe he'd broken it with his foul shouting and I called it a lucky break for me. I squirmed a finger into the coin return and it would barely flip open.

It was full of coins!

I stretched my t-shirt underneath the phone and dug out the coins until they stopped tinkling into the return slot. I snuck from the booth and across the station lobby, cradling the bulging stash of coins against my belly, and found my mother resting in a chair with her head leaned back and her eyes closed.

"Mom," I whispered, "Mom wake up, wake up!"

Her head bobbed forward and her eyes opened up behind her glasses. She sounded sleepy, but not angry or annoyed with me.

"What, Richie? What is it?"

I stretched my shirt out and whispered. "Look, Mom...we're *rich*."

She saw all the coins I had bundled up in my shirt and she pulled me close to her and whispered,

"Hurry, Richie, dump 'em in Momma's pocketbook." She held her purse open wide on her lap and I funneled my telephone booth treasure in among the balled up tissues, loose sticks of gum and tubes of lipstick.

"Where did you get this, honey?" she asked me quietly.

"Some man broke the phone. Can't I keep a little bit of it, Mom?"

She grinned at me, kissed me hard on my cheek and said, "Why don't we save it for the dime pitch? How's that sound, Richie?"

I thought that sounded just fine and I sat down next to my mom and rested my head on her shoulder until the crackly announcer called the 5:15 southbound with stops in Trenton, Atlantic City and *Wildwood*!

Eighteen - Down the Shore

We spent the early, hot part of the day on the beach, playing on the shore and in the surf, while Mom sat on a blanket, reading a romance book, occasionally looking up from the steamy pages to holler at us (*Don't go out too far! Watch out for the undertow! Come and let me rub some more Coppertone on your backs!*) and all day long, I could hear the sounds of the carnival up on the boardwalk.

Gary met a girl with long red hair and a yellow bathing suit and they splashed together in the shallow water, but I guess my big brother was too romantic for her because when he pulled her hair and pinched her arm, she ran off up the beach and plopped down on a blanket with her folks.

Tommy and I caught tiny crabs in the tide and we built a castle in the sand, far back from the threatening waves, but Gary came along and trampled it down.

We sat on a blanket and ate lunch, cold fried chicken and macaroni salad and deviled eggs (*not as good as Gramma's, but still delicious*) and washed it all down with bottles of pop. Mom made us wait an hour before she let us go back in the water, but when we did, she came in, too, splashing and chasing us through the shallow surf.

She walked with us along the smooth, wet shore and we collected seashells and when we gathered up our things and left the beach in the late afternoon, all of us were sunburned, sandy and salty.

We went back to our room at the Sandpiper motel and everyone showered and napped until Mom woke us up in the early part of the evening and we walked across the road to the boardwalk.

Mom loved carnivals as much as we did and she bought the biggest book of tickets and we used every single one and then she bought some more. She was afraid of the snapping, crackling electricity that powered the bumper cars, but she climbed in one with Tommy and chased Gary and I around the track, laughing loud and long whenever our cars collided.

We threw so many dimes at the dime pitch booth that people must have thought we were rich and we won Mom a set of glasses that almost matched and a big blue plate with a mermaid on it. Gary bragged about his pitching arm at the milk-jug toss, but he didn't knock them all down and he scowled when I did and won a stuffed tiger.

On the Sky Wheel, Tommy and Gary rode together and I went with Mom in a blue gondola. She squeezed my hand at the top and I thought of the night I rode the Ferris wheel with Cheryl Bozart at the rinky-dink dog and pony show.

Mom's favorite ride was the tilt-a-whirl and we rode it three times in a row, spinning around and around until we were dizzy, and Mom flirted a little bit with the man who ran the ride. She said he looked just like James Brolin and Tommy said, "But, Mom, I thought we weren't supposed to talk to carnies." Mom laughed at that and said that the men who worked on the boardwalk weren't the same as the carnies who traveled around from town to town.

We stayed on the boardwalk all evening and late that night, when some of the food carts and games started shutting down, Mom said she was tired and that it had been a very long day and we had to go back to the motel.

"You boys can swim in the pool for a little while, but we've got to catch the bus back home early in the morning."

I looked across the boardwalk at the giant skeleton of the *Jackrabbit* roller coaster and I could hear the riders screaming as the cars clicked and whooshed along the track. I looked up at my mom, hoping her happiness hadn't all been spent, and I asked her if I could ride just one more ride.

"It's so late, Richie," she said. "Didn't we ride them all?"

"Not all of 'em, Mom. I think this year I'm tall enough to ride the *Jackrabbit*. By myself."

Mom sighed. Every time we had come to Wildwood over the years, I had measured myself against the sign at the coaster's gate (*you must be this tall to ride this ride*) and been too short to ride, but I'd grown a lot in the two years since we'd last been to the boardwalk.

"Please, Mom," I pleaded. "Can we just go see if I'm big enough now?"

Mom gave in, we walked across the wooden planks, and my family sat on a bench while I walked up to the gate of the *Jackrabbit* and stood against the sign. I asked the man who took the tickets if I was tall enough to ride and he said, "Yeah, kid, you can ride the coaster."

"All by myself? I don't gotta bring my mom?"

He grinned at me, winked, and said, "All by yourself, kid."

I ran back to my mom and I told her I could ride and she frowned up at the tracks. "You sure you wanna ride it alone, Richie? It looks scary. Why don't you go on it with Gary?"

"Aw, c'mon, Mom... the man said I was big enough to go by myself."

Mom looked at Gary and he said, "I don't even wanna ride it." She sighed, handed me the tickets, and swatted me lightly on my butt as I turned and ran back to the roller coaster gate to get in line.

I was nervous as I shuffled along in the line and my palms were sweaty when I handed the man my tickets. I climbed into one of the coaster's cars beside a teenaged boy in a *Daffy Duck* t-shirt, pulled the lap-bar down across our thighs and a whole swarm of butterflies hatched in my tummy.

A man in a booth pulled a lever and the train rolled forward slowly and the boy next to me looked at me and smiled and said, "You scared?"

"Yes!" I shouted and the coaster picked up speed and banked, rose, and fell, clacking along the rails, rushing through the night and I imagined that the *Jackrabbit* was a train, speeding through a tunnel to the end of summer.

The train climbed a long, steep peak and I stared up at the stars and wished that the *Jackrabbit* could fly right off its track, straight into the sky and carry me away to heaven-up-above or far across the ocean, to a place where best friends and grammas never went away.

When the train neared the top of the peak, everyone raised their arms above their heads, but I squeezed mine beneath the lap-bar and stuck a hand into my pocket for the secret I had almost forgotten and left home in a dresser drawer. I pulled out the small cardboard carton that had once come with a Matchbox racer inside, but now held a small handful of cemetery dirt.

The *Jackrabbit* crested the peak and I felt my cheeks flapping as the coaster rushed down the track and I held the little box in both of my hands, slid it open and shook it in front of my face.

"I love you, Gramma!" I shouted into the Wildwood night and the dirt that I had stolen away from Gramma's grave on that miserable day in July rushed out of the box and onto the wind and straight into my eyes, and might have struck me blind if I hadn't already lost my sight to the blurring sting of tears.

Epilogue
Everything After

One - Ohio Sucks

Summer wasn't over, not just yet, but it was fading fast into autumn and every kid on the block knew it. Already, the days were beginning to shorten and the early evening heat that had lingered over the neighborhood all summer long gave way to September cool. School would be starting up again soon and our mothers had only a few days to tame their wild summer kids with haircuts and new clothes and shoes from Buster Brown.

Mom took us downtown on the city bus and we shopped for school clothes at K-Mart, two pairs of jeans and four shirts for each of us. At the shoe store, I had a small argument with Mom, but she let me get the waffle stomper boots with the zip-up sides that I wanted instead of the sneakers that she said I should have.

"You can't run around and play in boots, Richie," she said, kneeling down to squeeze her thumb against the toe of one waffle stomper, "And they don't look very comfortable, either."

"Aw, Mom, I always wanted boots like this. I can wear my old sneakers when I play anyway."

My sneakers were worn at the soles, the laces were knotted where they had broken and there was a hole in the left one just round enough that my big toe poked out of it. I figured they were good for another three months and I could ask for a new pair for Christmas.

Mom sighed and I hugged her and walked out of Buster Brown in a pair of shiny black boots that clopped on the sidewalk and my ratty old Converse high tops smelling up the shopping bag.

I'd won my battle for the day and wasn't likely to win a second, so at the barber shop, I didn't argue when Mom told the barber how to cut my hair and when we walked out of *that* shop, I looked like a total square and so did both of my brothers.

We had lunch at a little café downtown and I ordered my favorite sandwich, a B.L.T. with no tomato.

The waitress stopped writing on her pad, stuck the end of her pen between her lips and said, "It ain't a B.L.T. if it doesn't have tomato, kiddo."

She stared down at me and when I didn't say anything, she said, "That's what the 'T' stands for: Tomato. It's a bacon, lettuce and *tomato*. Get it?"

I looked at her, surprised. I'd never had any trouble getting a B.L.T. without tomato at any of the diners in our township, but this café was in Newark and maybe they did things differently in a city café or maybe this waitress just had her own way of ordering sandwiches.

"Well, what kind of sandwich only has bacon and lettuce and lots of mayonnaise?" I asked her.

"That's a bacon sammich."

That made sense. "Okay, I'll have that," I told her, "And a coke, please."

She wrote on her order pad again and when she had all of our orders, she turned around fast to go give it to the fry cook, but I stopped her.

"Ma'am? Can you ask that cook to cut the crusts off my bread, please?"

She sighed and Tommy said, "Mine, too, please."

I heard the cook grumbling behind his grill and when the waitress brought our food, the crust was still on my sandwich and it had tomatoes on it.

Mom reached across the table, pulled the red slices out of my sandwich, and put them on hers and when I asked her to cut off the crust she said, "Just eat it, dammit."

When we got home, Tommy ran to check the mail and he brought back two envelopes. One was a long envelope from the juvenile court and the other was a letter from Jesse. Mom said we would talk about the court notice later, after she had a chance to read it, and I took Jesse's letter to my room.

I tore open the envelope and pulled out a single sheet of notebook paper, unfolded it and smiled. Jesse had drawn a cowboy at the top of the page.

Sept 2, 1976

Dear Richie,

Well we got here and we moved into my aunt's It's a lot like the old neighborhood except there's no train tracks or bog I don't have any friends except my cousin Teresa. Mom says I'll get used to it if I give it a chance.

Did anyone move into my apartment? I hope some kids do I left a secret in my bedroom closet Make friends with them and you can find out what it is School starts next week I'm gonna be THE NEW KID!

Well, write back to me soon

Your BEST pardner,

Jesse Gwinn

p.s. Ohio SUCKS!

I read it twice and wrote a long letter back to Jesse that would catch him up on everything that had happened in the neighborhood since he moved away. I told him no one had moved into his old apartment yet and I asked him what the secret was, even though I knew he wouldn't tell me.

At supper, Mom said she would give me an envelope and a stamp so I could mail the letter the next day. I'd never mailed a letter out of town before or even wrote one to anyone besides Santa Claus and I thought if there could be even one good thing about Jesse moving to Ohio, it was that we could write letters back and forth.

After we finished eating our meat loaf and mashed potatoes, Mom told me about the letter from the juvenile court. The Bicycle Witch had agreed not to press charges as long as her new bike was paid for and no one from the Railroad company had reported any damage to any of its trains so I didn't have to go to juvenile hall, or even to court to see the Judge.

Mom was angry that she and Miss Brenda would have to pay for a brand new bicycle when Jesse and I were innocent, but she said it was still better than going to court and she would scrape up her half of the money somehow.

"But you're gonna have to help, Richie," she said, "Tomorrow morning I want you to go to that old lady's house and ask her if you can work off part of the bicycle doing chores."

Gulp!

"Mom! You're gonna make me go to a witch's house?"

Mom frowned and said, "You know she isn't a witch, Richie. She's just an old lady. You ride your bike over there tomorrow first thing."

Two - The Witch's Garden

I'm sure I don't have to tell you how hard it is to get a good night's sleep dreaming about white-haired witches on flying bicycles and when I woke up early the next morning, like mom said I had to, I was just as tired as I was when I went to bed. The sun was barely up and no one else in the apartment, maybe even on the whole block, was awake, so I moved quietly from the bedroom to the bathroom and then the kitchen. I was halfway through a bowl of Lucky Charms when I remembered that my sneakers were still in the shopping bag in Mom's room.

There was no way I could face a witch today if I had to face my angry mother first so I didn't risk waking her up by sneaking into her room for my high tops. I couldn't come home later in the afternoon with my brand new school boots all scuffed up from bike riding and chores, either, so I crept out the door and pedaled barefoot over the big Grand Avenue Bridge and into the neighborhood where the Bicycle Witch lived.

The nearer I got to her house, the slower I pumped the pedals and by the time I rounded the corner onto her street, the wheels of my bike were hardly turning at all and the Topps baseball card I'd attached to the frame with a clothespin sputtered between the spokes like a motor in a bad used car.

I put my feet on the ground, stopped my bike in front of The Witch's house and stared at the crooked white fence, the shaggy front yard and the empty flowerpots on the wide, dusty porch. The gate hung open and the sidewalk up to the front door seemed very long, but I leaned my bike against the fence and found myself standing at the front door sooner than I would have liked.

I took a deep breath and was about to ring the bell when I remembered something Jesse had said one Halloween when our moms had let us cross the river to trick-or-treat in this neighborhood.

We had been standing on the sidewalk in front of this very house, both dressed as cowboys and dragging around old pillowcases stuffed fat with candy, daring each other to trick-or-treat The Bicycle Witch.

"No way, Richie," he'd whispered, "Don't you know you never, *ever* ring a witch's doorbell?"

I yanked my finger back from the little white button and wished Jesse were here with me at the witch's house *now*. He wrote in his letter to me that Ohio sucks, but I bet he was glad to be there when the notice from the juvenile court showed up in the mailbox.

I paced and fidgeted on the porch, sat down on the steps with my head in my hands, and paced and fidgeted a little more before I decided to use the big brass knocker hanging from the door. I tugged on the screen door and it swung open with a loud, creepy squeak and I let out a long startled gasp and just as I reached up to bang the knocker, the door swung open and The Bicycle Witch stood looking down at me with a teacup in one hand and the Star-Ledger in the other. A cat circled around her house shoes, rubbing against her legs and swishing its tail. At least it wasn't a *black* cat, just an old grey tom.

The Witch wished me a good morning and I blurted out, "You knew I was out here!"

She smiled and, though I had never actually seen one to say for sure, her smile didn't look like a witch's grin at all.

"Of course I knew you were out here," she said, "You've been standing and stomping out here for ten whole minutes and that old screen door makes a bigger racket than any watchdog ever could." She took a breath and so did I. "Now that we both know you're here, why don't you tell me why a barefoot boy is at my door so early in the morning?"

I was too shy to tell her. She hadn't been mean, acted like a witch, or even winked at me yet, but she might not be so nice once she found out that I was one of the boys being blamed for stealing her Schwinn. I stayed quiet as long as I could, but when she drew the door open a little wider and bent toward me, I told her my mother had sent me to ask if I could pay for her new bike by doing some chores.

"But you're not the boy who took my bike," she said.

"I'm not?"

She laughed and waved the newspaper at me and said, "Honey, don't you know whether or not you stole a bicycle?"

I was embarrassed and I could tell by the sudden warmth in my cheeks that I was blushing. "Oh, sure, *I* know I didn't steal your bike," I said, "I just didn't know you knew I didn't steal it."

She told me to come inside the house so an old lady could sit down and when I hesitated, she said, "Oh, come on, boy....you don't think I'm going to bake you into a pie, do you?"

I *hadn't* thought that until she mentioned it, but I took a brave step across the threshold and followed her into a nice room with old furniture and lots of doilies and books on the tables. There were old black and white photographs framed on the wall, most of them of a little boy with blonde curly hair, and in one of them, he wore a baseball cap and held a bat across his shoulder.

The Bicycle Witch sat on a big soft chair, the cat curled up in her lap and purred and I sat on a fancy sofa and fidgeted. She asked me if I wanted milk or juice and I told her I didn't, but when she added a cookie to her offer, I said I did want one and asked for a glass of milk, too.

I got *three* cookies, homemade oatmeal raisin, and dunked them in the milk to soften them up before each bite while The Witch told me that she would call the police station and tell them that I wasn't the bicycle thief. I reminded her to tell them that Jesse wasn't a bicycle thief, either, and she said, "Of course. We'll clear Jesse's name, too...pardner."

Jeezly crow!

I had almost convinced myself that she wasn't any kind of witch at all, but she'd known I was at her door before I knocked, she'd known I wasn't the bicycle thief and now she called me 'pardner.' Only Jesse ever called me that.

I must have been wearing my suspicion all over my face because she said, "What's the matter now, child? You look like you've seen a ghost!"

No. Just a witch.

I took a deep breath, pretended to be brave and chose my words oh so carefully. "Are you a magic lady?"

She laughed again and rocked in the chair, disturbing the sleeping cat. "Oh, no, I'm afraid not," she told me, "There's more arthritis and rheumatism in these old bones than magic. When you go back to your neighborhood, you can tell all your friends that The Bicycle Witch isn't a witch after all, just an old lady who bakes hard cookies."

I leaned back on the sofa and drank the last of my milk. "But how do you know all that stuff," I said, "You know I didn't steal your bike."

She nodded and smiled. "I know who stole it because I saw them do it; that boy with the long hair like a girl and some other, new boy. I was watching right out my kitchen window when they took it out of my yard"

Hmmmmmm.

I *wanted* to be satisfied, but I wasn't. "How'd you know that Jesse called me 'pardner' then?"

Let's see her try to wriggle her way out of this one.

"Well, you *are* a suspicious little boy, aren't you?" she said with a sighing smile, "You kids rode those bikes of yours all over town, dressed up like little cowboys, whooping and hollering and making the worst kind of a racket shooting off cap guns. How many times do you think I must have heard him shouting out at the top of his lungs? Pardner this and pardner that!"

I couldn't deny that probably half the township had heard Jesse call me by my cowboy nickname at least once over the years, so I believed her, *still* there was that night at the baseball park when she'd winked at me and landed a foul ball at my feet and a free coke in my hand.

"What about that foul ball?" I said, "How'd you make that baseball foul off right straight to me?"

She smiled, but her eyes were serious and she said, "Oh, I just felt like your luck was due to change," she said, "Anyway, having a little idea that a baseball *might* come along is an entirely different thing than *making* one come along, don't you think?"

I was confused. She said she wasn't a witch, or even a magic lady at all, but that was still a kind of magic, wasn't it, knowing something was going to happen before it happened?

"Didn't you have other balls come over the backstop that you could have chased down if those bigger boys hadn't run you off them? Maybe the spooky old Bicycle Witch standing so near and winking at you was just enough to make those boys hesitate about bullying you, and there wasn't anything magic to it at all."

She told me that sometimes, only every once in a long while, she would get a little idea about things. Sometimes she knew when her favorite Frank Sinatra song was playing on the radio, even when she wasn't *listening* to the radio, and when she turned it on to check, sure enough, Ol' Blue Eyes would be crooning 'Luck Be a Lady.' Sometimes she might get "just the tiniest tickle of a notion" and know that she would have a lucky night at the bingo hall or that it was going to rain in the afternoon even though the sky was clear in the morning. Sometimes, she told me, she might even know when a good boy was going to catch a lucky break.

I decided that she probably wasn't a witch, but she would have been a great carnival fortune-teller. She didn't even need a crystal ball. I wasn't afraid of her anymore and, whether I could believe it or not, I actually *liked* her. She was around the age that Gramma had been and she had a nice crinkly smile and her cookies weren't as hard as some others I'd had.

I couldn't call her The Bicycle Witch anymore so I asked her what her name was. "My name is Olga Jean Pataki," she said, reaching her wrinkled, spotted hand across the coffee table to shake my smooth, deformed one, "Pleased to meet you."

"Do you already know my name?"

Her eyes twinkled and she said, "Of course I know your name, Richie, and now that we've agreed that I'm not a witch and you're not the boy who stole my bicycle, I suppose you can go on home and not waste a sunny day pulling weeds in a witch's garden. Unless you'd like to earn a little pocket money?"

I thought that over and said, "Well, I *do* need a dollar to pay Ray Laws for the dead kitten."

Olga Jean Pataki's eyes widened and her mouth crinkled up at the corners the way Gramma's used to do.

"Why in the world would you pay a dollar for a dead kitten?"

That made me laugh and I said, "No, no, no! Ray Laws paid *me* a dollar for a kitten, but it wasn't dead when he bought it, only when it came time to give it to him."

"I see," she told me, "Well, then, isn't that just a shame?"

She nudged the cat out of her lap and pushed herself out of the chair. "Come along, Richie," she said, "Let's go out in the backyard and if you work hard and don't trample my flowers, we'll see if you can earn a little more than just one dead cat dollar."

She led me through the house and out a back door that didn't squeak and I couldn't believe my eyes. The backyard was everything the front yard wasn't. The grass was neatly mowed and there were flower gardens on both sides of the lawn and I'd imagined tall, wild weeds like the ones growing up through the sidewalk, but all I saw in the rich brown soil were small sprouts that I could tug out easily. There was a white bench; the kind that swings, under a big tree and there was even a birdbath fountain.

Olga stooped in the garden, among the flowers, and I got down on my knees beside her and she showed me how to pull the weeds and put them in an old potato sack. When she saw that I could yank out the weeds without trampling her flowers, Miss Olga left me in the dirt and sat on the swinging bench in the shade of the biggest tree in her neighborhood.

Miss Olga was a lot different here in her backyard than I had thought she was when I only knew her from seeing her riding her bike around the township. She did burst into abrupt, kooky laughter every now and then or stop what she was saying and look off into the sky, but mostly she was nice and funny and not nearly as crazy as everyone made her out to be.

I worked through the morning and right up until lunchtime and I might have cleared all the weeds out of the flower beds sooner than that, but me and Miss Olga talked a lot and sometimes when I was listening to her especially close, I'd stop tugging weeds at all until I remembered what I was supposed to be doing.

Miss Olga had a real sundial in her garden and when its shadow silently struck 11, she got up from the bench and told me to come inside and eat some lunch. My knees were stiff when I followed her out of the garden and dark soil caked my bare feet, but I washed them off at the hose before we went inside to have lunch in the cool of her little kitchen.

She sent me to wash my hands with soap and when I came back, there was a tall glass of milk on the table and Miss Olga was standing in front of her open pantry with one finger in her mouth.

She laughed suddenly, the way she did sometimes when she rode her bicycle around town, and I got a little nervous, but then she smiled and said, "I bet you like peanut butter. I never met a little boy who didn't like a peanut butter and jelly sandwich for lunch."

"Do you know how to make 'em with peanut butter on both breads and the jelly in the middle?"

She brought a jar of peanut butter and a loaf of bread out of the pantry and a jar of peach jam out of the refrigerator. "I've never made one that way, no," she told me, "But I'm not too old to learn it."

She brought me a plate with a pretty decent Jesse Special and two of her hard cookies and when she sat down across from me with her own sandwich, I saw that she'd cut the crust off.

"Could I have mine without crust, too?" I said, "Please."

Miss Olga laughed and said, "Of course you can! I didn't know you liked them like that, too."

She must not have got a tickle.

After lunch, she said I should go on home, but not until she paid me. She reached into her purse and brought out a single bill. When she put it in my hand, I thanked her and folded it in my palm. I didn't look at it and Miss Olga said, "Aren't you even curious if you made a fair wage?"

"A little bit," I admitted, "But I don't want to look right in front of you. That might be rude. Anyway, I know it's at least one dollar and that's what I needed."

Olga Jean smiled at me. "Well, sure, that's all you *need*, but if you look at it outside my door and it only is one dollar, would you want to come back and pull weeds in my garden ever again?"

I gave it a thought and said, "Well, I might...if you put a little more peanut butter on the sandwiches next time."

She tossed her head back and laughed and this time, she didn't sound off her rocker. "Well, let's see if we can think of another job for you to do and you can come back in the morning, if you want to."

"And I'll get paid again? Or just the extra peanut butter?"

She laughed again and her eyes sparkled. She sat in her big soft chair and the cat slunk out from behind the sofa and hopped up on her lap. "Now, let me see," she said, "What would be a good job for tomorrow?"

"I know!" I told her, "We can fix that crooked fence out front. We can cut the grass, too."

She shook her head and said, "No...we wouldn't want to do anything out there in the front."

"Why not?" I asked, "I can swing a hammer real good!"

"Oh, I bet you can, Richie," she said, "But I like to keep the front yard just the way it is."

It didn't make sense; at least, I didn't think it did. Why would Olga Jean Pataki let her front yard get so crooked and tangled, but keep her back yard so perfect and pretty?

"But why do you want to leave it like that?" I said, "I know it's not nice to say, but your front yard looks worse than Blackberry Bog in spring."

She just crinkled up her smile and her eyes and said, "When you get a reputation that suits you, young man, you can't go wrong by keepin' up appearances."

I had no idea what she meant and I told her so, but she said I was plenty smart enough to figure it out if I thought on it a bit, then she shooed me home and told me to come tomorrow at eight o'clock. I said I would and I left her sitting in her chair with her lazy cat, but she called after me and stopped me with my hand on the doorknob.

"You don't come barefooted tomorrow," she told me, "You be extra sure to wear shoes. Don't forget."

I nodded at her and stepped out on the porch and when the door closed behind me, I snuck the corner of the bill she gave me out of my pocket for a peek.

Sheeshomighty!

Going home, I stopped in Ratto's market for a chocolate bar and got nineteen dollars and eighty cents back in change.

Three - The Fistfight

All the way home, I thought about what Miss Olga had told me, but I couldn't figure out what she meant about keepin' up appearances because her reputation suits her. Of course, I had to tell Mom all about The Bicycle Witch; how she wasn't *really* a witch and mostly not even scary.

I saved the best news for last and when Mom found out that Olga Jean was going to call the police this afternoon and tell them me and Jesse were innocent, she smiled big and wide. When I told her about the twenty dollars I had earned working in the garden, her big, wide smile almost split her face in half. I thought she might take the money from me and put it away somewhere, but she let me keep it if I promised not to spend it all at once on candy and toys.

I promised and got my torn out sneakers from Mom's room so I wouldn't forget them in the morning. I put them on and went outside to find the gang, but in the courtyard, out on the sidewalk and all the way down the block, the street was weirdly quiet.

This late in the summer, with only a week until the first day of school, the whole gang was usually scattered up and down the block or huddled together on the lawn playing a game.

I figured everybody must have gone down to the bog or over to the train tracks while I was off pulling weeds and I ran up the sidewalk to find them all.

Wait until I tell 'em that I'm takin' us all around the corner to the strip mall for ice cream cones!

I pounded pavement up the block and there wasn't a kid in sight. The neighborhood, at least our street, was as still and empty as a ghost town. I caught a stitch in my side from running too hard and I stopped at the end of the block and leaned over with my fingers dangling over my toes, breathing hard and sweating on the sidewalk. I opened my eyes and had an upside down look at the block and I saw Ross Hodges on his bike, leaning over the handlebars, standing on the pedals and pumping furiously, hauling hell-bent up the block and shouting my name.

"Rich-eeeee! Rich-eee-eeee!"

I stood up straight on the corner and waved my arms over my head, even though it hurt my side to stretch like that, and Ross pointed his front wheel at me and came on fast, power skidding on the blacktop right in front of me.

"Richie! C'mon! Come quick!"

We were both huffing and puffing, me from running, Ross from trying to break the land speed record on a bicycle.

"Where? Why? What *happened*?"

Ross settled on the seat of his bike and rested his right foot on the pedal, ready to roll. "Nothin' *yet*," he hollered right in my face, "But there's gonna be a fight!"

I felt my eyes widen in excited surprise. "A fight? Who's gonna fight?"

"Your brother Gary," Ross huffed, "And that new kid with the freckles!"

"Let's go!" I shouted and I climbed up on the front wheel of Ross' Huffy and planted my butt on the handlebars. I put my feet on the fender and held on tight and Ross gave it all he had and got us zooming through the apartment complex.

"Where they fightin' at?" I hollered over my shoulder.

Ross was riding so hard he could hardly answer. "Puh...play...ground!"

There was a run-down playground, just a sandbox and a rattrap pair of swings and a slide, that none of our gang ever used because stray cats pooped in the sandbox and the landlord's apartment was right across the street. Mr. Dollasso was the grouchiest man in the whole neighborhood and he kept a grumpy eye on the playground to make sure no kids had any fun. Sometimes the little kids played there early in the morning and the high school kids loitered around late on Friday nights, smoking cigarettes and even drinking beer. I don't know how Mr. Dollasso didn't hear those teenagers with their loud music late at night when he could hear an eight year old fart from his doorstep.

Ross took the shortcut, skidded into the playground and I hopped down from the handlebars as he let his bike drop to the ground and we hustled our way through a gathering crowd of fifteen or twenty kids. Most of the kids from the nearest blocks were there: all of our gang, older kids and even some of the littlest ones. All of the kids were gathered in a loose circle around the sandbox, some chanting "fight, fight, fight" and choosing sides, and Gary and Kenny, the crew-cut bully, were squared off in the middle of it all, taunting each other.

They both had their fists up in front of their faces and they were doing the schoolyard waltz around the sandbox, taunting each other. The spectators were thirsty for blood, the chanting grew louder, and one of the teenagers hollered, "Hurry up and fight already before Ol' Man Dollasso gets out here!"

Gary squinted his eyes into narrow slits like an alley cat and growled, "Well, you gonna fight or not?"

Bobby Bozart shouted, "He's scared of you, Gary!"

Kenny's face blushed so red you could hardly see his freckles and he puffed out his chest and squinted *his* eyes down even narrower than my brother's were. "I ain't scared of him!" he shouted, looking around at all the faces, "I ain't scared of *any* of you."

A few of the older kids cheered him on, but everyone else jeered and his face blushed brighter and he looked at me for just a second or two and I saw in his eyes that he really *was afraid* and I felt bad for him.

He set his jaw and squinted into Gary's squint and said, "All you gotta do is throw the first punch!"

I knew that was a mistake and Gary cocked back his fist fast as lightning and punched the bigger boy right on his nose. Kenny didn't fight back at all. His eyes went wide and brimmed with tears, a little blood trickled out of his nose, and his big, meaty fists fell open at his side.

He stumbled backward in the sand and Gary stayed on him, landing another punch on his nose, one hard in his belly and another solid one straight on the mouth.

Big, mean-looking Kenny, so new to the neighborhood that most of us didn't even know his name, burst into tears and fell on his butt with his hands spread open flat in front of his face. Gary pounced on top of him, straddled his chest and pummeled him, and most of the kids in the crowd started laughing and calling the new boy names, but none of that violent noise seemed as loud to me as the sound of the big boy crying.

I broke rank with the crowd, scrambled into the sandbox and grabbed two handfuls of my brother's t-shirt, tugging hard until he noticed me.

"Stop, Gary!" I told him, "Just stop hitting him, okay? He's not fighting you back."

Gary smirked at me and smashed his fist against the big boy's head once more before he stood up and gloated over him. "Don't come around picking on my brother and his friends anymore!"

Kenny was hurt and embarrassed, but he found his feet and skulked off alone, still crying, and some of the kids shouted mean things as he went, but most of us were very quiet. I looked at Gary and I was proud that he had taken up for me and the gang and I knew he'd only given the new kid what he had coming to him, but I knew he was going to get in a lot of trouble when Mom found out he had a fight in the playground.

"Landlord!' a few of the kids hollered.

I looked around and saw Mr. Dollasso hurrying out his apartment door, shouting at us, but he was old and very round and all of us kids scattered home before he made it across the street.

Back on our own block, I caught up to Gary as he fell out on the lawn, out of breath from fighting and running and I sat down alongside him.

"Thanks for stickin' up for me, Gary," I told him, "But Mom's gonna be so mad at you."

Gary looked up at me and grinned and said, "Mom ain't gonna be mad, Richie. Mom told me to beat that kid up."

I looked over my shoulder and saw Mom standing on the stoop with her hands resting on her hips. She was too far away for me to judge the weather in her eyes, but I could tell just by the way that she was standing, just by the almost unnoticeable grin on her face that she was as proud of Gary for defending me as she was of him for playing baseball.

Four - Humble Pie

That evening, Mom made our favorite tuna casserole for supper and at the table, no one mentioned the fistfight. Mom knew that Gary had done what she had asked him to do and taught the new kid a lesson and I knew she wouldn't bring it up, because she didn't want to encourage us to fight. Mom had her own ideas about justice, though, and she always said it was best to handle problems right here on the block and not get the cops involved.

After supper, I remembered that I had meant to spend some of my witch's garden wages treating the gang to ice cream cones, and I went outside with Tommy to round up all of our friends. The first kid we saw was our own big brother, sitting on the front stoop by himself, reading the new issue of *Mad Magazine*. Gary *loved Mad Magazine*, especially the *Spy vs. Spy* and Don Martin strips.

He had taken up for me today and tamed the new bully, even if he only did it because Mom told him to, so I wasn't going to ditch him out on ice cream.

"Hey, Gary, come on for ice cream," I said and I'm a little embarrassed to admit that I felt like a bit of a big shot when I told him it was *my* treat for the whole gang.

Gary looked up from the magazine and closed it on his lap. He scowled at me and I wasn't surprised. I had expected his newfound heroic good grace would fade fast in the afterglow of his street fighting victory.

"Jeez, Richie. You think I wanna hang around the ice cream shop with that bunch of geeky friends of yours? I'm too old for that."

I sighed. Gary used to be fun, even if he wasn't always nice, but here he was, retired from childhood at the ripe old age of thirteen.

"I got an idea," I said, "How 'bout I bring you one back? A triple scooper!"

For just a second, Gary's eyes, earthy brown just like Mom's eyes, sparkled and I knew he wanted that ice cream cone, but he turned it down with his usual charm. "Um, thanks but no thanks. By the time you bring it back, it'll just be all melty."

I got a little mad and decided I sure wasn't going to try to *force* a free ice cream cone on anybody, especially my own grouchy brother, but I got an idea. I dug in my pocket and brought out my money. Tommy's eyes almost exploded when he saw all the money I had and Gary watched out the corner of his eye as I peeled a dollar bill out of the stack and held it out to him.

"Here, Gary. Have a dollar. You can go get a triple scooper without all us geeks hangin' around."

I think I sounded a little meaner about it than I meant to, but Gary didn't notice because he wasn't embarrassed at all to take the dollar from my hand and shove it down in his pants pocket.

He *did* thank me for it, though.

Tommy and I made the rounds and gathered up most of the gang. The girls turned me down flat, but I didn't argue and I didn't peel off any dollars for them like I had for my brother. I was sad that Cheryl and Brenda were both angry with me, but I was glad they didn't want to go for ice cream if they weren't my friends anymore.

At the ice cream shop, the high school boy working the fountain got flustered because there were six of us all at once and we all wanted triple scoopers, all asked for different flavors and none of us was very patient when it came to ice cream.

He was scooping and cursing, scooping and cursing and when Ray Laws wouldn't stop tapping his finger on the display case and saying, "*French* vanilla, not regular," he mixed up the flavors on the cone and got mad. He stood straight up behind the counter and almost shouted at us, but he held his temper and just hissed at us instead.

"Okay, that's it, you kids," he said, "Do the math, you boneheads! Six triple scoopers. That's *thirty-six* scoops I gotta scoop! Not to mention about 14 different flavors."

We all shut up and stared at him when he raised his voice, except Tommy and Ross because they had already gotten *their* cones.

"Good," he said, "Now...the only way I'm scooping anymore ice cream for you guys is if you can order one at a time." He looked down the line at each of our faces and glared at Ray. "And no tapping on the dang glass!"

Burt Hodges raised a finger in front of his face and said, "You know, you make a very good point. That *is* a lot of ice cream to scoop."

The kid behind the counter grinned and said. "Well, that's more like it, then. Now who's next?"

Ray Laws stepped up to the fountain. "Me. All vanilla. French, not regular. I don't think the regular is very good if you can get French."

We sat on the low wall at the end of the strip mall parking lot and ate our ice cream cones. The evening was cool, but we were all in our summer shorts and the ice cream was a perfect end of summer treat. It had put a considerable dent in my sudden wealth, but I knew that I was going to make some more money working for Miss Olga the next day, and I was happy to share it with my friends.

CLANG!

That was the big bell that hung over the door of Ratto's Junior Market and we all looked up from our shrinking ice cream cones to see who was coming out. It was the freckle-faced crew-cut bike thief and when he saw us, he stuffed his hands in his pockets and went the other way up the sidewalk.

Ray Laws shouted after him. "Hey, look! Isn't that the Cowardly Lion?"

I elbowed Ray and said, "Knock it off, Ray."

"Are you kiddin' me, Richie," Ray whined, "He's the one who came around being a bully!"

"Ray," I said, "Just...just stop in the name of the *goshdanged* Laws!"

I hopped off the wall and followed the big kid up the sidewalk. I almost caught up to him outside the donut shop and I said, "Hey, Kenny, wait up! Hey, kid!"

He stopped walking and turned around. His lip was fat, both of his cheeks were puffy and red, and there was a nice shiner spreading out underneath his left eye. He didn't look mean or mad anymore. He just looked lonely and defeated and I felt bad for him again and thought it was probably somehow better to be mad and mean all the time than to feel the way he must be feeling now.

"What do you want?" He said, glancing over my shoulder to see if my friends were watching.

I didn't answer right off because my ice cream was melting and I had to lick all the drips off the cone before it got on my hands and ran all the way down to my elbow.

"I dunno," I told him, "I'm sorry you got beat up."

He smirked at me, but it was the doubtful kind of smirk, not the bullying kind. "Oh, *really*? Why would *you* be sorry about it? It was your brother who done it to me."

I wanted to tell him that I was sorry because the fight shouldn't have had to happen and that things didn't have to be the way they'd been in the neighborhood since he'd come around. I wanted to tell him that we were all friends around our block and we stuck together, and if he just tried to get along, he could be a part of the only valuable thing any of us had; our friendships. I wanted to tell him that I knew he was sad, but instead of all that I made him an offer I thought no one could refuse, though three people already had that very same day.

"You want an ice cream? I'll pay for it."

For a moment, I thought he was going to take me up on it, but his face fell a little bit and he shook his head. "Nah...I don't want any ice cream."

Before he turned away, I said, "Why are you so mean?"

I didn't expect an answer, really, and I didn't get one right away. He stared at me and I stared back at him, but I didn't walk away because I really wanted to know why he was so mean when he could have friends, and just when I thought I might blink, his lip trembled and he lowered his face and I knew that he was crying.

In a very soft voice, almost a whisper, he said, "My mom and dad died."

I had no words, only a hollow pit in my tummy and an out of season chill down my spine. I tried to think of something to say, something besides all the stupid things I heard grown-ups say when somebody died, but before I could find the words, he found some more of his own.

"They got killed in a car crash in June. I came here to live with my uncle. He's the only relative I have, but he don't like me much. He beats on me some."

I felt my own lip tremble. Just a little.

"I wasn't ever a bully back in my town," he said, "Heck; I never even had a fistfight before in my life."

I felt bad that his first fight had to be with a kid who knew how to punch as hard as Gary could.

"When I came here, everyone just made me out to be a bully 'cause I'm so big. I know I got a mean lookin' face, but that's just how we look in my family. My dad looked kinda mean, too, but he was nice to everyone."

I forgot about my ice cream, felt it dripping onto my fingers and gave up on it I tossed it into the wastebasket outside the donut shop.

"Sheesh," I said, "Why didn't you just act nice and make friends so everyone would know you weren't a bully."

"I dunno. I was mad and sad and I guess I kinda liked it, everyone thinking I was mean and tough when everything hurts *so* much." His face was wide open and honest and I thought he really didn't look so mean when you could actually see him. "I could hide behind myself real good when everyone thought I was tough."

He turned and ran away up the sidewalk and I didn't follow.

In that moment, I understood why Miss Olga let her front yard grow over so creepy and didn't argue back when everyone around town called her a crazy old witch. She was hiding behind herself, just the way this big freckled boy was hiding behind *himself*. Miss Olga was on *her* moon and this sad boy was on *his* moon and I realized that if I wasn't very careful with the pain in my heart, then one day, I'd get exactly the wish I'd made and I'd end up all alone, on a moon of my very own.

five - Broken Windows and Hearts

In the morning, Mom was already up, making pancakes in the kitchen when I woke up to go to Miss Olga's house. Mom always cooked pancakes the way Gramma had taught her when she was a little girl, in the big cast iron skillet with just enough oil in the pan to turn the edges of the cakes golden and crispy. Mom's pancakes weren't thin like the ones we got when we went out to eat, but thick and fluffy. I could never get pancakes like hers in a diner, even when I tried to order them that way.

"How come you're up makin' pancakes so early, Mom?" I asked her, sitting down at the table in front of a glass of cold milk.

She brought a plate stacked with steaming hotcakes in one hand and her coffee mug in the other and sat down beside me at the table.

"Well, a workin' man should have a good breakfast," she said, using a fork to load three cakes on to my plate. She took the remaining three and we both fattened them up with lots of butter and syrup.

"Richie," she said, "Are you sure you wanna spend the last day of summer vacation working in the witch's yard? Wouldn't you rather play with your friends. School starts tomorrow and it's back to regular rules, regular hours."

I didn't tell my mom, because I could hardly believe it myself, but I had just about had my fill of the gang for the summer. I loved them all, even Ray Laws and the girls who didn't love me back anymore, but since Jesse had been gone, I'd somehow become the unofficial leader of our gang. That was almost exactly like being the captain of a pirate crew, except without the ship, treasure or glory - *just* the pirate crew.

"Yeah, I wanna go work," I said, "And, mom? Do you think, maybe we could stop calling her The Bicycle Witch? She's really not one. She's nice...and I think she's sad."

Mom took a sip of her coffee and lit a cigarette. "She's really nice, huh? Okay, Richie, what do we call her then?"

I smiled. "I know it's a funny one, but her name is Olga Jean Pataki."

Mom laughed and I laughed, too, but she said, "Olga Jean Pataki it is then. It's familiar. I think she may have known your Gramma back when I was a little girl"

"She was at Gramma's funeral."

Mom sighed. "Was she? I didn't even notice her."

She kissed me and I rushed out the door, but before I hit the sidewalk, I remembered what Miss Olga had told me the day before.

You don't come barefooted tomorrow. You be extra sure to wear shoes.

I hurried back inside and put on my old sneakers and when Mom saw just how ratty they had gotten over the summer, she said, "Richie, I want you to take a little bit of that yardwork money and buy a new pair of sneakers."

"Okay, Mom, I will."

I rode my bike hard all the way across the river so I wouldn't be late and when I got to Miss Olga's house, I waited on the sidewalk for five minutes so I wouldn't be early. When my cheap Radio Shack watch read 7:59, I leaned my bike against the fence and went up the weedy sidewalk. I stepped up on the porch and stopped short. Broken glass littered the porch, big sharp shards and dangerous shattered bits that were almost too tiny to see, and I was reminded again of Miss Olga's words.

You be extra sure to wear shoes.

The front door opened and Miss Olga was there with a broom and dustpan. She stepped out, closed the door behind her so her cat wouldn't get out and step in the glass, and handed me the broom.

"Well, child," she said, "Looks like we found your job for today. There's plenty more glass inside on the floor, too."

I looked up at her and smiled. "You *knew*."

Olga Jean Pataki raised an eyebrow and put a finger to her chin. "What did I know?"

"Oh, come on," I grinned, "You knew the windows were gonna get broken!"

She laughed and it only sounded a *little* kooky. "Nonsense," she said with a dismissive wave of her hand, "I never got a tickle of this until it happened."

"But yesterday," I reminded her, "You told me to not come barefoot. You said I had to be *extra sure* to wear shoes."

She smiled. "Oh, yes, I did," she said, "But that was because you got dirt between your toes and all the way up to your ankles working in my garden, that's all. Nothing more, Richie. Nothing magic."

Coincident, Tommy had called it that night at the ballpark.

I swept up all the glass on the porch and after I finished with the broom inside, Miss Olga told me to run the vacuum over the floor, just to be sure no broken glass was left behind.

"I wouldn't want Mr. Mulligan to get glass in his feet," she frowned.

I put the vacuum cleaner back in the closet and said, "Who's that? Who's Mr. Mulligan?"

She laughed and nodded at the big overstuffed chair where her old grey cat lay curled up around himself, purring in his sleep.

"Miss Olga," I said, "Do you know who broke your front windows? Was it the same boys who stole your bike?"

When I first saw all the broken glass on Miss Olga's porch, I'd thought it must have been Kenny who had done it, but the kid I saw at the donut shop the night before didn't seem like he had much heart left for making trouble.

"I don't know which boy did it," Miss Olga told me, "But I know which boys *didn't* do it. It wasn't *those* boys."

I was glad it hadn't been Mike Renfro or Kenny who vandalized Miss Olga's house. I wanted that new boy to turn out okay. I knew he would if he could stop being so mad and sad about his folks being killed in a car crash.

"You saw them?"

Miss Olga sighed. "I don't sleep so good these last years, Richie. I was awake and right in that kitchen putting on the kettle. I heard a crash that almost shocked me to death and when I came in to see what happened, that's when the second window shattered. A big rock came tumbling right inside and nearly hit my Mulligan. But when I got to the door and looked out, all I saw was a boy I didn't know running away."

I asked her if she called the police and she said she had, just as she had promised.

"No, Miss Olga," I said, "Not about me and Jesse and the bicycle. Did you call the cops about the windows?"

"Oh, heavens no," she said, "I'm the scary old witch. Do you wanna know how many times I've had a rock through a window in the last forty years? So many, I get a discount from the glass man."

After we cleaned up the glass, Miss Olga gave me a ten dollar bill and told me I didn't have to do any other work since the man would be coming to fix the windows. She told me to go on home and enjoy my last day of summer freedom, but before I left, I said, "I figured it out. I know why you let the front yard go so bad and why you let people call you a witch."

She smiled at me, ever so softly. "I knew you would. I can tell a smart boy. Tell me why, then."

I grinned, but it felt sad on my face. "You *like* being the witch. You like it because people stay away from you. And they're scared of you, but really, *you're* scared."

Her smile remained, but her eyes brimmed with tears. "Well, now! You're even smarter than I thought. And do you know why I'm scared, Richie?"

I did.

"Because you're hiding behind yourself. But...I *don't* know why you're doing *that*"

She gasped, just the tiniest gasp, and her smile fell down. She shooed Mr. Mulligan out of her chair, settled into the cushions and waved me over to sit beside her on the sofa.

"Sit quietly, Richie, and I'll tell you a story," she said, "It's a true story, but it isn't a happy one. Not at all."

She told me a story about the boy in the pictures on her walls, the curly haired boy in the old fashion baseball uniform. His name had been Danny. It was a story I had heard bits and pieces of before, the kind of bits and pieces of truth that are handed around until, over the years, something true and tragic becomes just another ghostly local legend.

All of us kids knew at least one version of the story about the boy who drowned in the river back in 1934, when the banks were flooded over after a storm, but none of us knew that the boy had been The Bicycle Witch's son or even that she had ever been somebody's mother.

She told me that he had bothered her all that day, once the rain had passed, to let him go out and explore the flood. She hadn't wanted him to go outside, but after three days cooped up together in the little house, listening to the thunder and watching the lightning flash outside the windows, she had finally given in and told him to wear his slicker and galoshes and be home by supper, sooner if it started to rain again.

She never saw him alive again. When it got dark and he still hadn't come home, she had called the police and when they still hadn't found him by morning, she had known he was dead, even though they didn't find his body until three days later, floating near the bank of the river two townships south.

The police never found out how he had ended up in the river, but it had always been assumed that he'd simply slipped down the muddy bank and been carried away by the rushing, swirling storm waters. She finished with an echo of the legend we had all heard, telling me that some people liked to say that on particularly stormy nights, his ghost could be seen, trying helplessly to crawl up the muddy bank, out of the deadly water. They said the ghost always wore a bright yellow rain slicker.

I leaned forward on the sofa, and I whispered, "But that part isn't true, is it Miss Olga?"

She smiled and it was a welcome thing to see beneath her teary eyes. "Of course that part isn't true," she told me, wiping the corners of her eyes with a tissue, "You can only see Danny's ghost at the baseball park."

I didn't realize I was going to do it until I had, but I got up from the sofa and hugged Miss Olga tight around her shoulders and I didn't stop hugging her until she wasn't crying anymore. When we turned each other loose, she smiled at me again and said, "That's the first hug I've had from a little boy since the spring of '34."

"That's a long time to be sad, Miss Olga," I said, "Do you think you might ever get over it?"

"I got over Danny's death a long, long time ago," she said softly, "I just never stopped *blaming* myself for it."

"But you didn't know he was gonna get drowned," I told her, "Why do you think it was your fault?"

"Because," she whispered, "I had a funny little tickle about it that day, but I let him go out in the storm anyway."

I learned being friends with Jesse that a heart can break from someone else's hurt and just then, mine broke a little bit for Olga Jean.

"Miss Olga," I said, "How come you gave me that foul ball? And don't say you didn't 'cause I won't believe you. And how come you told me about Danny and your secret about not bein' a witch?"

Olga Jean sighed.

"I knew your grandmother," she said, "A long time ago. Did you know that?"

I shook my head. "I didn't know it, but I thought that might be why you went to her funeral."

"Anna and I worked together, on the switchboard," she told me, "Until Danny drowned. I stopped working after that. Well, I stopped *living*, really."

The cat, Mr. Mulligan hopped into her lap and curled himself up for a nap and Miss Olga stroked his fur absently. I thought he was a very handsome cat.

"I'm not so crazy now as people think I am," she said, "But I was crazy then. I know that. After a while, I didn't see my friends anymore and when they saw me, they only saw the Bicycle Witch."

I felt sad for her and I wished that losing Danny hadn't caused her to lose all of her friends, too.

"I saw Anna downtown once, though," she said, "Must have been in, oh...1968 or '69. We nearly bumped into each other on the sidewalk that day and I almost spoke to her, but she had a little boy with her and she hurried and led him by the hand into the drugstore."

The little boy was me. I know it was me.

Olga Jean nodded her head just like I was nodding mine. "That's right, Richie," she said, "It was you. You looked up at me with *such* big blue eyes. Dreamer's eyes"

"*That's* how come you told me everything?" I asked her, "Because of my *eyes*?"

"Oh, no, not because of your eyes at all," she said, "I guess I took a little shine to you because of the tickle I got when you looked up at me that day,"

Oh, my gosh!

"You had a tickle about me?" I said, "One of your *bad* tickles?"

She smiled.

"No, child. It was a *very* good tickle."

She told me that was enough talk for one day and sent me home, but she also told me to come back any Saturday I felt like it and she would find a job for me to do. Until I moved away from the township when I was sixteen years old, that's just what I did, and I never told anyone, except Mom and now you, that Olga Jean Pataki wasn't really a witch, not only because I wanted to protect her hiding place, but because I've never quite convinced myself of it.

Six - A Little Night Dancing

That night, Mom made us go to bed early so we would be rested and get to school on time in the morning. It was still a little light out when I crawled under the sheet and I couldn't fall asleep that early, not after three months of staying up almost as late as I wanted. Even after it got dark outside, I knew I wouldn't sleep well that night. I had too much on my mind, and so much in my heart.

I had been sad since the day before when the freckle-faced boy had told me about his parents being killed and why he had to hide behind himself and pretend to be a bully. I was sadder still after hearing a second tale of death and mourning from Olga Jean Pataki and learning that she had wasted forty years hiding behind *herself* and her overgrown front yard.

I had learned a thing or two about loss that summer and I was afraid that I would end up hiding behind myself, wearing a mask that only looked like who I wanted people to see. I didn't want that to ever happen to me, but in my heart's imagination, I could already see the features of the mask that I was carving for myself to wear one day. It was more than just frightening to imagine myself, years and years later, hiding behind the face of a little boy who refused to grow up. It was terrifying.

I wondered if it would happen to all of our gang, if all of us would grow up, not to be racecar drivers and firemen and presidents, but just pretenders, trapped behind the masks that the neighborhood expected us to wear, strangers to ourselves and everybody else.

When Mom went to bed after ten, I was still awake, and when I heard her snoring a half hour later and knew she was asleep, I slipped silently out of bed and got dressed in the dark. I put on a warm shirt and jeans and my new boots because it was chilly outside, and I crept through the apartment, quiet like a burglar, and snuck out the door.

I had been sneaking out at night ever since I was small, but I never went farther from the apartment than our tree out on the curb, and I never stayed out long enough to press my luck about getting caught, but that night I walked my bicycle out to the sidewalk, took the baseball card out of my back spokes, and pedaled silently down the block.

Out on Grand Avenue, I looked around for any cop cars, and pumped my bike across the road, but instead of following the sidewalk, I detoured into the darkness and rode in the dirt along the railroad tracks. I rode along for almost an hour, cutting into the woods at Ferry Street and swerving between the trees by the light of the moon until I came out the other side, beyond the outskirts of town, on the two-lane stretch of blacktop that everyone called The Bone Road.

I pedaled my bike up the center of the road, watching for the glow of headlights, even though I didn't expect to see any cars out there so late at night. If I saw a car coming either direction, I would hurry off the road and hide in the cover of the trees until it passed, in case it was a State Trooper out on patrol.

The night was cooler now and it was so quiet out there beyond the town that the sound of my bike tires treading over the asphalt seemed loud enough to wake the dead. For my own sake, I hoped and prayed the dead stayed fast asleep.

I didn't see a single car and in another ten minutes, I was stashing my bike in a culvert and doing something I never thought I would do, even on a double dare. I climbed the iron fence on Tranquility Hill and dropped into the cemetery, with midnight only minutes away.

I wasn't afraid, of any ghosts or graveyard curses, only of being caught out. I crept cautiously across the well-kept lawns, extra careful in the dark not to step on any graves, and I snuck among the shadows of the headstones and crosses until I came to the far side of the cemetery and found the marker with Gramma's name on it.

"Hi, Gramma..."

I had come all that way in the dark, against every lick of sense that I had, because I needed to talk to Gramma, even if she wouldn't answer back, but standing there in the darkness at the foot of her grave, the weightlessness of summer fled from my soul and when I opened my mouth for the words I had planned, they were lost to the night and replaced with soft sobs.

Mom hadn't brought us back to the cemetery to visit Gramma's grave and bring flowers since the funeral, because we didn't have a car and it was such a long way from home. Seeing her marker for the very first time, my heart ached over the chiseled stone that all of our lives would wind down to when we died.

I cried until I could see clearly again and when my tears had subsided and my chest rose and fell peacefully again, I found the words I'd meant to say, closed my eyes in the dark and hoped that my whisper was loud enough to be heard all the way in heaven up above.

"We went to Wildwood, Gramma. We found the money you saved and Mom took us. I rode the *Jackrabbit* all by *myself*."

I listened for her then, in the trees and even in the blades of grass, but there was only nature there and not a sign of anything beyond it. I listened to the sky, but only silence fell, not a single star to light my faith and prove my prayers, and in the earth beneath my feet, there was no sound up from the ground, just the endless silence of a thousand sleeping bones.

Are you there?

"I did a silly thing. I think you'd laugh if you could know it. I stole some of your dirt, Gramma, and I spread it on the wind when I rode the coaster. I know it's not sacred like spreading ashes, but you loved Wildwood as much as I do and I wanted a little bit of you to be there, too."

My tears were coming back, the night was growing thick and I knew now that Gramma couldn't answer, but I didn't know that she wasn't listening. Maybe the people in heaven hear every word we say. Maybe it's *we* who can't hear *them*, so they answer back with sunlight and twinkling stars, with rain and breezes, too.

Please answer.

I talked until I had told Gramma all that had happened since she had died, all the deep summer hurts that I knew marked me now, and the happiness, too, that I could not deny. I hoped that she had been watching me all summer long and that everything I told her was just second hand news, and the last thing I said was the one thing I was certain that she already knew.

"I love you, Gramma."

I left her behind, but I promised I'd come back, next time with flowers, and I snuck out of the graveyard and over the fence and all the way back the same way I'd come. When the railroad tracks brought me home to the Grand Avenue crossing, it was after two in the morning and I was finally tired and ready for sleep.

I pedaled up our block, past the buildings where my friends were sleeping, and when I got to my own front porch, there was a light on in our apartment. Mom was awake! I was afraid to stay out and afraid to go inside so I sat on the stoop and cried.

"Gramma..." I whispered, "If you're there, if you're *really* there like Jesse said you are, please...don't let Mom hit me tonight."

Silence answered back, as I expected it would, and I wished my tears away and willed my fears to let me loose and went inside.

Mom was on the couch, wide-awake and waiting, and Elvis Presley was on the stereo, singing 'Love Me Tender'. I stood still inside the doorway, afraid to speak or move and my mother looked at me with eyes gone red from crying.

"Where've you been?" I had never heard her voice so small and Elvis went quiet, too, his song fading into the soft pop and crackle of the record's end.

"I went to see Gramma."

Mom sighed, then just the very corners of her mouth crinkled up and I saw Gramma in her slight smile and wondered why I'd never noticed her there before. I waited for her eyes to flash, but they only looked sleepy and brown and she didn't raise her hand or even her voice.

"I thought that's where you went," she said, "Richie, that's too far away in the middle of the night."

"I know a shortcut."

She got up from the couch, leaned over the stereo cabinet, dropped the needle on the record's edge and 'Love Me Tender' began to play again. I remembered all the nights I had stayed up late with Mom, watching Elvis movies on television, all those times she had played his records and taught me how to dance to them, and when she shuffled across the carpet, her arms stretched open wide for me, I knew just what to do because I had learned the steps from her.

She held me close in her arms, I rested my head against her belly and we twirled slowly 'round and 'round, dancing to a song that I'd known all my life, one that she had taught me when I was just small and sang to me softly when she used to love to sing. I could feel myself fading into the softness of her fuzzy blue robe, falling asleep on my feet, dreaming that it was still June, but we went right on dancing to The King.

We danced until I felt myself, weightless and free, carried off to bed in her arms and tucked in with a kiss on my lips. I almost woke up just then, but the dream was too nice, and I knew if I opened my eyes that the music would stop and summer would be gone and, when it returned for me in time, the way it always did, it would never *ever* feel the same again.

Made in the USA
San Bernardino, CA
14 June 2018